Daniel and the "Lion"

"She smiles too much," Daniel said in a scoffing tone.

Nick considered this; he hadn't caught Dana Morgan smiling too much in his own direction.

"She works too hard—and she's too pretty," Daniel went on, in this peculiar catalog of Dana's faults.

"I hadn't noticed about the pretty part," Nick said gruffly.

"Sure." Daniel glanced at Nick with disfavor. "You look at her all the time."

"So she's pretty," Nick acknowledged.

"She acts like she wants to be my friend or something. I don't trust that."

"Maybe she wouldn't be such a bad friend to have."

"Is that how you feel?"

"I'm not in the market for friends," Nick said after a moment.

Daniel almost looked relieved. "I'm not in the market for friends, either."

ABOUT THE AUTHOR

When Ellen James was ten years old, she moved with her family to Central America. This was the beginning of a seven-year adventure—new schools, new friends, new culture. Learning Spanish became a matter of "do or die," but she soon fell in love with the exotic landscapes and with the people. She also developed a fascination with the area's Mayan culture and ruins, which helped inspire her writing of *Forbidden*.

While *Forbidden* is Ellen's second Superromance title, it's actually this exceptionally talented writer's eleventh romance novel. As popular author Debbie Macomber says, "I love Ellen James's stories! Her wit sparkles and her full-speed-ahead heroines are sure to capture your heart—as they do mine."

Ellen James
Forbidden

Harlequin Books

TORONTO • NEW YORK • LONDON
AMSTERDAM • PARIS • SYDNEY • HAMBURG
STOCKHOLM • ATHENS • TOKYO • MILAN
MADRID • WARSAW • BUDAPEST • AUCKLAND

ISBN 0-373-70641-3

FORBIDDEN

Forbidden

CHAPTER ONE

NICHOLAS PETRIE WAS like the island shore itself: lean, craggy, windswept—more than a bit weatherworn. Dana had a few moments to observe him as he came striding toward her at the boat landing. She recognized him from photographs she'd seen in his books. Dr. Nicholas Petrie...archaeologist. The photographs, however, had shown a vibrant young man gazing at the camera with a cocky devil-may-care grin. The individual approaching her now didn't look cocky. Instead, he seemed grim, and absorbed in his own thoughts. Although he could be no more than forty or so, his face showed grooves that seemed etched by some deep pain. No...this wasn't at all the brash man Dana had seen in those photographs. What had happened to change him?

Dr. Petrie wore dusty jeans and his faded shirt was stained with sweat in this humid heat. The tropical breeze had rumpled his dark hair, and as he drew nearer Dana saw that his eyes were a blue as startling and crystalline as the Caribbean Sea. Still unsmiling as he reached her, he ignored her offer to shake hands.

"Ms. Morgan?" he asked. "I'm Nick Petrie."

"Yes...Dr. Petrie." An unfamiliar mixture of excitement and apprehension swirled through Dana. She'd both dreaded and looked forward to this meeting. Dr. Petrie had once been a well-respected expert in Mayan archaeology. Yet, by all accounts, he had lost his respectability along with his youthful, debonair looks. Nowadays Dr. Petrie was rumored to be a grouch—at best.

"Is this all?" he said dryly, motioning toward the pile of duffel bags that surrounded her.

Dana eyed the bags, too. Perhaps she *had* packed more items than were strictly necessary, but her research indicated that Mexico's Isla Calamar offered few amenities. With a six-month supply of toothpaste, every brand of insect repellent she could lay her hands on and tapes of her favorite music—along with the requisite clothes, reference books, photo equipment and her special field glasses, Dana reasoned that she'd be ready for any adventure.

She hefted one of her duffel bags, ignoring just how heavy it was. "I believe in being prepared," she said, her own tone dry.

Nick Petrie didn't offer so much as a ghost of a smile. Easily taking a duffel in either hand, he turned and strode back along the landing. Dana hurried after him, hauling the other two bags. They reached a battered old Rover, so mud streaked Dana could only guess at its original color. Dr. Petrie slung all the bags in the back, then climbed in and started the engine. Apparently he was a man of few words. Make that a man of *no* words at the moment. That was fine, though. Dana hadn't come here to chat. She'd come to this small island so she could finally work at something that really mattered to her. No more being stuck in a lab, analyzing soil samples. For once she was actually going to get some real dirt under her fingernails.

That heady excitement swept through Dana again. For too many of her twenty-nine years, she'd followed the safe, predictable route. She'd attended the local ag-

ricultural college because she knew it would afford her
a secure future. She'd graduated with her master's and
then taken a job with Simonson Labs in Saint Louis
because it, too, promised a good future. And then, for
an interminable four years, she'd dated Alan, a man
who at one time had seemed both dependable and ambitious....

But after the recent debacle with Alan, she'd given up
on dependability, security—all of it. By traveling to
Mexico like this, Dana was finally doing something
unpredictable, and it felt downright exhilarating. Exhilarating—but scary, too.

Now Dana climbed into the Rover beside Dr. Petrie,
and in short order they were rattling along a coastal
road. The view was spectacular: to one side the shimmering Caribbean, with its waters of jade and reefs of
coral; to the other side the lush beginnings of jungle—
the coconut palms and the zapote trees with their sup-
posedly sweet-tasting sap. Dana had read all about the
plant life of this Mexican island, for she definitely believed in being prepared.

Unfortunately, nothing could have prepared her for
the queasiness that assaulted her stomach. The road was
rutted and unpaved, and the old vehicle's shock ab-
sorbers were clearly not up to the job. As Dana clung to
her seat, every jounce made her feel like a tennis ball
slapped by a racket. She wasn't going to be sick, was
she? Absolutely not! She could control this sensation if
she breathed deeply and calmly. She had to stop being
so keyed up. Too much unaccustomed travel, that was
her problem. The day before she'd flown down from
Saint Louis to the Mexican resort of Cancún, and this
morning she'd experienced the choppy boat ride from

Cancún to Isla Calamar. Add to that, bouncing around on this primitive road...

Dana took another deep breath and glanced at Dr. Petrie. Somehow the sight of his stubborn, unyielding profile had a calming effect on her. Maybe he wasn't prone to conversation, but she found that she needed to talk, after all—anything to keep the queasiness at bay.

"Dr. Petrie, I've read both your books," she said. "I found your explanation of Mayan script very... fascinating." She had difficulty getting the last word out. Just then the Rover lurched to skirt a boulder in the road, and she pressed a hand to her stomach.

Nick Petrie returned her glance. "It's been quite a while since anyone bothered trying to flatter me."

His bluntness stirred Dana to speak her own mind. "I wasn't trying to flatter you," she said through clenched teeth. A film of perspiration had broken out on her forehead, adding to her discomfort. "I was just trying to—to make friendly conversation."

"That's not necessary, either," he said, and for the first time she heard a reluctant hint of humor in his voice. "I'm sure the people at the Mesoamerica Institute told you I was foul tempered and difficult to work with. It's all true."

"Actually, they were a little more specific than that. They said you were a royal pain in the ass."

Nick surprised her with an actual smile, and she thought she saw a glimpse of the cocksure young archaeologist he must have once been. Only a glimpse and then it faded, replaced by a stern demeanor. No matter what, he was still an attractive man... very attractive. He appeared seasoned, matured by hardships she could only guess at. That was somehow appealing, too.

Dana forced herself to stare straight ahead, through the grimy windshield. She'd never intended to feel attracted to her new boss. It certainly wasn't part of the plan for her new life! Hadn't she learned anything after what had happened with Alan?

Nonetheless, Dana's thoughts strayed to the sparse facts she'd learned about Dr. Petrie from the Mesoamerica Institute of Saint Louis. The Institute funded a number of archaeological sites in Mexico and Central America, albeit on a shoestring. At first Dana had been overjoyed when she'd been granted a position on the excavation of Mayan ruins at Isla Calamar. However, the Institute staff had warned Dana that the archaeologist in charge of the project, one Nicholas Petrie, was irascible and dictatorial in the extreme. It seemed both his career and his good humor had gone into sharp decline over the past ten years. Dana would have her work cut out for her, establishing herself on the Calamar dig while at the same time finding a way to get along with her bad-tempered supervisor. The previous soil scientist had quit in disgust over conflicts with Dr. Petrie.

Beyond sharing this warning, the Institute showed discretion. It did not elaborate on further aspects of Dr. Petrie's personality, nor did it explain why his promising career had faltered to the point that only a struggling organization like the Institute itself would hire him.

In preparation for her new job, Dana had promptly attempted to find copies of Nicholas Petrie's books on ancient Mayan culture. Both volumes had gone out of print, and she'd finally located dog-eared copies of them at two separate libraries. It was all a mystery, really. The books were excellent, written in a lively, insightful style. At this stage of his career, Nicholas Petrie should have produced even more insights into the Maya. What had reduced him to second-class status, heading a minor dig on the insignificant little island of Calamar, Mexico?

Dana forced herself to stop speculating. She'd come to this island for herself. Perhaps the Calamar dig was a minor one, but she didn't care about that. This was her chance at last to break out of the stifling mold of her old life.

And so she was excited. And nervous. Her emotions were pent-up. All these sensations roiled inside her.

"Please pull over," she said in a very distinct voice.

"Ms. Morgan, I'm sure you'd like to admire the view, but—"

"You'd best pull over, Dr. Petrie."

Thankfully, something in her tone prevented him from further argument. He brought the Rover to a halt. Dana clambered out her side of the vehicle and stalked off toward the underbrush. She had a vague notion of preserving some dignity for herself, but a second later she was doubled over in an ignoble fashion.

Nick Petrie knew exactly what to do. Without saying a word, he followed Dana and supported her head during the humiliating episode. His hand was cool and firm against her clammy skin. When it was all quite over, he held a canteen of water to her lips for a blessedly refreshing sip or two. Then he moistened a serviceable white handkerchief in the water and pressed it matter-of-factly against her face. She was trembling, and he held her steady with one arm. Giving up all hope of dignity, she leaned against him, silently accepting the strength he offered her.

"I usually don't cause such a strong reaction in people," he said. "I make them run away, yes—but I don't make them sick. This is a first."

She couldn't even bear to look at him. Dana hated feeling out of control, the way she did right now. When she was quite sure she could stand alone, she moved away from him—although she'd ended up clutching his handkerchief and couldn't seem to let go of it.

"I feel fine now," she declared. "It's all very embarrassing, what just happened—but it was the excitement, you know. I've been that way ever since I was a kid. I'd go on a trip, and I'd get so worked up about the adventure I'd be sick...." Her voice trailed off. She realized she was only making matters worse, conjuring up an image of herself as a spindly little kid who couldn't even handle the anticipation of going to Disneyland. She could tell from the disgruntled expression on Dr. Petrie's face that he didn't want to hear any more about her childhood.

And yet, just a few moments ago, he'd been... compassionate. There could be no other word for the way he'd helped her. Gruffly compassionate. Maybe only the gruff part remained now, but she hadn't imagined the other.

"I'm ready to go on," she said.

"I doubt you're up to working," he answered brusquely. "I'll take you into the village and let you rest for the day." He made it sound as if he wanted to be rid of her, and that only strengthened Dana's resolve.

"Absolutely not. I'm fine—really I am. I'm more than ready to work."

He studied her with a skeptical expression, the harsh lines of his face hardening still further. There could be no doubt that he disapproved of her. But then he gave an abrupt nod, and led the way back to the Rover.

Dana clambered in beside him. He drove more slowly now, making the ride smoother. Dana suspected he was doing it out of consideration for her, but she didn't know how to thank him. He probably wouldn't appreciate her gratitude; he still maintained a beleaguered expression.

But at least they were on their way again, the road turning and making a path among the vine-draped trees. The jungle of Isla Calamar engulfed them. Branches scraped the sides of the Rover as the road grew more narrow and rutted. Now Dr. Petrie couldn't avoid bouncing along, and Dana's stomach clenched in protest. She willed herself to remain calm; she simply would not disgrace herself again.

They traveled for half an hour, perhaps more. Nick didn't speak to her. The silence seemed a brooding one, broken now and then by the shriek of some exotic bird. The green shadows of the forest pressed in on the Rover, but at last Nick came to a halt. And that was when Dana saw it—the Mayan temple.

It jutted up amid the jungle with all the majesty of its thousand years. Mossy stone upon stone rose in narrowing terraces to the very pinnacle of the pyramid. Underbrush still tangled about the steps, and here and there gnarled tree roots had broken up the dark gray stone. Dana climbed out of the Rover and went to stand at the very base of the temple, craning her neck upward. She was filled with a sense of awe—and gratitude that she could witness this remnant of a vanished civilization. She knew there were more impressive ruins: the great Mayan cities discovered at Palenque, Tikal, Copán. That didn't matter. This was *her* ruin, this temple hidden among the forest of mangrove and cypress.

At last she turned to Nick, who had come up beside her. "It's wonderful," she murmured. "I've never seen anything like it."

He said nothing in return, but merely studied her in that disconcerting manner of his. In the mysterious shade of the jungle, his eyes were an even more intense blue than before—and his features even more stern. His gaze might be disapproving, but that didn't stop her from feeling oddly drawn to the man, as if they shared something unspoken in common. For the space of several heartbeats she gazed back at him. His features had gone taut—perhaps a sign that he, too, felt this odd connection between them. Dana knew it didn't make sense. Nicholas Petrie was a stranger to her. How could she therefore feel this disturbing sense of closeness to him?

She was the one who glanced away first. Firmly she reminded herself of the disaster with Alan. She couldn't afford to be attracted to Dr. Petrie, of all people.

She turned from him, and saw a black-striped iguana dart across a rock. Insects buzzed around her. So far this morning her repellent wasn't doing the job, and she had to resist the urge to slap her arms.

"What types of artifacts have you uncovered in the vicinity?" she asked, needing to fill the silence between herself and Nick. "Monuments, stelae, that sort of thing."

When she ventured to glance at him again, she could swear she saw a restrained humor hovering in his expression now. His change of mood annoyed her. What did he find so funny, dammit? She slapped her arms after all, as a swarm of whining bugs strafed her. Why didn't any of them seem to be attacking Nick?

"We're excavating for remnants left by the Mayan farmers who lived near this temple," Nick said. "But don't get too worked up, Ms. Morgan. We're not likely to make any stunning discoveries. I'm not the first archaeologist to descend on the island. Different groups were here during the 1920s and 1950s. They didn't find anything particularly noteworthy. We're here as follow-up."

His impassive tone made her glance at him more sharply. "You're not excited about this place?"

"The capacity for excitement is something I lost a long time ago." He seemed to lapse into his own thoughts then. The silence felt more strained than ever to Dana, but she didn't know how to fill it this time. She was almost startled when Nick spoke again a few moments later.

"This was once a shrine to the goddess Ixchel," he said. He still seemed lost in his own contemplations as he gazed at the temple. "Superstitions about it have circulated the island for centuries now."

The air was heavy, like a shroud of heat wrapping itself around Dana. "What superstitions?" she asked.

Nick seemed to stir from his reverie. "There've been stories about the temple ruins being haunted by a woman of the ancient Maya. You know the type of thing—people out to scare each other with talk of a ghost, and evil curses if anyone dares to climb the temple steps."

Dana was not prone to superstition herself, but she supposed this jungle was the place for ghost stories, all right, with its gloomy shade and aura of deep isolation.

"Exactly what do the stories say?" she asked, trying to evince nothing more than scientific interest.

"Ixchel was the Mayan goddess of fertility, and women once came to the island on pilgrimage to worship her. The story goes that one of these pilgrims knelt to beg Ixchel for a baby and then died mysteriously while still at the temple. They say her ghost haunts the place, refusing to leave until she obtains her child. People also say that the ghost curses anyone who ventures near the temple to disturb her mourning."

"Hmm...a ghost and the goddess Ixchel." Now the temple rising up before her seemed more grand than ever to Dana. She could almost picture a young Mayan woman climbing the steps reverently and hopefully, going to petition her goddess, unaware of the fate that awaited her....

"Does the story frighten you?" Nick asked, making Dana start.

"No—of course not. It's just sad, that's all. I feel sorry for the woman who never got her baby. But you aren't trying to scare me off, are you, Dr. Petrie?"

"And why would I try to do that?" he asked gravely.

"I don't know. Maybe you like to scare people off."

He surprised her again, this time with just a flicker of a smile. Then he glanced beyond Dana. She followed the direction of his gaze and saw a young boy sitting at the far end of the temple steps, quietly observant. It was disconcerting to see the boy; surely he hadn't been there a few moments ago. He looked to be no more than eleven or twelve, with dark tousled hair, dark eyes and the sun-burnished skin of an islander. At Nick's glance, the boy came over to stand beside him. The two exchanged no greeting, no acknowledgment of any kind, yet seemed accustomed to each other's presence. They stood there together, apparently satisfied with the silence between them. Dana got the feeling that if anyone was going to speak, it would have to be her.

"Hello," she said to the young boy. "I'm Dana Morgan."

The boy stared at her, as if she'd breached some obscure code of etiquette by actually introducing herself. But at last he gave a brief nod in return.

"I'm Daniel," he said, his pleasing Spanish accent at odds with his grudging tone.

The conversation threatened to die there, but Dana had always been good with kids. She tried again.

"My grandfather was a Daniel," she said. "I was christened for him, in fact."

This tidbit of information didn't seem to inspire young Daniel in the least. He continued to look disapproving. As for Nick...well, he observed Dana with that subtle hint of amusement she already found annoying.

She refused to be daunted by two such closemouthed individuals. As she searched for a more fruitful line of discourse, at last Nick spoke.

"Daniel works with me part of the time. Come along, Ms. Morgan, we'll show you where we're excavating." Nick strode away, the boy following him like a small shadow. Dana brought up the rear, wondering why Daniel seemed so prickly and difficult. Maybe he was just trying to emulate Nick Petrie's charming demeanor, she told herself ironically.

Almost immediately the jungle engulfed the three of them. Ferns and vine tendrils brushed Dana's face. Orchids and other bright flowers she couldn't identify clung to the trees. Patches of bamboo reeds impeded her progress, but she fought her way through. Already her cotton shirt had grown damp with perspiration in the tropical heat.

Nick held aside a tangle of stalks so she could pass. "Half the time I carry a machete with me. A lot of my work involves cutting back the jungle, as well as digging in the ground."

There was an image: austere, forbidding Dr. Petrie wielding a machete. But those darn bugs were following Dana everywhere she went, pesky little dive-bombers that had identified her as their target. She pulled down the floppy brim of her canvas hat, realizing just how damp her skin had become. If she was this sweaty and buggy after only a few minutes, what would she be like at the end of the day?

Dana reminded herself that it was all part of her unpredictable new life. Adventures didn't come with air-conditioning or other such comforts. Adventures were messy, difficult things. That was what made them so satisfying.

Nonetheless, Dana felt relieved when they came to a small clearing and at least she no longer had vines swatting her in the face. She saw an excavation laid out before her, alternate squares neatly chiseled from the dirt. The effect was rather that of a three-dimensional checkerboard.

Dana gazed at it in fascination. Her specialty had always been soil science, not archaeology itself, but she'd done enough research to know exactly what she was looking at. Archaeological sites required a great deal of care. All digging had to proceed slowly and cautiously, information collected in an orderly manner so that no detail was lost. Hence the grid pattern, with alternate test pits chosen for excavation. It allowed the archaeologist to cover a fair amount of ground, while still maintaining proper control of the entire project.

Dana turned to Nick. "It's wonderful," she said enthusiastically.

He raised his eyebrows just the slightest bit. "That's what you keep telling me."

The boy Daniel looked skeptical, too, as if to add emphasis to Nick's words. Dana grimaced, realizing that she must sound like a gushing schoolgirl. But it *was* wonderful. With an effort, she refrained from further superlatives, taking in the rest of the site. Across from her, where the jungle strained to encroach on the clearing, two palm-thatched huts sprouted like mushrooms. A plump, white-nosed burro was tethered near the huts, munching on some hay. It was all remarkably picturesque, but just then a low moan disturbed the tranquillity.

"What was that?" Dana asked, glancing around.

Already Nick was striding away, skirting the edge of the excavation. With a muttered oath, he knelt down next to one of the pits. Daniel caught up and knelt beside him as Dana hurried over to stare into the pit for herself. She gasped at what she saw there—a man sprawled on his side, blood trickling down his face.

CHAPTER TWO

DANA COULD HONESTLY SAY that she'd never been in a real crisis before. In fact, that was one of her complaints about her old life: no real crises of any kind, no true tests of character. It meant she had no way to predict how she would react in a given emergency. And this definitely constituted an emergency—a wounded man splayed in front of her, bleeding from an ugly gash to the head.

Dana slid down into the shallow excavation pit, bumping against Nick as he leaned over the wounded man. She reached out her fingers and felt the man's throat.

"My God—I can't find his pulse."

Nick edged her aside and placed his own fingers at the man's throat. "His pulse is fine. Daniel—"

Before Nick even finished, the boy seemed to know what was required. Dashing to one of the huts, he emerged a few seconds later with a metal box, its bright red cross identifying it as a first-aid kit. And then, while Daniel produced gauze bandages and antiseptic, Nick deftly stanched the flow of blood from the man's wound. With Dana crowded in beside them, it made for rather cramped quarters. Nick treated her to an impatient glance, and young Daniel frowned as if in echo.

"Ms. Morgan, could you give us a little elbow room?" Nick asked.

"There must be something I can do to help," she muttered. "Who is this man, anyway?"

"Jarrett Webster."

That didn't tell her anything useful, but a moment later Dana noticed a jagged rock lying just outside the pit—a rock with a smear of blood on it.

"Look!" she exclaimed. "Someone must have hit him with that. Who would do such a thing?"

"I don't know," Nick said harshly, "but I intend to find out. Daniel, did you see anything unusual this morning?"

The boy shook his head emphatically. "I wasn't here, Señor Petrie. I waited for you at the temple."

Nick took the antiseptic from him. "Never mind—we'll get to the bottom of this somehow."

Meanwhile, the injured man opened his eyes and smiled weakly up at Dana. "You must be Ms. Morgan. So glad to have you with us...."

"Please don't talk," Dana murmured in concern. "You'll waste your strength."

"I so wanted to welcome you properly, Ms. Morgan. Do hope you had a good trip in . . ." His eyelids drifted shut. The poor man had been bashed over the head with a rock, yet here he was politely inquiring about Dana's journey. She examined Jarrett Webster more closely. He appeared to be in his late thirties and had a pleasant-looking face, even under these conditions. His light brown hair was so long that it touched his shoulders. Altogether, his appearance seemed oddly bland in contrast to Nick Petrie's. But perhaps it wouldn't be fair of Dana to judge him until she saw him in more favorable circumstances. At the moment Nick was in charge, demonstrating skill and quick thinking, while Jarrett Webster was completely vulnerable.

Nick finished bandaging the wound. "We need to get him out of the sun," he said tersely, lifting Jarrett by the shoulders.

Once again Daniel moved with alacrity, awaiting no further instruction as he took hold of Jarrett's legs. The load was obviously too much for him, however, and Dana added her own efforts.

"I can do it," Daniel said, no doubt wishing to dismiss her. But Dana saw that his thin arms strained at the job. She realized just how much this boy wished to prove himself strong and capable ... exactly like Nick, it seemed.

Under other circumstances, Dana might have obliged the boy's pride, but right now there were more urgent concerns. She continued grappling with her part of the load. She hadn't known a human being could weigh so much. Jarrett was only a medium-size man, but all her muscles strained at the burden of lifting him from the pit. Nick, in contrast, moved masterfully, hardly showing the effort.

All three of them managed to haul Jarrett up and began making their way through the excavation site. Dana lurched unexpectedly and saw a corresponding wince on Jarrett's face.

"Sorry," she said.

"No, no. Quite all right," mumbled Jarrett, eyes still closed.

He really was amazingly polite. Dana glanced at Dr. Petrie, only to receive a laconic glance in return. She knew one thing. "Polite" was not a term she'd ever use to describe Nick Petrie. Virile, rugged, competent, in charge ... yes. Polite ... no.

They entered the first of the huts and deposited Jarrett on a low cot. He seemed to be unconscious now.

Perhaps they'd removed him from the sun, but the air was still heavy with humid heat. Dana mopped the back of her hand across her forehead, droplets of perspiration clinging to her skin.

"He should go to a hospital," she pointed out.

"There is no hospital on the island. We'll get him to the village soon, though. For now he's probably better off here, not moving. Try to get him to drink something and Daniel and I will have a look around." With that, Nick strode out the doorway of the hut, followed by his diligent shadow.

Dana stared at Jarrett Webster's recumbent body, feeling suddenly at a loss. It wasn't a familiar sensation for her. In the dim light of the hut, she found a crate of orange and lime soda next to a sizable jug of water. Dana picked up the jug as well as a soda, then turned back toward Jarrett.

His eyes were wide open and he was staring right at her. Dana started a little.

"How are you feeling?" she asked.

"Not too bad. It's just a bump on the head."

"I'd say it's a bit more than that. Here, I want you to drink this." Moving over, she held the jug of water to his mouth and he managed to take a few sips. She remembered the way Nick had held a canteen to her own lips earlier this morning, and realized that she far preferred to be the one giving help than receiving it.

"You should try to get some rest," she told Jarrett.

"I feel pretty damn stupid. I didn't see who attacked me. I was engrossed in my work—didn't even hear anything."

Dana settled onto a camp stool beside Jarrett. "Maybe it would be a good idea if you told me what you do remember."

He reached up a hand to his head and gingerly felt the bandage there. "Not much to tell, I'm afraid. I was alone here, but that's nothing unusual. I was kneeling down with my trowel, digging.... Next thing I knew..." Jarrett's voice trailed off and he seemed to drift into sleep again. Dana watched him, making sure that he was breathing steadily. Then she relaxed enough to drink some lukewarm orange soda. It tasted too sweet, but at least it soothed her throat. She thought about Dr. Petrie and the young boy Daniel, off in search of Jarrett's attacker. She doubted seriously that anyone could take Nick Petrie by surprise... but she felt worried, nonetheless. She supposed anyone could be lurking out there in the jungle.

Jarrett slept on, leaving Dana to her own musings. So far today, nothing had been as she'd expected it to be: the humiliating drive from the docks, the attack on Jarrett, the hot, humid discomfort of the island—the discomfort from Nick Petrie. That unwelcome attraction to Dr. Petrie, that was the worst of it. From the moment she'd met him, some essential buffer had seemed lacking between them. Her reactions to him were too immediate, too close to the surface. He both irritated and intrigued her....

In a short while, Dana heard a murmur of voices outside the hut. She hurried to the doorway and saw Nick immersed in discussion with two of the native islanders—a man and a woman. The woman's black hair was plaited into a thick braid and she wore a beautifully embroidered blouse over her gathered skirt. The man seemed protective of the woman, standing close beside her. He spoke in Spanish to Nick, gesturing occasionally to make his point. Dana had begun studying Spanish, but she wondered if it was doing her any good.

She couldn't understand a word the man was saying. Often the woman broke in to add something, and Dana couldn't understand a word she said, either. It was possible to guess, however, that the man and woman were married, or at least had been together for some time. The woman seemed to keep finishing the man's sentences for him.

Nick was talking now. Unfortunately, Dana couldn't understand a word *he* said, either. He spoke Spanish easily, fluently, the language surprisingly melodious in his deep voice. He didn't seem aware of Dana's presence, and neither did the other two. She was reluctant to interrupt, not wanting to distract them in case they were solving the mystery of Jarrett's attacker. But it made her feel like an outsider, standing here in the shadows of the hut, listening to words she couldn't comprehend. An unfamiliar loneliness seeped through her.

The conversation went on another moment or two, and then the man and woman hurried away, disappearing among the dense foliage. Dana stepped from the hut.

"Were you able to learn anything?" she asked. "I'd like to say I caught all that, but I didn't."

Nick rubbed the back of his neck, frowning at Dana as if he'd forgotten about her and didn't like being reminded of her existence.

"That was Anton and Elena Montano. They live nearby and they both work for me from time to time, but they were away from the site all morning. They didn't see anything unusual."

The conversation had gone on for quite a while, and Dana suspected it had been more informative than Nick allowed.

"You don't suppose one of them—Anton or Elena—could have sneaked up and conked Jarrett on the head?"

"Hell, I could have sneaked up and attacked him myself, then still made it in time to meet your boat. But why would I want to do that? Don't try to play detective, Ms. Morgan."

She stared at him in exasperation. "We have to find out who did it before it happens again. We have to conduct an investigation, contact the police—"

"I'll handle it, Ms. Morgan. It's not your concern."

"Right. Someone is running around, walloping people with rocks, and I'm supposed to forget about it?"

He stared back at her, as if to quell her with one of his silences. Dana refused to be quelled. She confronted Nick Petrie's ice blue gaze—and experienced once again that bewildering and completely unwelcome sense of connection to him. He wasn't touching her at all, yet she felt the beat of her pulse in an elemental rhythm that suddenly seemed unfamiliar to her. Too much had seemed unfamiliar today....

"I'm surprised Daniel didn't return with you," Dana said quickly. "He seems to like being around you."

A wry look crossed Nick's face. "Daniel is very much his own person. He comes and goes as he pleases."

Then the sound of voices interrupted Nick, and a moment later a man and a woman came striding out of the forest into the clearing. They appeared to be in the midst of some disagreement.

"You didn't listen to a thing I—"

"On the contrary. I have been the soul of attentiveness."

"Like hell—" The woman stopped herself in mid-curse as she saw Nick and Dana. "Oh. Well...Daniel told us what happened," she said in a brisk tone. "How's Jarrett?"

"He'll live," Nick answered tersely.

The woman now concentrated on Dana, her glance assessing. "I'm Pat." She said her name as if she expected Dana to know all about her. She was tall and athletic in build, sandy hair curling haphazardly at her shoulders. Her grip was firm as she shook hands with Dana.

Now the man stepped forward. He was distinguished looking, with a reddish beard cropped close to his resolute chin. In spite of the heat, his khaki shirt looked fresh and crisp. Dana wondered how he managed that. He, too, shook hands with her and introduced himself.

"Robert Lambert, Ms. Morgan. It's too bad you're joining us under such disturbing circumstances." He didn't sound disturbed—merely perfunctory. Dana thought she could identify his accent as French, but she wasn't entirely sure.

Nick, however, left no time for speculation. "I'm taking Jarrett into the village. Robert, Pat, have a look around—but stay together!" He glanced at Dana. "Ms. Morgan, I suppose you'd better come with me."

Dana disliked being treated like unwanted baggage. She thought she'd detected a slight resentment flicker across Robert's and Pat's faces, too—perhaps they weren't particularly pleased about following orders, either. But clearly Nick was the one in command.

"We'll see what we can find," Robert said.

"Yeah, right," Pat added, and a few seconds later they disappeared back into the jungle, their conversation resuming all the intensity of their prior argument.

"Are they always so friendly toward each other?"

"Of course," Nick said matter-of-factly. Then he turned and began walking back to the hut. "We'll take Jarrett to the village. After that, there are a few things that need checking out."

"Sounds good," Dana said with determination. "Just tell me what we're looking for."

"I'll do the investigation, Ms. Morgan. On my own." He gave Dana a look sufficient to suppress all arguments. Goodness . . . was this entire expedition comprised of grouches?

NICK PETRIE NEEDED a drink. Hell, he always needed a drink. Wearily, Nick wondered if the craving would ever let up on him. He just didn't know. He fought a battle every day, every minute of his life. Lord, it could make him tired sometimes.

The waiter at the café stood in front of Nick, looking bored. He'd probably go right on looking bored, even if Nick ordered some whiskey or tequila. The guy didn't realize how easily Nick could flush his life down the toilet again.

"*Una* Coca-Cola," Nick said. The waiter nodded blandly to Nick and left. Nick turned to stare across at the village plaza. He'd chosen one of the outdoor tables, as usual, but he couldn't seem to get comfortable in his rickety chair. It had been a lousy afternoon, which didn't help his mood any. No matter who he'd talked to, he hadn't been able to learn more about the attack on Jarrett. Either the islanders didn't know anything—or they just weren't talking.

Now the heat of the day had lessened with dusk, and teenagers were starting to congregate in the plaza for the nightly ritual of courtship. A cluster of girls gathered at the wrought-iron gazebo like a flock of restless doves, while the boys hovered at the outskirts. In a little while, the males would start mingling with the females, becoming more bold as the shadows of twilight fell. Maybe clothes and hairstyles had changed, but this same scene had been taking place on the island for the past two hundred years or so. It would probably go on for another two hundred years.

Nick shifted in his chair, still unable to get comfortable. When the waiter brought his soft drink, he took a good swallow but it did nothing to slake his thirst. Somehow this evening, watching the kids in the plaza, he remembered how long it had been since he'd allowed any woman to get close to him. It had been well over a year, in fact, since he'd botched things with Kathryn. Since then, he'd left mating rituals and such for younger men. The truth was, getting and staying sober had taken all his energy. He hadn't even been tempted by a woman....

Until today. Today he'd met Dana Morgan, with her gold hair tumbling halfway down her back and those dark brown eyes of hers that had seemed to gaze straight into his soul. His reaction to her had been completely unexpected, and it had happened almost the first moment he'd seen her down on the landing waiting for him. It had been something about the way she'd held herself—standing very straight, as if she believed good posture was essential for an archaeological dig. He'd almost wanted to say "at ease," but he wasn't much into joking these days. Then he'd looked into her eyes and he'd felt lost. Disoriented...

Nick drained his drink and thumped the bottle down on the table. It was going to be damned inconvenient, working with the woman. But he had a hunch she wouldn't last long. She looked like someone made for happiness, sunniness, not someone willing to hang around a crabby ex-drunk. Nick smiled grimly. He enjoyed his ill-tempered reputation. It kept people at bay. No doubt it would keep Dana Morgan at bay—and next thing he knew, she'd be off the island, boating her way back to more civilized society. If nothing else, she wouldn't want to stay around in a place where people were assaulted with rocks.

Nick drew his eyebrows together. The whole incident with Jarrett was an unsavory one and a puzzler. Isla Calamar was not known for violence. Who the devil had been behind the attack this morning?

"Dr. Petrie," said a woman's voice, as rich and mellow as a thread of honey. Damn. It was her voice... Dana's. A few hours earlier he'd left her in her room at the local hotel and he'd assumed he'd be free of her until tomorrow. But he'd been thinking about her, and it was almost as if he'd conjured her presence by the very insistence of his thoughts.

Reluctantly Nick glanced at Dana Morgan. She stood beside his table, looking both refreshed and determined. She still wore khaki pants, but she'd changed into a sleeveless denim shirt. Nick's gaze lingered on the curves of her body. It was happening again, that unsettling awareness of everything about her: the silken waves of her hair, the faint flush on her cheeks, the creamy skin of her bare shoulders... He wished once more, futilely, for a stiff drink.

"Ms. Morgan," he said. "I'm surprised you were able to find me in the teeming metropolis of La Ceiba." It seemed he still knew how to joke, after all. The town was so small that you didn't have to look very hard to find anyone.

Dana pulled out a chair and sat across from him without waiting for an invitation. "Jarrett's sleeping again," she announced. "I think he's doing much better. The village doctor said you did a good job of treating Jarrett yourself. At least, that's what I think the doctor said."

Nick shrugged noncommittally. The village doctor was a seventy-eight-year-old man who'd retired to the island over a decade earlier, but his opinion was probably as good as anyone's.

"I'm surprised you left Jarrett alone," Nick remarked. "You seem to think the attacker will be back."

"It's a very strong possibility, isn't it? But I managed to communicate with the lady at the hotel. She promised she'd keep the door to Jarrett's room locked and that she'd watch out for him."

Nick was impressed. The lofty proprietress of the village's one hotel rarely did favors for anyone. "So you have everything under control, Ms. Morgan. You should try to get some rest."

She didn't take the hint, but simply went on gazing at him with earnest intensity. "I need to know more. Did you talk to the police yet?"

He stifled a groan. She was still gung ho, determined to crack the case herself. "Yes, Ms. Morgan, I spoke to the police. Correction—I spoke to Inspector Maciel, the one policeman on the island. He's a rather elderly friend of the doctor's, by the way, but he still takes his job seriously in spite of his gout and nearsightedness. He's looking into the matter."

Dana made a restless gesture. "Are you trying to be funny? But there must be something more we can do."

"Not 'we,' Ms. Morgan. I'm the one in charge."

"I see." She gave him a disdainful glance. "That's why you're sitting here...doing nothing."

"I figured I'd start rounding up suspects any second now."

Dana sighed and propped her elbows on the table. "Dr. Petrie, at least talk to me about what's going on. Why would someone want to harm Jarrett Webster? Does he have any enemies?"

Against his better judgment, Nick eased back in his seat and answered her question. "Jarrett doesn't have any enemies that I know of. He's been working at the dig as long as I have—almost seven months. In that time, he seems to have charmed just about everyone on the island." Nick couldn't keep a little sarcasm out of his voice. In his opinion, Jarrett overdid the charm bit. Dana, however, didn't seem to think so.

"He does seem like quite an affable person, even with a wound to the head," she remarked.

Nick felt a distracting sensation, and it took a moment for him to identify the fact that he resented Dana's approval of Jarrett. Lord, maybe he should have his own head examined.

"Okay, so we've established that Jarrett is a wonderful guy," he said sardonically. "No enemies, just admirers. The next logical conclusion is that the attacker is angry about the dig itself."

Dana looked interested and leaned toward him. "Why would anyone be angry?" she asked.

Nick wondered if she knew what a sexy voice she had. Here she was trying to sound professional and businesslike, and all the while her voice held a hint of natural huskiness. He rubbed the back of his neck. For one reason or another, he'd gone hot under the collar.

With an effort, he concentrated on the subject of Jarrett's attacker. "Many people on the island don't like the fact that we're excavating. There are different reasons. Some islanders are afraid we'll disturb the goddess Ixchel or the ghost who haunts the temple. They say the whole island is in danger of being cursed. Others just plain dislike outsiders prying into their heritage. And still others..." Nick paused, then went on. "Let's just say that certain traders in the island's black market might resent our dig."

"Black market—what do you mean?"

Nick figured he might as well explain; it was something Dana would hear about sooner or later. "If you know where to look, this entire island is littered with Mayan artifacts—pottery, clay figurines, simple jewelry and the like. Over the years, the islanders have taken to selling these items illegally to tourists—who, for a few measly pesos, can sneak pieces of Mayan heritage out in their suitcases as souvenirs. Unfortunately, it's all become part of the island economy." Nick shook his head. "Once these antiquities get into private hands, they're lost forever."

"Can't something be done?" Dana asked.

"Ms. Morgan, I don't like it any more than you do. If I could stop the smuggling, I would. But I'm also realistic. I don't have the power to stop it. And besides, if you took away the illegal trade from this island, the already fragile economy would be threatened. The place barely survives as it is."

Dana glanced around the plaza. "It's a shame people have to sell off their past to pay for their present...."

"I'd call it a tragedy. Still, I've done the best I can under the circumstances. I have an unspoken agree-

ment with Inspector Maciel. He makes certain the illegal traders stay off my turf and I don't raise a fuss about
what they do elsewhere. At least, that's the way it's
supposed to work. Perhaps this attack on Jarrett..."
Nick stopped, preferring to keep the rest of his thoughts
to himself.

"Well, there must be someone we can question about
Jarrett—someone who knows something."

"Ms. Morgan, think about it. No one is going to
come out and admit they bashed Jarrett with a rock.
Sure, I've spoken to people—and they all deny knowing anything about what happened."

Dana tapped her fingers on the table. "I hate to feel
useless like this. Are we just going to sit around and wait
for it to happen again?"

"We'll take precautions. Meanwhile, I'll continue
investigating... without the benefit of your own for-
midable sleuthing abilities."

She seemed determined to ignore his sarcasm. She
also seemed determined to stay here and needle him.
"I'm afraid we might be missing something that's right
under our noses," she declared. "Who else works at the
dig?"

"Aside from the Montanos, other islanders pitch in
at times. Then there's Tim Reese, a university student
getting summer credit for helping. He's on the mainland right now, buying supplies."

"Anyone else?"

"You've met the rest of them. Daniel has been hanging around the dig almost from the beginning. He's a
sharp kid—maybe too sharp for his own good." The
subject of Daniel was something else again. Nick had
some worries about the kid... several worries, to be
exact. But Dana didn't need to know about those. Nick

went on. "Robert's a volunteer of sorts, Pat just got her Ph.D. in anthropology, Jarrett's the resident ethnographer and I'm the...resident pain in the ass."

Dana gave a sagacious nod. "That much I believe. But there's no one else?"

"That's it."

"I knew the dig was understaffed, but still..." She kept her musings to herself as evening darkened into night. Across the street, the lights of the gazebo glittered over the plaza. And from the windows of the café, light spilled over Dana, turning her hair a deep burnished gold.

"Ms. Morgan—" Nick began.

"You may as well call me Dana."

He gazed at her. Someone had started to thrum a guitar in the plaza, the melody carrying plaintively. The warm island breeze was sultry, stirring strands of hair against Dana's cheek. Nick had a sudden urge to touch her cheek himself, to see if her skin felt as soft as it looked.

What the hell was wrong with him? He didn't even know this woman...and he didn't want her to know *him*. What would she say if she learned how he'd messed up his life? She'd probably get up and walk away. She wouldn't sit here gazing back at him, her lips parted slightly, as if he'd caught her off guard....

He couldn't act on this raw attraction he felt, that was for sure. He had to work with Dana Morgan for as long as she remained on the island, not fantasize about her.

She dropped her gaze from his, impatiently pushing the hair away from her face. "Anyway," she said, "you can't shut me out of this thing. I want to know who attacked Jarrett—and why."

"If you're so concerned about Jarrett, go nurse the guy or something. I'm sure he'd be delighted."

She didn't budge. She remained seated stubbornly right where she was. The bored waiter, finally realizing that he had another patron, appeared with a menu for Dana. She opened it and perused it with great concentration.

"I'm famished," she announced. "This sounds good...*ceviche.*" She probably had no idea it meant marinated fish.

"That wouldn't be wise," Nick said. "Especially after your...uh, indisposition today."

Even in the hazy light, he could tell her face was turning red. "What happened this morning—it was just an aberration. My stomach's usually as—as solid as a rock."

"Except when you're contemplating an adventure," he reminded her. "That's what you told me, anyway."

She slapped her menu shut. "Everyone has...peculiarities."

He couldn't argue with that. He had his own peculiarities, for that matter. He called to the waiter and ordered a more reasonable meal for Dana—tortillas and rice. She looked put out, although she didn't object. He knew it wasn't any business of his what she ate, but he didn't want her to be sick again.

Eventually Dana's food came. "It looks delicious," she said. "Aren't you having anything to eat?"

"No." Breaking bread with her would be going too far. He was accustomed to solitary meals, and he didn't intend Dana Morgan to get any ideas otherwise.

She seemed to have exhausted all conversation and Nick didn't help her any. He tried concentrating on the activity in the plaza, but it wasn't easy. Even when he

wasn't looking at Dana, the uncomfortable awareness
of her remained. She was like some beautiful painting
he wanted to study again and again, seeking nuances he
hadn't noticed before. His gaze strayed to her. She
looked young to him, young and clear-eyed and confident. She ate with good appetite, regardless of everything that had happened today. Nick tried to remember
the last time he had enjoyed food with that type of zest.
He tried to remember the last time he'd enjoyed anything with zest. It had been a long while ago...too long
ago.

The combination of his silence and scrutiny finally
seemed to discourage Dana. She pushed her empty plate
aside, slapping some money on the table to pay for her
meal—as if to advise Nick she considered herself his
equal and didn't expect any favors.

"Good night...Nick." She stood and glanced at him
one more time. She'd used his name defiantly, emphasizing once again that she considered herself his equal.
Then she turned and strode away.

He'd succeeded in running her off, after all. She
moved with that graceful posture of hers, and Nick
suspected her mother had made her walk around with
a book on her head. Dana Morgan seemed like the type
of woman who would have adoring parents somewhere, beaming over her accomplishments. She'd
probably even grown up in a house with a white picket
fence and some happy mutt of a dog.

She turned the corner toward the hotel, and he could
no longer see her. Feeling vaguely dissatisfied, he ordered another Coke. He just hoped Dana didn't last
long on the island. For his own peace of mind, he hoped
he could make her leave.

CHAPTER THREE

LATE NEXT MORNING, Dana sat cross-legged under the shade of a palm, drinking another lukewarm orange soda. If there was one thing she'd learned so far, it was that the tropical heat of Isla Calamar produced an endless thirst in her. It made her long to go find the beach and jump into the waters of the Caribbean. However, Dana's busy schedule with Dr. Petrie allowed no time for frivolous activities such as swimming. It was surprising that he had permitted her even this short break. She'd spent the entire morning with him at the excavation site, learning her duties. Robert and Pat were off together, making preparations to open a new site. Apparently young Daniel had business elsewhere today, and none of the other islanders had appeared—which left Dana alone with Nick. Not the most comfortable of situations.

Jarrett, meanwhile, was recovering well, but the kindly old village doctor had advised complete bed rest for the next few days. Dana had taken it upon herself to make sure the doctor's orders were strictly observed. Ignoring Jarrett's protests, she'd left him under the charge of the hotelkeeper. From the beginning, the hotelkeeper had seemed to enjoy allying herself with Dana. In spite of the language barrier, they were both women, after all, out to convince Jarrett they knew what was best for him.

Nick, however, had followed his own agenda. Dana seriously doubted anyone could tell *him* what to do. He had spent the night camped out at the dig, lying in wait should the attacker return. Nothing untoward had happened, and Nick had come back to the village to announce that work would proceed as usual. He'd seemed determined to have the excavations progress— no matter what.

And so he had made sure that Dana was very busy all morning. They'd thoroughly gone over the charts of stratum analysis she'd be updating in minute detail, as well as other complex field notes that would be her responsibility. Nick had also introduced her to the actual tools she'd be using. Screens, brushes, plumb lines, rods, trowels, shovels—and yes, her bare hands. Archaeology was definitely a hands-on experience.

All in all, it had been a most instructive morning— but a tense one, too. Dana couldn't seem to relax around Dr. Nicholas Petrie. His presence was simply too... forceful. At the moment, for instance, he sat across from Dana, frowning over the rim of his own orange soda, lost in thoughts she couldn't even begin to imagine. She felt edgy in his proximity, yet her gaze kept straying to him, tracing the bold, hard lines of his face. Dana didn't understand her confusing reactions to Nick. She far preferred more straightforward feelings. Usually, either she liked someone or she didn't, and that was that. But with Nick Petrie, the words *like* and *dislike* were much too tame. After all, Dana couldn't very well say that she merely *disliked* the uneasiness that Nick caused her, or that she *liked* his unquestionable virility. More potent words were needed....

Dana shifted uneasily at the direction of her thoughts, and this seemed to prompt Nick from his own musings. He gave her a disparaging look.

"Why the hell didn't anyone tell me you'd never worked on a dig before?" he asked.

"I can't be responsible for the lack of communication between you and the Institute," Dana said, immediately on the defensive. "Besides, you need a soil expert—and I'm a soil expert."

"The way you tell it, you've spent the last six years cooped up in a lab. That's no experience for the type of work we do here."

The disgust in his tone rankled her, and she treated him to a frown of her own. "Look, I have the knowledge you need. I received my master's from Adams College in Missouri, a very respectable school. And the Simonson Labs in Saint Louis are at the very forefront of agricultural research."

He didn't say anything, but he didn't need to. His expression was more than eloquent, seeming to convey the opinion that her stint at the labs had been one step above a jail sentence.

Maybe Dana was so annoyed because that was how *she'd* felt at her job. She'd been simply one more employee in a large impersonal firm, facing the same routine day after day. Yes...it had been a jail sentence of sorts.

Dana tightened her grip on the soda. "You should be aware that I also grew up on a farm in Missouri. I know soil as well as anyone you'll find—farm soil. Considering that you're trying to prove Mayan farmers actually made a go of it on this island—don't you think I'm qualified for the job?"

He didn't answer. He just went on studying her. For some reason, all he wanted to do was point out her deficiencies. He wanted to think the worst of her.

"Why did you decide to come here?" Nick muttered at last. "You just wanted some type of diversion, is that it? An adventure, as you keep putting it."

Dana cursed herself for growing too voluble during the course of the morning. She'd confided in Nick her need for new experiences in her life...in other words, adventure. But maybe it was time to give him something else to think about.

"Do you want to know why I really tossed everything aside and came flying down to Mexico? I'll tell you why. It's because...because I proposed to a man and he turned me down flat."

She certainly appeared to have captured Nick's interest. He stirred a little. "You're here because of your love life?"

"Exactly. I asked Alan to marry me, he said no—and here I am." She took a thoughtful sip of her soda. "I wasted a lot of effort on that proposal, you know. I planned everything out so carefully. The flowers, the candles, the music. Scented beeswax candles, of course, and a centerpiece of blue clematis."

"I suppose you're going to tell me what kind of music you used to serenade the guy," Nick said in a long-suffering tone.

Dana sighed. "Alan's always been partial to country music. Not that it did me any good. He simply ate his chicken fricassee and told me he'd be perfectly happy if he went on sleeping over at my place four nights a week. I suppose after that I just snapped. I knew I had to change my life. I applied to the Mesoamerica Institute, quit my job at the lab, dumped Alan. Pretty much in that order." Dana started to wish she hadn't blurted this out, after all. It was rather a pathetic story—proposing to a man and having him turn you down. It didn't make her sound particularly on top of things, and Nick was contemplating her as if he couldn't believe what he'd just heard.

Yet breaking off with Alan was one of the best things Dana had ever done. It was proof that she knew how to start a new life...a better life. She was proud of herself for that, but she didn't know how to explain it to Nick Petrie. Maybe, where Nick was concerned, it would be better *not* to explain. Everything she said only seemed to make him more skeptical about her.

She tried to be businesslike. "I think I've had enough of a break. We ought to get back to work—and I want to return to the village as soon as possible to check on Jarrett."

Now Nick's expression became inscrutable. "Jarrett again," he commented. "You keep mentioning him."

"I have to admit he's foremost on my mind. After what happened to him yesterday, it seems we have to be aware of danger."

"There are dangers on this island, all right," Nick said quietly. His tone of voice seemed ominous to her, and she gave him a quick glance.

"What do you mean?"

"For one thing, Ms. Morgan...you're sitting under a coconut palm. A stiff breeze and the hazards should be obvious."

Dana glanced up and saw the cluster of coconuts dangling fifty feet above her head. Nick Petrie's unexpected sense of humor manifested itself at the most exasperating times. She scrambled to her feet and stalked away from the palm.

"Dammit, I wonder if you take the attack on Jarrett seriously at all."

He rose to stand beside her, his face suddenly grim. "I take it very seriously, Dana. Until we know what happened, I want you to be careful. Stay aware of what's going on around you."

"Yes . . . of course I will." But it was another type of awareness that concerned her at the moment. Much to her dismay, she was feeling it again—that connection to Nick. All her senses seemed attuned to him. She saw the steady rise and fall of his chest under the sweat-dampened cloth of his shirt and suddenly she knew that she had to get away from him. She didn't understand why he affected her this way. She didn't want to understand.

And then it happened. Nick raised his hand and touched her cheek. His fingers were very warm, his skin roughened from digging in the earth. And so his touch was warm and rough and gentle all at once. But there was nothing gentle about her reaction. Heat rippled through her, a heat that had nothing to do with the tropical weather.

Nick's gaze held hers—intense, uncompromising. And she knew of a surety that he, too, felt what she did: an attraction that was sexual and yet something more, as if they'd met in some other lifetime and only now had stumbled across each other's path again.

Dana felt afraid in a way she'd never known before. She pulled away from Nick and hurried to find work to do—any work.

There were dangers on this island, indeed. The greatest danger of all was Nick Petrie.

SEVERAL DAYS LATER someone stole Nick's machete. Nick went through the tools one more time, just to make sure. But he already knew it wasn't there: his machete, the only one he used. He always brought it back to the hut, along with the other tools. This project operated on such a meager budget that he couldn't afford to lose anything, no matter how basic. And there was something else to consider. After the unexplained attack on Jarrett, any unusual incident had to be noted and investigated.

Nick straightened up, trying to stifle his irritation. A few minutes earlier, he'd questioned the others. Everyone, including Dana, said they hadn't seen the machete.

Nick felt something tighten in his gut, just thinking about Dana Morgan. She'd now been on the island almost two weeks, and she'd proven herself to be a hard, efficient worker. Maybe she'd never been on a dig before, but she was a quick learner. He couldn't fault her there. No... what really bothered him was the way her presence permeated the damn place. No woman had ever had quite this effect on him, not even his ex-wife. It was an aberration. Lord, they always said alcohol killed your brain cells. Maybe that had happened to him, after too many years of drinking. He'd killed off any sense he had, and now he spent his time daydreaming about his soil scientist.

There was another possible explanation. He hadn't had sex in so long, no wonder he was overreacting to Dana. She was beautiful and innocently sensual enough to disturb all his concentration. He couldn't figure out why she seemed untouched in some basic way. She'd made it clear that she'd had at least one lover—the guy who hadn't been swayed by her marriage proposal. Therefore she wasn't inexperienced. . . .

He had to stop speculating about Dana, sexually or otherwise. He had enough problems as it was. Then it occurred to Nick. He couldn't remember the last time he'd had sex and been sober at the same time. For all he knew, he couldn't even function without alcohol in his bloodstream. That was a joke, all right. Not a humorous one, but he almost laughed.

Daniel poked his head into the hut just then. "I've looked everywhere, Señor Petrie. No machete."

"Figures. Thanks for checking, anyway, Daniel. Have a seat." Nick tossed the kid a can of pineapple juice and popped one open for himself. He settled down behind his rickety field desk, while Daniel appropriated one of the camp stools and they shared several moments of companionable silence. Daniel was only thirteen, but already he'd learned the art of keeping his mouth shut. As far as Nick was concerned, it was a skill more people needed to master.

Nick studied the boy. Daniel claimed to live in the village, although he was always vague about his family's identity. Nick suspected the kid was on his own. He was too darn skinny, for one thing. And every day he wore the same clothes: a rumpled plaid shirt with two buttons missing, a pair of threadbare shorts and sandals with frayed straps.

Nick tore open a bag of potato chips and offered some to Daniel. The kid shook his head. Maybe he'd drink some juice now and then with Nick, but he seemed to make it a point of honor to decline food. Evidently being too skinny was part of his independence.

"I had breakfast before I came," he said.

"What did your mom fix for you?" Nick asked casually. "Or maybe your dad does the cooking."

Daniel looked wary. "I had *plátanos fritos*—fried plantains. They were pretty good."

The kid was smart, all right. He didn't overexplain, didn't invent elaborate stories about a family—stories that might be too easily detected as falsifications. Instead he offered as little information as possible, stubbornly and persistently protecting his own privacy.

Nick tried another tactic. "You do good work around here, Daniel. I could use you more often, if you have the time."

The boy's expression grew more wary still. "I'm busy, Señor Petrie. I come here as often as I can." Now Daniel made it clear *he* was the one who required silence, swigging his pineapple juice with concentration.

Nick drained his own juice and aimed the empty can at the wastebasket across from him. He tried to respect Daniel's pride and independence, sensing an affinity with the kid. Hell, Nick understood the need for privacy better than anyone. But at the same time, he sensed an underlying need in Daniel.... Still, the kid just wouldn't let anyone get too close. He wouldn't let Nick get too close, that was for sure.

Daniel pitched his juice can at the wastebasket, his aim as accurate as Nick's. Then he stood and went to stare out the door of the hut, hands jammed into the pockets of his shorts.

"There she is—*la rubia*," Daniel said in a scoffing tone. "She smiles too much."

Nick considered this; he hadn't caught Dana Morgan smiling too much in his own direction.

"She works too hard—and she's too pretty," Daniel went on, in this peculiar catalog of Dana's faults.

"I hadn't noticed about the pretty part," Nick said gruffly.

"Sure." Daniel glanced at Nick with disfavor. "You look at her all the time, Señor Petrie."

The kid was observant, along with everything else. "So she's pretty," Nick acknowledged. "But I have a feeling she won't be around this island for long. She'll get tired of ornery people like me—and like you, Daniel. Whenever she tries to talk to you, I've noticed you don't even give her a chance."

Daniel shrugged. "I don't have time." That was his usual convenient excuse for withdrawing from other people, and he used it now. "Have to go, Señor Petrie."

"Wait—aren't you forgetting something?" Nick asked. "It's payday."

Daniel stood reluctantly as Nick fished in his pocket, extracting more pesos than he could well afford. But he always gave Daniel a generous rate of exchange. It was the only way he knew to get around the kid's stubborn pride.

Even so, Daniel eyed the money distrustfully, and it was only grudgingly that he finally stuffed it into his pocket.

"*Adiós,*" he mumbled.

"Daniel, be careful out there. We still haven't caught Jarrett's attacker—"

But already the kid was gone, as elusive as ever. An unwelcome thought occurred to Nick. Maybe Daniel had been the one to take the machete; it was something he'd be able to sell. At the same time it was a relatively small item, easily concealed. And no matter what Daniel said, he was obviously struggling just to survive....

Nick moved restlessly to the door of the hut. He didn't like the way he'd become suspicious ever since the attack on Jarrett. He preferred to rely on what his instincts told him. Daniel would do everything he could to make it from one day to the next, but he possessed certain rigid standards for himself. He wouldn't stoop to stealing that machete. The kid needed a break, more than anything else.

Nick emerged from the hut into the dazzling sunlight. It seemed that whenever the sun had a chance to break through the jungle canopy, it burned all the brighter. He shaded his eyes and glanced around. Pat was in the midst of talking intently to Robert and Tim— Pat was always going on about something or other. Robert listened with an air of detached amusement and Tim listened with a mournful expression on his face. No one could accuse Tim of enthusiasm. Nick still hadn't figured out why the guy was studying archaeology, or why he chose to spend his summer on a dig; he seemed to have no true affinity for the work. Once again, Nick cursed his meager budget and his meager crew.

Now his gaze strayed to Dana and Jarrett. Dana was working, using one of the sifters, but Jarrett simply watched her as she sorted a soil sample. Jarrett seemed taken with Dana. But who wouldn't be taken with her? She was *la rubia*—the golden-haired one, as Daniel had called her. Nick himself seemed capable of nothing more than standing here, watching the way the sun lit up her molten cascade of hair and the way khaki and denim traced the curves of her body so enticingly.

Just then Dana glanced up and saw Nick. She waved cheerfully, pushing up the brim of her hat. Jarrett turned and waved, too. He didn't seem perturbed to be caught standing around, doing nothing but ogling a pretty woman. Under Dana's influence, Jarrett appeared to be prolonging his recuperation as much as possible.

Nick didn't want to watch the two of them together anymore. He turned abruptly and forged his way through the brush. When he came out near the temple, it was like entering a different world. Here the trees cast a dense shade, as if seeking to reclaim the shrine and cover it once more with vines and moss. Nick paced off the base of the shrine, reaffirming the calculations he'd made a few days earlier. Lately he'd developed a notion about the temple that wouldn't let go of him. Wishful thinking, maybe that's all it was. No doubt he was looking for a way to jump start his career again. But, still, the notion had taken hold of him and wouldn't let go....

In his reports to the Institute, he continued to assert that his main goal was ascertaining the viability and extent of Mayan farming on the island. He hadn't yet mentioned anything about his theory in regard to the temple. This was his idea alone for now, whatever its worth might be.

He heard a rustle in the bamboo stalks nearby, and swiveled around to see Dana striding toward him. Nick frowned at her.

"What the hell are you doing, traipsing around by yourself? I told you to be careful."

"I am being careful," she said imperturbably.

"Jarrett shouldn't have allowed you to wander off alone."

"Jarrett is very chivalrous, but I declined his company. I decided that it's time for me to...well, it's time I climbed the temple steps."

She had a determined look that he was already coming to recognize. "Remember what the superstition says," he cautioned. "Anyone who ventures here is subject to misfortune."

Dana only looked all the more determined. She faced the temple and slowly climbed the first few steps. She appeared almost reverent as she reached the first ledge, but then she seemed to gain confidence. She climbed to the next ledge and then the next, until she'd reached all the way to the top. For a moment she gazed inside the altar room. Then she turned and sat down.

"There," she called to Nick. "It's too late now. I did it...and I don't see any lightning in the sky. I don't hear any thunder."

He climbed up and sat beside her. "Didn't I tell you the rest of the story? It takes a while for the misfortune to strike. Your chances of escaping it are a whole lot better if you leave the island."

"You can stop hoping, Nick. I won't leave." She took off her canvas hat and rested it on her knee. Perspiration had curled strands of hair next to her face. Nick studied her profile, lingering on the decisive outline of her features. Dana had mentioned that she'd grown up on a farm in Missouri, and she did look like someone who'd spent years riding horses, milking cows and such. She was wholesome and seductive all at once. Lord, what a combination.

"I saw Daniel hurrying away, as usual," she said, treating Nick to her clear, straightforward gaze. "He seems to trust only you—he never stops to talk to anyone else."

Nick's own gaze dropped to Dana's mouth. Her lips were tinged a natural shade of rose. He rubbed the back of his neck distractedly. "The kid's already advised me in so many words that you're trouble, Dana. Big trouble.'' He heard the thickness in his voice and felt that clench of need in his gut.

Dana stared at him, a rose color tinting her face as well as her lips now. "I'm doing my job, Dr. Petrie. Nothing else should matter to you."

She was right about that much, but it was already too late. The need, the wanting in him took over...and without another word, he drew Dana into his arms.

CHAPTER FOUR

NICK WAS OUT OF practice with this sort of thing, and it didn't go well. Dana was stiff and unyielding in his arms, as if he'd caught her by surprise and she didn't know what to do about it. Hell, he'd caught himself by surprise. But he went on holding her a second longer, moving his cheek against hers, feeling the softness of her skin. She smelled faintly of soap—clean, fresh soap. It made Nick imagine her bathing under the hot island sun. It made him imagine too much....

The way he figured it, they both pulled away from each other at the same time. Dana frowned at him, her cheeks flushed.

"Darn it, Nick—what do you think you're doing?"

"You tell me," he muttered, running a hand through his hair. "Look ... just forget it happened."

She stood quickly, and her silly canvas hat went tumbling down. Nick bent to retrieve it.

"Thank you," she said acidly and she jammed the hat back on her head. It was the kind of hat straight out of a safari movie. Nick could imagine Dana marching into a store and requesting a full complement of adventure gear, right down to the patch-pocket shorts and mosquito netting. For a moment, that almost made him smile. He had to get a grip on himself.

"You shouldn't have come looking for me," he said.

Her flush deepened. "If you think I wanted this to happen—dammit, I didn't want anything from you. I didn't intend for anything to happen!"

"Neither did I."

She took a deep breath. "It was a mistake."

He didn't say any more. He just went on standing there with her in front of the altar room of the temple. Against his will, his gaze lingered on Dana's face...on the creamy rose of her skin, the deep brown of her eyes, the sensual curve of her mouth....

"Don't look at me like that," she said, almost in a whisper. She turned and hurriedly began making her way down the temple steps. She didn't seem to be watching where she was going. Nick came along beside her and halfway down he reached out to steady her.

She pulled away from him. "Don't."

"You're overreacting just a little, don't you think?" he said gruffly.

She stared at him, a variety of emotions seeming to cross her expressive face. That she was angry, there could be no doubt...maybe even a little embarrassed. In the end, Nick had the feeling that pride won out.

"I didn't come looking for you, Nick," she said in a cool voice. "All I wanted to do was climb the temple steps." With that, she descended the rest of the way, refusing any assistance from him.

When they'd reached the base of the temple, Dana started veering off toward the trees. "Goodbye," she said.

He didn't allow her to escape, falling into step beside her. "You're not going anywhere alone—remember?"

"I wish you'd realize that I can take care of myself," she muttered.

"Just follow orders, Ms. Morgan, and you'll make it easier for both of us."

He could tell she was still fired up. She made a point of striding ahead of him, finding her own path. Even as she pushed through the thick undergrowth of the forest, she moved with that graceful posture of hers. When they reached the excavation site, she stalked over to the knapsack she'd left propped near one of the huts. She pulled out some insect repellent and slathered herself with the stuff, glancing defiantly at Nick. Maybe she was trying to send him a message. Then she went back to work at the sifter.

Nick got to work himself. He wanted to forget what had happened with Dana.... He just wished it was that simple.

DANA HAD NEVER REALIZED that her body possessed so many muscles—and that they could all ache with such simultaneous insistence. By now she'd spent two weeks on the island, and her main activities seemed to be crouching to dig in the soil, crouching to carry the soil, crouching to sift the soil. This morning, her knees hurt. Her elbows hurt. Her back hurt. The insides of her thighs hurt. Hell, her whole body hurt. Perspiration trickled down her back. And she thought she'd throttle Pat if she had to listen to the woman one more minute.

Today Pat and Dana were working at the new site. Pat was marking off measurements on the ground while discoursing on her career prospects—clearly a favorite topic.

"I've applied to every Ivy League school—including a few with poison ivy." Pat gave a smirk. "The job market is very tight, let me tell you. That's why I'm here. *This* job is only a stopgap...."

Dana did her best to tune out Pat. She pulled the brim of her hat down lower, squinting at the grid chart she was trying to map. The sun seemed to bounce right off the page and into her eyes. She was learning just how precise and nitpicky archaeologists had to be. Findings of any type had to be categorized down to their minutiae. Pottery shards, scraps of obsidian, bone fragments, traces of ancient seeds and kernels—these were the treasures accumulated on the dig. No discovery was too small to go unrecorded. Dana's own particular skills as a soil scientist also required precise documentation. Soil profiles, soil maps, soil surveys and chemical analysis charts all fell within her purview. When Dana wasn't crouching and digging and sifting, she was writing and graphing and cross-referencing.

But who was she kidding? No matter how she occupied herself, her thoughts kept returning to Nick Petrie. *Dr.* Nicholas Petrie, her irascible boss.

Two days earlier she had sat beside Nick on the temple steps and he'd taken her into his arms. It had been the briefest of embraces, and they hadn't even kissed. Why, then, did Dana keep replaying those few seconds in her mind, over and over? It was almost as if Nick had imprinted himself on her senses. Even now she remembered the feel of his arms around her, his gentle strength, the touch of his cheek against hers, the warmth pervading her body at his nearness....

She stared unseeing at the grid chart before her. Vaguely she tuned in to Pat's voice.

"You really have to watch yourself," Pat was saying. "You can't get desperate. I mean, if you take the first job that comes along, you could be making a *big* mistake. I still tend to wonder if I made the right move, signing on at this—"

Dana simply didn't have the patience for one more word. "You're an archaeologist. You're doing archaeology. What's the problem?"

Pat seemed nonplussed for a moment, but then she started up again. She was hardly ever at a loss for words. "You have to understand, Dana. It'd be wonderful if I could just forget about everything else and enjoy what I'm doing. Really, it would be. But I have to think about my future. Who doesn't? The academic world is such an incredibly narrow-minded place, and you have to take careful steps while building your career." Whenever Pat mentioned the academic world, she did so with a mixture of reverence and scorn.

"And make no mistake about it, Dana. That's why I'm here—I'm building my career. Despite the relative unimportance of this dig, Nick's name still carries with it a certain amount of weight—although even that's starting to wane...."

Nick again. Perhaps in the larger world his influence had waned, but here on this island he dominated. His crew members might resent his autocratic methods, but they invariably obeyed his instructions. He demanded the best from people and he worked the hardest himself. For all his apparent cynicism, this project had to mean something to him.

Dana glanced around the small clearing, where they'd barely started the preliminaries for the new excavation—the surface survey and the plotting out of test pits. If they were very lucky, eventually they'd find evidence of Mayan crops—maize, beans, squash. This would tell them more about ancient settlement patterns on the island, but it would probably not add significant new information to knowledge of Mayan farming. In many ways, it was tedious, thankless work. That couldn't be denied....

"This island *is* important," Dana said. "All you have to do is think about the people who walked here a thousand years ago. And now we're trying to re-create their lives—it's very exciting."

Pat gave Dana a condescending glance. "I suppose I sounded like you on my first dig. Overexcited, overenthusiastic. You'll get *over* it—trust me." Another smirk. Then, in an emphatic manner, Pat tied a string to a marker in the ground, her sandy hair falling into her face. Pat always looked as if she'd grown impatient halfway through the task of straightening her collar and combing her hair; she was perpetually a bit rumpled and scattered in appearance.

"Nick's the one who really had it made," Pat remarked after a moment. "With everything he'd accomplished on Mayan hieroglyphics, he had tenure before he was thirty—can you believe it? At Deacon University, no less. A very exclusive, very pretentious school. Anyway, Nick was on top of it. He was set for life...and then he just tossed it all away. Of course, after what happened to him, I guess it's understandable."

Dana gritted her teeth in frustration. Was there no way to shut Pat up? Was there no way to escape the subject of Nick? It was bad enough for Dana to be dwelling on the man, but now Pat was making mysterious comments about him. Dana had to erase a few lines on her page and start over. She resisted for a short while, but then at last she gave in.

"Okay, out with it. Exactly what happened to Nick?"

Pat shrugged. She obviously enjoyed having the inside story, as well as dangling her knowledge before the less informed. "Family tragedy," she said enigmatically.

Tragedy... Dana thought of the pain she'd seen shadowing Nick's face now and again. "What was it?" she asked, almost fearful of hearing the answer. But now Pat was hedging.

"His wife left him over it, that much is for sure."

"Just spit it out, Pat!"

"I'm not aware of all the details," Pat said defensively. "That wasn't the point I was making. The fact is, whatever the reason, Nick threw away his career."

So Pat didn't really have the inside story—she just liked to pretend that she did. Dana felt like an idiot for taking the bait. She reminded herself firmly that Nick's private life was none of her business and tried to concentrate once again on the grid sheet in front of her.

Pat went back to her measurements, but nothing seemed to dampen her zeal for conversation. "I'll bet Jarrett knows more about Nick. Jarrett's always dropping little hints about people. You know the type of thing—nasty little gibes, backhanded compliments."

Dana glanced up in surprise. "I've never heard him say anything like that. Jarrett strikes me as...courteous. That's really the only word to describe him."

"He must be trying to make a good impression," Pat said shrewdly. "I think he's sweet on you."

"Not likely," Dana muttered. But Jarrett did seem to pay her a lot of attention, helping her with her work, making sure all her questions were answered.

Pat placed another marker in the ground. "Tell the truth, Dana. Jarrett's a good-looking guy, and there isn't much entertainment on this island. Can't you see yourself and him—"

"No."

"How about one of the others, then?" Pat sat back on her heels; obviously she'd embarked on a subject of real interest. "Okay, there's Tim. A little wet behind the ears, unfortunately. He must be what—all of twenty?"

"More like eighteen, I'd think."

"No, he's been in college too long," Pat pronounced. "The way I understand it, anthropology is at least his third major—he just can't make up his mind what to study. He lives off some kind of trust fund, can you believe it? Just a monthly stipend, of course, but still—"

"Pat, I'm trying to draw this damn grid."

"You're as curious about the guys as I am," Pat said imperturbably. "But you're right, Tim isn't much of a prospect. As for Nick...well, he *is* very sexy, with all that brooding disillusionment. Suppressed intensity, that's Nick. It might be interesting to be around when he stops suppressing—don't you think?"

Dana made a great effort to concentrate on her graph sheet. She needed to replicate on paper what Pat was marking off on the site. All measurements would be checked for accuracy against their original calculations....

It was hopeless, of course. Dana now had a more vivid image than ever of Nick imprinted on her mind. According to Pat, he was a man who had endured some type of family tragedy, and that only made him seem more...compelling. A man who guarded some deep sorrow behind that gruff exterior....

"The way I understand it, Nick's ex-wife is completely out of the picture," Pat went on inexorably. "There's no other woman in his life that I can tell. In a manner of speaking, he's available—in spite of that don't-touch attitude of his."

Dana tightened her grip on her pencil. "I'm not interested in Nick or anyone else," she said, keeping her voice carefully neutral.

"You will be. After you've been on a dig for a while, you find out things get pretty chummy. It's the isolation, and all of us being stuck together like this."

Dana finally gave up on her graph, tossing her clipboard down. "It won't happen to me," she declared. "I won't let it. I've had enough of men for a while."

"This sounds intriguing," Pat murmured, clasping her arms around her knees. "Let me guess. You're here to escape a broken heart."

"Hardly anything so melodramatic." Dana paused, but something about Pat inspired confidences. Maybe it was just the possibility of shutting her up for a moment. "The truth is," Dana continued, "I wasted too many years on the wrong man. When I finally woke up to that fact, I got rid of him. And now I'm finally free. Why ruin that?" Just saying the words out loud gave Dana much needed perspective. After all, she'd practically lived with Alan four long years. If she'd been able to get him out of her life, then certainly she could control this very inconvenient attraction to Nick Petrie, a man she'd known only a short while. Nick had certainly made it clear that *he* wanted to dismiss this attraction between them. The past two days he'd spoken to Dana only when absolutely necessary—and he was outright grouchy whenever they did encounter each other. So obviously the best thing for both of them would be to forget their embrace on the temple steps....

Pat was following her own line of thought. She sighed exuberantly. "I broke up with someone a few months ago myself," she said. "The whole thing was bad news.

One day he'd act like he worshiped me, the next he'd say I drove him nuts.... Go figure."

Not a difficult scenario for Dana to imagine, not difficult in the least. "Do you mind if we change the subject?" she asked. "I'd just as soon not talk about men."

"Let's see," Pat went on unabashedly. "Tim, Nick, Jarrett...that only leaves Robert. A Frenchman with a beard. I don't think I've ever met a more argumentative person in my life. He challenges everything I say about archaeology, always insisting on relevant facts and empirical evidence to support my ideas. He's annoying, aggravating, pestering.... Is it any wonder that I'm so in love with the guy?"

This last statement caught Dana completely off guard. In the blink of an eye, the expression on Pat's face had turned from cocky to defenseless, and suddenly she looked like a very young woman as she knelt there with her topographical map and large spool of string...very young and very vulnerable.

"Why, Pat. Have you told him how you feel?"

"Are you nuts?" Pat exclaimed. "The guy's a complete mystery to me. I just can't get a handle on him, no matter how hard I try. I don't even know if he's married or single. I don't know if he's actually *French*, for that matter. Wouldn't you say his accent is a little off?"

"It seems totally natural—nothing overdone about it."

"That's just it," Pat said darkly. "It's too perfect. Everything about him is perfect...especially the beard. That really does something to me, you know—a man with a beard." She positioned another marker in the ground and for a few moments actually seemed lost in her own thoughts. The unexpected silence was almost disconcerting as Dana picked up her clipboard again. But then a rustle came from the nearby forest and both Tim and Robert appeared.

"Speak of the devil," Pat whispered to Dana. Then she called out to the two men in her usual strident manner. "We were just talking about you...both of you, in fact. We were compiling a dossier, so to speak."

Robert strolled through the clearing, hands tucked casually into the pockets of his crisp khaki pants. He addressed Dana. "Pat is convinced she'll discover some fascinating secret in all our pasts. Has she been entertaining you with her speculations?"

Dana smiled noncommittally. "You'd be surprised how much work we've accomplished this morning."

"You're discreet, Ms. Morgan—an admirable virtue." Robert smiled back at her with a striking glimpse of charm. Dana supposed he was handsome, with his reddish hair, neatly trimmed beard and aristocratic bearing.

Tim, meanwhile, had brought along some fresh mangoes. Without saying a word, he handed the fruit to the others and then moved to sit hunch shouldered in the dirt. Tim was pale complexioned, with a bony, angular frame. There was a rawness to him, as if he hadn't yet settled into his own body.

"We thought it was time for everyone to take a break," Robert said, playing the part of host. "We've all been working hard, and it's an exceptionally hot day." Robert didn't look as if the heat disturbed him in the least, however. He seemed entirely cool and composed. He even ate his mango with neatness and control, although everyone else had juice dribbling down their chin. Mangoes were notoriously messy fruit—but not for Robert, it seemed.

"What about Jarrett? And Nick?" Dana added before she could stop herself. Here she was, bringing up Nick's name and wondering about him again.

"Haven't you figured it out yet, Dana?" Pat said. "Nick and Jarrett are management. Head honcho and number-two honcho. The rest of us are just the hired help. Now and then they have to make that fact clear to us, so they refuse to socialize."

"Nick perhaps likes to keep his distance," Robert observed. "But not Jarrett. He is always amicable."

"Why is everyone defending Jarrett today?" Pat asked. "He's not a saint. He can be downright nasty when he chooses."

"I haven't seen that," Dana said, putting in her two cents' worth. "I really don't know what you're talking about."

"Bravo, Ms. Morgan. We don't want to encourage Pat. She wishes to believe she is an authority on human nature."

Pat frowned at him. "I *am* an observer of human nature. I see things other people miss. Take you, for instance, Robert. I can tell you're hiding something. You want us to believe you're some wealthy French businessman, but you won't even say what business you're in. If that's not suspicious, what is?"

Robert seemed to enjoy provoking Pat, and by the looks of things he was particularly adept at it. He smiled again—an economical sort of smile, as if he didn't believe in wasting too much amusement at one time. "I've asked you to believe nothing about me—you draw your own conclusions. Next you'll accuse me of being the one who hit Jarrett over the head with a rock."

"Well, it could have been you," Pat argued. "I mean, you weren't working here with me the entire morning. You went off by yourself for a while, I recall. And you didn't tell me where you were going...."

"An obvious sign of guilt. Tell me, Pat. What would be my motive for the attack? If you are such a perspicacious observer, you will have a theory."

"Anything's possible."

"I believe that is what is known as a cop-out, Pat."

"Oh, stuff a sock in it."

"I do so enjoy these colloquialisms of yours."

Dana took another bite of mango, her fingers sticky with juice. She recalled what Pat had just told her about being in love with Robert and tried to picture the two of them actually getting together. Somehow that didn't seem a likely prospect. It wasn't just the fact that they were always at odds with each other. They looked nothing alike. Pat was pretty, but she gave a flyaway rumpled impression next to Robert's elegance. Even her athletic build contrasted with his compactness.

At any rate, Dana felt she'd had enough of listening to the two of them. She moved over to where Tim sat in self-imposed solitude.

"How's it going?" she asked in a conversational tone.

"Okay," Tim muttered. He stared at his half-eaten mango as if he had neither the energy nor inclination to finish it.

"It does seem hotter than usual today, doesn't it?" Dana remarked. "It's a sort of closed-in feeling...as if there's a storm pressing."

Tim exerted himself enough to glance up at the sky. "It's sunny."

"Yes, but even so I think a storm is coming. I knew days like this in Missouri.... My dad always liked to

joke that I could predict weather better than the weath-
erman.''

This elicited only a shrug. Despite Dana's efforts to
draw him out, Tim was short-winded in the extreme. It
became a challenge to get anything out of him at all.

Dana wondered wryly if she was losing her touch with
younger people. She'd made no headway in her at-
tempts to befriend young Daniel so far, and now Tim
resisted her endeavors.

"So—I'm from Missouri," Dana tried again. "How
about you?"

Tim gave her an indifferent glance. "Colorado."

"Hey, Tim. Tell her about that trust fund of yours."
Pat called out this remark from nearly a dozen feet
away. Evidently even distance couldn't contain her in-
quisitive nature. "What a shame you can't get at the
principal," she continued. "Then you could be vaca-
tioning in Cancún instead of sweltering away on this
poor excuse of an island."

Robert immediately began to chastise her. "You're an
incredibly nosy person, Pat. Tim's financial status is his
own concern."

"Nosy... I'm not nosy in the least. I just like to be
informed...."

As Robert and Pat started in on each other once
more, Dana tried to give Tim a reassuring smile. "She
doesn't mean to be rude. I think in her own way, Pat
believes prying into people's lives is a way to make
friends."

Tim's shoulders seemed to raise another fraction or
so. He was quiet for so long, Dana thought he might
have forgotten she was there. Then finally he looked
straight into Dana's eyes and spoke up. "I never wanted
my parents to leave me that damn trust," he said in a

low voice. "Sometimes I just wish they'd thrown the money away. And I wish they'd thrown away all their expectations along with it."

Tim rose to his feet with surprising agility and went to the forest's edge. He stood there, staring through the trees as if he longed to lose himself among them. Dana wondered just what expectations his parents had bequeathed to him. They must be heavy, indeed. Even now his shoulders were still hunched, as if he actually carried some invisible burden on them.

But then the vine-laden branches nearby rustled again, and this time it was Jarrett who emerged into the clearing. He looked worried.

"Something's happened," he said without preamble. "Something unfortunate. Nick wants to see all of you—right away!"

CHAPTER FIVE

DANA COULD TELL THAT Nick was very angry. He paced back and forth in front of the huts, his expression grim. The entire crew had trooped back from the new site and now stood clustered before him. Young Daniel had also joined the group, but he stood slightly apart, his expression guarded as he watched Nick.

"Someone has stolen artifacts from the lab," Nick bit out at last. "The painted water jugs we found last week are missing—as are the two unbroken grindstones and remnants of seeds."

Dana listened in growing dismay. The larger of the huts served as a field lab, where finds and records were kept in careful order. Even the slightest disturbance could mean a loss of essential information. But actual theft... The ancient grinding stones and water jugs had been some of the most precious discoveries made at the dig—surviving unharmed all these centuries. And recently Nick had unearthed a pit that had contained carbonized seeds and maize cobs surely at least a thousand years old....

"It's clear someone is trying to send a message," Nick said harshly. "First the attack on Jarrett, and now this."

"Are we sure the incidents are related?" Robert asked. "They are disparate in character, after all."

Robert didn't seem overly disturbed. He showed merely curiosity.

"Malice was involved each time," Nick said, his voice dangerously quiet now. "I intend to find out exactly why these things are happening. If any of you has something to tell me, you'd better do it now."

"It could have been done by anyone on the island," Dana said. "Anyone at all."

Nick gave her a cutting look. "I'm well aware it could have been anyone," he said, his voice still quiet. His eyes were an icy blue. But surely he couldn't suspect her.... She stared back at him, her own resentment beginning to spark.

Apparently Pat had been silent too long, and words began to spill out of her. "Robert doesn't know what he's talking about—of course the incidents must be related. They could be an expression of resentment, or—"

"I'm not asking you to speculate. I'm just asking you to tell me what you know." Now Nick's repressive gaze centered on Pat. She made as if to say more, but then clamped her mouth shut.

Jarrett spoke in conciliatory fashion. "I'm sure all of you are distressed by what's happened. But no one is accusing you of anything. We just want to get to the bottom of this in the best way possible—"

"I don't need an interpreter," Nick said impatiently. "And they can handle this, Jarrett."

The flash of hostility across Jarrett's face was unmistakable. It was also quickly replaced by Jarrett's usual obliging demeanor.

"Of course," he said. "Just trying to help, Nick."

Pat gave Dana a significant nudge. "Look out," she whispered. "Dissension among the ranks of management." Maybe Pat was trying to be jocular, but she looked nervous and keyed up. Dana felt keyed up herself, and distressed over what had been lost. In its own way, the theft seemed as vicious as the attack on Jarrett.

Nick paced again. "Since no one is forthcoming, we'll do this the hard way. I'll need to know each of your whereabouts since last evening—starting with you, Ms. Morgan."

Dana stiffened. Nick was going too far now, treating all of them as if they were criminals. It was especially humiliating to have him treat *her* like that.

But did she really expect special consideration from him? Just because of that day on the temple steps when he had put his arms around her and drawn her close....

"Pat and I ate dinner together at the café in the village," she said coolly. "Afterward we walked around the plaza, then went back to the hotel for a game of cards with Robert. I went to bed around eleven, got up once to have a drink of water—no witnesses there—and then slept soundly till six. Since then, I've spent all morning working with Pat. Is that a sufficient alibi, or would you like me to elaborate?"

"As always, you're very thorough, Ms. Morgan." Nick's tone was dismissive and he moved on to Tim. "What about you, Mr. Reese?"

If possible, Tim paled even further under Nick's ruthless gaze. "Uh...I went back to the village with the others. I stayed in my room all night."

Nick continued his interrogation. No one escaped it— not Pat, not Robert, not Jarrett. Then Nick came to young Daniel, and he was just as brusque, just as rigorous in his questions as he'd been with the others. It was one thing to treat the adults so dictatorially—putting a child through the third degree was something else again. Daniel stood unflinching as he gave his answers, but at last Dana could tolerate no more. She stepped close to Nick and spoke to him in a low voice.

"Daniel's just a boy. Lighten up, will you?"

Nick gazed back at her with his most trenchant look. Daniel didn't seem to appreciate her intervention, himself. He'd stiffened, and he stared at her with an expression that could only be termed...well, it could only be termed as severe as Nick's own expression.

Dana's eyes locked once again with Nick's. It was the coldness in his gaze she wished to fight, as well as the domination he exerted over her.

"Really—haven't you asked enough?" she persisted. "Jarrett's right. We're *all* upset about what happened."

He seemed to consider her words in a disparaging manner. But surely he could see that his confounded inquisition had yielded little result. The day before, Daniel had left the dig by early afternoon. In the evening, Pat, Dana, Robert and Tim had all driven together to the village. Nick and Jarrett had remained behind to camp out at the excavation site. There was nothing unusual about that. At any given time, two or three people slept at the dig while the others went into the village to freshen up at the hotel. Last night had been no different. No matter how Nick had probed, he'd uncovered nothing untoward about anyone's movements.

Finally Nick gave Dana a curt nod, and then he addressed the entire group. "We're finished discussing this...for now. But I don't want anyone going around alone. Keep your eyes open. Always make sure you have at least a few of the others with you—your own safety might depend on it. And let's get back to work." With that, he disappeared abruptly into the large hut.

Dana moved over to one of the sifters and tried in vain to involve herself in her customary tasks. She fingered a mound of dirt. The confrontation with Nick had disturbed her. She'd tried to defy his remoteness, but it had done her no good. Why did she want to reach him at all?

She glanced up to see young Daniel approaching her in resolute fashion. This was a first; Daniel had never sought her out before. Usually *she* was the one trying to strike up a conversation with him. Not that she deluded herself. She didn't imagine Daniel wished an amiable chat. He reached her side only to frown at her.

"I don't need anybody's help," he said. "I can take care of myself. And Señor Petrie is right. If someone stole from me, I'd make everybody sorry, too. I'd make everybody afraid." It was the most Daniel had ever said to Dana. He paused now, still frowning, as if to make absolutely sure she got the point. What an irony—this thirteen-year-old boy deciding that he needed to defend the almighty Dr. Nicholas Petrie.

"Message received, Daniel," she said. "Loud and clear."

He gave her a sharp glance, as if not quite convinced. Then, with a brusque nod taken right from the book of Nick Petrie, Daniel turned and strode away.

Dana watched him go, experiencing a mixture of frustration and reluctant admiration. Daniel knew how to handle himself, all right, and she ought to have known he wouldn't take kindly to her interference—particularly where Nick was concerned. Daniel was a determined kid. From the little Dana had been able to gather, he'd taught himself English just by picking up whatever he could from the tourists who visited the island. Smart... and determined. He was also an adept student of Nick's. Dana had often seen the two of them engrossed in some job at the excavation pits, both dark heads bent together as Nick explained and Daniel emulated. But Daniel wouldn't let anyone else get close to him, least of all Dana. The boy disdained her, and she couldn't figure out exactly why....

She tried to get back to work, but now it was Jarrett who came up to her. "How are you doing?" he asked. "I know that none of this has been a pleasant experience."

"I'm fine. But thanks for asking." She glanced at him. In spite of the heat, Jarrett wore an old-fashioned paisley vest over his shirt. Combined with his longish hair, it made him look like one of the Victorian explorer gentlemen who had discovered the Mayan ruins of the Yucatán back in the 1840s. Jarrett seemed so open faced, so essentially good-natured. Yet, according to Pat, he was a bit of a back stabber. What was he really like?

As Jarrett often did, he lingered beside her. "Don't blame Nick too much for coming down hard," he said. "This has been a pretty big shock for him. For me, too, I'm afraid. We work for months, and then something like this can happen." Jarrett's hazel eyes seemed to reflect only concern. If anything, he was too quick to excuse Nick. But Dana knew she hadn't imagined that flash of hostility she'd seen earlier.

"Who do you think stole the artifacts?" she asked.

Jarrett raised his hand and pressed gingerly where the wound had healed on his head. "It still hurts sometimes," he said in a wry voice. "A reminder that someone doesn't want us here. I wish I knew who it was—I can't even make a guess."

"But you don't think it was one of us."

Jarrett gave her one of his engaging smiles. "I've ruled you out, Dana—me, as well. As for the others..." He hesitated, then went on. "I just don't see that, either. Pat's too wrapped up in her own life to bother with intrigues of any kind, Robert wouldn't care for the mess, and sometimes I think Tim is hiding from his own shadow. Daniel tries to act like an adult, but he's just a kid putting up a front. Nick has the kind of calculating mind to play us off each other like this—but what would be his motive?"

Jarrett's observations about the others could almost be called gibes, Dana supposed. "So there's only one conclusion that makes sense," she said. "It was someone outside our little group—perhaps one of the islanders."

"Don't forget that anyone can come to the island from the mainland. It doesn't necessarily have to be a native of Calamar."

"That's certainly reassuring," Dana muttered.

"I didn't mean to frighten you," he said. "But I want you to be on your guard. Be careful, Dana, just as Nick says." In a seemingly casual motion, Jarrett placed his hand over Dana's, there on the sifter. He gazed at her intently, anxious lines furrowing his brow. And she knew that, unfortunately, Jarrett was interested in her. Pat had been right about that much.

Dana slipped her hand away from his. "I'll be fine. You don't need to worry about me."

"I will worry," Jarrett said ruefully. He gazed at her a moment longer and then he left her. Dana watched him walk toward the huts and gave a sigh. On top of everything else, she'd have to deal with the problem of Jarrett. Quite how, she didn't know. She wasn't sure about much of anything anymore.

AT EVENING TIME, the air was still heavy and oppressive. Dark purplish clouds roiled on the horizon, and now Dana knew of a surety that a storm threatened. Nonetheless, she had escaped at last to walk on the beach. She and Pat had once again eaten dinner together in the village and it had taken some doing to get away from her. But Dana had managed it, and now she could enjoy some relative solitude. She took off her shoes and dug her bare toes luxuriously into the sand. The warm salt-laden breeze drifted over her. It couldn't exactly be called refreshing, but Dana would take what she could get. She wandered along, swinging her shoes by the laces, allowing the waves to lap at her feet. The waters of the ocean had darkened to an unusual murkiness, but still the rhythmic sound of the tide was soothing. For the first time all day, she began to relax a little.

"I told you not to go out alone." Nick's harsh voice came from right behind her. She swiveled around.

"Don't sneak up on me like that," she exclaimed. "You almost gave me a heart attack."

He looked at her, his gaze still a cold blue. "What if I'd been someone who meant you harm?"

She gestured to a point down the beach, where a few islanders also walked in the sand. "I would have screamed bloody murder and those people would have come to help me."

"Maybe they wouldn't have reached you in time. When will you realize there's someone unpredictable around, who's ready to target any one of us?"

Dana stared at Nick. Unpredictable...that was the best word to describe her emotions lately. Take right now, for instance. All she had to do was look at Nick Petrie and confusion swirled through her. In spite of everything, she craved his nearness. He was an obdurate man, and that quality showed in the bold angles and planes of his features. Even so...she wanted to be near him like this, as if there was something in his stubborn, unyielding self that commanded affinity with her. It didn't make any sense. Nick Petrie was hardly congenial or compatible....

She turned and began skirting the ocean again. "I had to get away. Call it emotional survival, if you will."

"I'm more concerned about your physical survival." Nick strode beside her. He looked tired and out of sorts. Dana couldn't really blame him for that. It had been a miserable day, all around. She knew that he'd spent a good part of it with Police Inspector Maciel, working on an investigation of the theft. But no clues had been uncovered, no leads established. All the inspector could promise to do was make inquiries, to try to determine if the artifacts had reached the black market. It seemed a necessary but inadequate step.

"I thought you'd be back at the site," Dana said now.

"I'll be there later. At the moment, Robert and Jarrett are standing guard."

"You actually trust them?" she asked mockingly.

Nick glanced at her. "I don't have much choice. But don't take any of my suspicions personally, Ms. Morgan."

"So I'm a suspect, too."

He uttered an oath under his breath. "I'd be pretty damn surprised if I found out you were involved. But I've been surprised by things before, Dana."

At least they were on a first-name basis again. She didn't know whether or not to be pleased about that.

"You can't suspect everyone," she remarked. "Take Daniel, for instance. You really grilled him this morning, right along with the others."

"Daniel's stronger than you think... and he would have been offended if I'd treated him any differently than the rest of the crew. This way he knows that he has my respect, and that's more important than anything to him."

"Respect..." Dana could have argued the point, but she suspected that if Daniel himself were here he'd take Nick's side, not hers. Besides, Dana wasn't in the mood to argue. She slowed her pace and noted that Nick adjusted his own accordingly. Perhaps he, too, needed to be out here on the beach, seeking some relief from the events of the day. Dana studied him obliquely. If anything, the outline of his features seemed even more stern than before. His dark hair stirred back in the breeze, but that only emphasized the rigid set of his face. Dana couldn't help comparing him to the other men she'd come to know these past few weeks. Robert's fastidious elegance, Jarrett's old-fashioned courtliness... No, neither one had Nick's rugged, uncompromising appeal. It was like comparing ordinary stone to flint....

Stone and flint—she was already starting to think like an archaeologist. But the attraction Nick held for her still made no sense. He drew her on some instinctual level she couldn't explain. Some primitive level...

She became aware that she'd tangled the laces of the shoes she held. With an effort she loosened her grip a little. She glanced down at the battered hiking boots Nick wore.

"You might as well take those off," she said. "The sand feels wonderful against bare feet, you know. Or maybe you don't know... I wonder if you've even walked along the beach the entire time you've been on the island."

His expression grew quizzical. He didn't answer, but he surprised Dana by bending down to take off his shoes and socks. She couldn't help giving his feet a quick perusal. They were long and lean, strongly formed and serviceable. Somehow Nick's feet being bare made him seem a little more accessible. Dana was glad when he knotted the laces of his boots together and carried them along as he walked beside her. The atmosphere between them was almost companionable for once.

"Nick... the theft of those artifacts is just a rotten thing. It isn't fair."

"Are you offering me sympathy?" he asked dryly.

"In a manner of speaking—yes. You try to act as if you're jaded, but I can tell how important the dig is to you."

"I'm doing my job, Dana. Don't try to turn me into a chipper version of yourself."

"Chipper is the last word I'd use to describe you," she muttered. They didn't say anything more for a while. The palm trees along the shore bent gracefully under the growing wind. The sky darkened toward restless night and Dana shivered, even though the air was still hot. So much for companionable—now Nick's presence seemed as ominous as the encroaching storm.

At last Nick spoke. "When I find out who attacked Jarrett and who stole from the dig...it won't go well for them." His tone was all the more threatening for being so matter-of-fact. Dana realized she would not want to be on Nick's bad side.

"You really do think it was one of the crew," she said, pushing back the hair that had whipped into her face.

"Whoever committed the theft knew what was most valuable. A layman would dismiss the grinding stones as ordinary—too much like what the islanders use nowadays to grind their corn. A layman would also not understand the significance of those seeds and maize cobs. That points to one of the crew or one of the islanders who's worked with us—or one of the black-market traders."

His logic was irrefutable. To the untrained eye, those food remnants would have appeared only as so much garbage. Indeed, they *had* been garbage all those centuries ago, but they could reveal much about the Maya who had once discarded them. Only an expert would know this; only an expert would understand how crucial their loss would be.

"I doubt it's a member of our crew, though," Dana objected. "If one of us did it—well, it means sabotaging our own work. What would be the reason?"

"I'll find out." Nick spoke again in that dangerously calm voice.

As Dana turned to retrace her steps, her foot came down on something sharp in the sand, and she gave a yelp.

"Here, let me see," Nick said. Before she could protest, he had her sitting on the sand and he was examining the sole of her foot. "It was just the jagged edge of a shell," he said. "You didn't even break the skin. You'll be fine."

"Of course I'll be fine...." Her voice trailed off. Nick ran his fingers over the arch of her foot in a completely unnecessary caress. His touch was warm, as warm as the island breeze. He gazed at Dana for a long moment, his eyes darkened in the stormy dusk. She couldn't look away. Her heart seemed to pound in rhythm to the surf, and still Nick's touch tantalized her bare skin.

"Dammit," she said at last, her voice shaking. "I...I don't want this, Nick."

"I haven't even kissed you yet." His voice was soft now, and yet he sounded oddly somber.

"Let's just...keep it that way."

"What *do* you want, Dana?" His gaze was intent.

Somehow she managed to pull away from him. She curled her feet under her body. Without him touching her, she could think a little more rationally. "All I want is a different life than the one I had. A better life."

"And you think you've found it here, on this island?"

"It's a beginning. I don't know where it will lead. And that's the whole point. Before this I knew exactly where my life was headed. I knew it too well."

"That's right. You had the boyfriend who slept over regularly, four nights a week."

Dana bit her lip. Nick's memory was altogether too precise. "Alan was...predictable," she admitted.

"So now you want the unpredictable?"

"Yes, that's part of it."

Nick slowly shook his head. "I don't think so," he murmured. "You came to this island with your duffel bags full of precautions. You seem determined to be prepared for any circumstance. You haven't changed your life, Dana. You've only changed the geography."

She stared at him angrily. "I rejected everything in my old life. It scared the hell out of me, but I did it anyway. Who are you to tell me otherwise?" He didn't know anything about her. He didn't know how lost she felt right now, how ungrounded. She'd truly cast herself into an unfamiliar landscape. The only realities were the feverish ocean and sky, and Nick's implacable gaze upon her....

And then the storm broke. Large drops of rain pelted down on them. Without a word, Nick grasped Dana's hand, hauled her upward and ran with her along the shore. They were both drenched by the time they reached one of the beach shelters—nothing more than a roof of palm fronds lashed onto a few poles. And yet this *palapa* shelter did a remarkably good job of fending off the rain. Nick and Dana stood under it, the water streaming down all around them.

It was so dark now that Dana could see only the outline of Nick's face. Her wet clothes clung to her body and she wrapped her arms around herself. Nick was very close to her, not speaking...seeming to wait for something. Her awareness of him transformed itself into an actual physical sensation inside her. She was tempted to dart back out into the rain—anything to ease the aching sensitivity all along her nerve ends—

But then Nick took her into his arms. He bent his head and placed his mouth on hers. It was a kiss that did not demand—it simply took. It conveyed the most essential, most fundamental need and desire. Dana had no choice but to acknowledge her own need. She opened her lips to Nick, moving her hands up the muscles of his chest. Everything about him was lean and powerful, flesh whittled down to basic strength, basic truth. He did not prevaricate and neither did his kiss.

His tongue probed her mouth, titillating her senses. Dana tangled her fingers in his hair, pressing against him, taking what she wished, too. She could no longer deny herself. A heated longing radiated through her body, reaching from deep inside her. She couldn't question it—couldn't stop it. She molded herself to Nick and his arms tightened around her almost fiercely. The rain pounded down unheeded. The cast of the wind now sprayed water under the shelter. There was wet cloth between Nick and Dana, nothing more....

It was Nick who ended the contact, as abruptly as he had initiated it. He stepped back from Dana, leaving her suddenly bewildered. She couldn't read his expression, couldn't guess what he was thinking. But for a brief moment she had known surety in his arms—the surety of her own desire. That frightened her as much as anything, the conviction of her own physical longing for him. Her emotions couldn't keep pace.

Nick turned and stared into the night. Dana reached out a hand as if to touch him, but then stayed herself. She was trembling deep inside. Together she and Nick waited out the rest of the rain in tense silence, but Dana feared that the storm inside her would never be quelled.

CHAPTER SIX

NICK FOUND THE COMPANY of Anton and Elena Montano almost relaxing. He knew full well that he should view the couple as suspects, yet he had a habit of letting down his guard around them. Perhaps it was because they both seemed to have such a straightforward outlook and were not the type to keep their motivations hidden. They had been married almost twenty years. With no children, they focused primarily on each other and made no excuses for that. When Nick was with them, he felt accepted on the edge of their small family circle. Nick decided it was a good place to be—a place to get away from the tensions of the dig. That suited him.

Today Anton and Elena had invited him for lunch. He sat outside their hut, working on a plate of tamales. Anton sat beside him, silently eating his wife's food. Elena whisked back and forth between the men and the interior of the hut, bringing cups of soda, a plate of the sugary rolls known as *buñuelos,* an extra tamale for Anton. Nick had already learned that Elena grew affronted if anyone offered to help her with chores. She possessed the firm conviction that it was a woman's prerogative to wait on her man. She spoiled Anton shamelessly, and he spoiled her in his own way with his overprotectiveness. Anton and Elena were fussbudgets, and they fussed over each other. Nick almost envied the two of them. His own marriage had been a rocky one, even before what had happened with Josh.

Always in the past, Nick had blotted out memories of Josh with a drink.... At least, he had tried to blot them out. Even large amounts of alcohol hadn't been entirely successful. But now he could not make even the attempt to escape his memories. Sobriety had brought with it a ruthless clarity of mind. When he least expected it, he would see Josh's face before him: freckled cheeks, a shock of dark hair falling over his forehead, that goofy and endearing grin of a seven-year-old....

Nick clenched his plate until he was in danger of cracking the fragile china. That wouldn't do—Elena had served him on her best dishes. But now Nick realized one of the reasons why he most liked the couple. They were always so wrapped up in each other that they never seemed to notice these lapses of his. At the moment Elena perched on the edge of her chair and peered over at Anton's plate in a proprietary manner.

"I put a little garlic in the rice this time. It's good. Why don't you eat it?"

"I'm eating the rice."

"I see what you're doing. You're pushing it over to the side there. You think I won't notice? Garlic, it's good for your stomach. Eat it up."

"I'm eating," Anton said patiently. "I'm eating."

Gradually Nick found himself relaxing again, and he took another bite of spicy tamale. Maybe he didn't envy Anton and Elena so much, after all. He didn't know if he could live the way they did—no boundaries allowed between them, no spaces where the other couldn't enter. Nick needed barriers where a woman was concerned. He'd learned that with his ex-wife, and then later with Kathryn.

He gazed off toward the beach, the sands shimmering white in the sun. Anton and Elena lived a secluded existence on this small, beautiful cove. Anton earned a living in a piecemeal sort of way: tending his cornfield, doing a little fishing, hiring out for odd jobs in the village, assisting Nick at the dig. Then Anton came home each night to his solitude with Elena—except that he would probably protest that it wasn't solitude. He and Elena had each other, after all.

Nick idly tried to picture Dana and the ex-boyfriend who had refused to marry her. He wondered exactly what Dana had wanted from the guy—all boundaries abolished, barriers tumbled down? It was obvious that the boyfriend had wanted at least some boundaries left intact. Four nights at Dana's house, and the rest of his life to himself.

Nick smiled faintly. Dana claimed that she now wanted adventure and freedom. But she also possessed an undeniable homeyness. . . .

"You look perturbed, Nicolás," pronounced Elena. "What is your trouble? You don't like my garlic, either?"

Nick grimaced to himself. So much for Elena's sharp eye missing anything in her vicinity. "The rice is fine. It's not that."

"You are still worried about the thief."

"Yes—I am." Nothing untoward had happened on the dig since the loss of the artifacts five days earlier. Nick, however, harbored the uneasy conviction that someone was only waiting for another opportunity to cause trouble. He'd therefore established a rotating-guard system at the dig. He tried to make sure no one was ever alone there. This would protect everyone's safety and at the same time inhibit any crew member who might actually be the culprit. Nick himself tried to be at the dig as much as possible, allowing himself only the occasional reprieve—such as accepting this invitation today.

But he had not come here merely to share lunch with the Montanos. He needed to talk to them away from the others on the dig. Nick set down his plate. "Have your inquiries produced any results at all?" he asked.

Anton continued to push the rice around on his plate. "Many of the people I speak to are resentful. They say you are accusatory in manner, Nicolás. They also believe bad things are beginning to happen on the island. They blame you."

Nick made an impatient gesture. "They can blame me all they like. I'm just trying to find out if anybody knows anything useful."

Elena deliberately scooped up a forkful of rice and tasted it. "The garlic is good," she said assertively. Then she glanced at Nick. "I have been speaking to people, too. They exaggerate, they spread rumors, but they know nothing. They say only that they are afraid of going near the temple. They wonder if they should work for you anymore."

"Are you afraid?" Nick asked gently.

Something flickered in Elena's eyes, but then she shook her head vigorously. "I will allow no one to make me afraid."

Anton moved his chair a little closer to his wife's. "Nothing will happen to Elena," he said with conviction. "I will see to that. We will continue to ask questions and perhaps we will learn something."

Nick was grateful that he could still count on their assistance, but he wondered for how long. If Anton came to believe there was any threat at all to his wife's safety, he would justifiably put her first. Without Anton and Elena, the other islanders would hesitate to work at the dig. Nick's crew would become more and more isolated.

Feeling dissatisfied, Nick nonetheless finished his tamales. Elena was an excellent cook—except when she laid on too much garlic—and he appreciated her hospitality while he still had it.

Now it was time to return to the dig. Nick rose and took his leave of the Montanos. "Thank you," he said simply.

"*De nada*—it is nothing," answered Anton.

"You will come again," said Elena. "And next time you will show my husband how a man is really supposed to eat."

"I'm eating," Anton grumbled. "I'm eating."

Nick smiled as he left them. He moved into the forest, unerringly choosing his way. Against his will, his thoughts returned to Dana as he went along. He had not touched her since the day of the storm. He'd barely even spoken to her. But he remembered kissing her, that was for damn sure....

He really was out of practice with this kind of thing. That day of the storm, he'd taken her into his arms without observing any preliminaries. He'd forgotten how to be casual, how to be easy with a woman.

And so now he stayed away from Dana—kept his distance. He couldn't think of any other solution. Where Dana was concerned, he couldn't really think at all.

Nick heard a rustle among the trees to his right and immediately stopped, straining to see through the dense foliage. Many small animals lived in this jungle—armadillos, foxes, even deer. But if it had been an animal, it had already scuttled to safety. Nick continued on.

And then the rustle of branches came again, farther ahead. It was almost a taunting sound. Nick placed his hand on the hilt of his new machete. His intuition told him that it was not a deer or a fox disturbing the branches.

Nick refrained from calling out. He waited for another rustling noise, heard nothing, moved forward once more... and then the sound came, still taunting. Someone wanted to play a game of cat and mouse, that much was clear.

Deftly, efficiently, Nick unsheathed the machete and held it in readiness. He moved swiftly in the direction of the sound—so swiftly that he seemed to have surprised his stalker. Now a thrashing noise sounded in the brush. Nick hurried in pursuit, but still the source of the mysterious noise eluded him. Suddenly there was silence again... a waiting silence.

Nick scanned the tangled brush. A jewel-winged parrot flew among the trees, then all was quiet again. Whoever hid there in the jungle was clever—at least clever enough to remain hidden.

When Nick moved forward again, this time no answering rustle came. Apparently the game was over. Nick uttered an oath to himself, knowing that he was at a disadvantage. The dense foliage would continue to protect anyone who did not wish to be seen.

Nick scouted carefully the rest of the way among the great mahogany and ceiba trees, jungle vines dangling all around and brushing against him as if to impede his progress. He found nothing. Eventually he reached the dig and stood beside the huts to assess his crew.

Everything seemed to be in order. Robert and Jarrett were discussing a topographical map while Tim worked desultorily with a shovel. Pat, Dana and a few of the islanders were lugging baskets of dirt along. Daniel sat cross-legged inside one of the shallow excavation pits, chipping away at the earth with a spade. From this viewpoint, the kid looked even younger than usual, his head bent, his dark hair tousled. Daniel worked with concentration, as if focusing on his task was of prime importance at the moment. Sometimes the kid almost seemed too intense. Yet Daniel was also becoming more elusive than ever. These days he arrived at the dig when least expected and was apt to disappear just as suddenly. Nick experienced a frustration that was becoming too familiar. He wanted to keep Daniel safe—but Daniel refused to be protected. The kid traveled to and from the village on his own, making it clear that no incursions on his privacy would be permitted. Nick sensed that if he pressed for something more, Daniel would stop coming here altogether. It was an unsatisfactory situation, but Nick didn't know what the hell to do about it.

Now, as he watched, Dana paused at her own tasks to lean down and speak to Daniel. Nick couldn't distinguish what she was saying—only the soft murmur of her voice. Apparently, no matter what she said, Daniel would have none of it. The kid gave only a shrug in response and wielded his spade with all the more concentration. Finally Dana straightened up and moved away, hauling another basket of dirt toward the sifter.

Today she wore shorts. They were no-nonsense canvas shorts, but she looked good in them, her legs shapely and sturdy at the same time.

As if sensing Nick's gaze, she glanced toward him, unsmiling. She didn't say anything. She, too, had been doing her share of avoiding.

Nick followed an impulse, not stopping to reason it through. He went to Dana and spoke to her in a low voice. "Tell me if anyone has left the site in the last hour."

She frowned at him. "What am I now—the camp spy?"

"Just tell me, Dana."

She sighed. "I haven't really been paying attention. In case you hadn't noticed, all I do is look at dirt...haul dirt...sift dirt. Dirt, dirt and more dirt." She sounded unusually irritable, but there was something more in her tone. Nick looked at her closely. Her skin had a grayish cast under a film of perspiration and she held her lips tightly together.

"Are you feeling all right?" he asked. "You look sick."

"Of course I'm all right. If you think I get sick every time I turn around, you're very mistaken."

"You need a break." He steered her along, grabbed a couple of sodas and led her through the forest until they came out beside the temple.

"I don't want to be here," she muttered.

Nick paid no attention, prodding her down until she was sitting at the base of the temple steps. "Drink this," he commanded, handing her one of the soft drinks. "Chances are you're dehydrated. It happens in this climate."

She took several long swallows and then clasped the bottle between her knees. She looked a little less shaky. "Actually I do feel...better. But I wasn't sick, you know."

"Is it such a point of honor with you, Dana?"

"After the first time we met . . . yes."

Nick sat beside her. "Drink some more," he said. "We're talking heat exhaustion."

"I'm perfectly fine—"

"Just drink it."

She sipped from the bottle. "It really bothers me, the way you order people around all the time. You behave as if you're the only one with any power here."

"That's because I am the only one with any power."

"Are you running a military camp or what?"

The color seemed to be returning to Dana's cheeks. Apparently complaining about him made her feel better.

"I recognize this stage," he said. "It's the stage where people get so fed up working for me that they pack their duffels and head home on the next boat."

"Don't count on it." Dana drained the last of her soft drink and looked speculatively at the bottle Nick held. He handed it over to her.

"Maybe you should think about leaving," he suggested. "With everything that's been happening, you'd be a lot safer off the island."

"That's not why you want me to leave."

He thought about this. "It's one of the reasons," he said at last.

She pulled off her hat, that long golden hair of hers tumbling down around her face. "I'm not leaving," she said. "Nothing is what I expected here . . . but I'm still not leaving."

She was an obstinate person, there could be no doubt about that. Some might even say pigheaded. Nick looked at her. Any softness of Dana's was deceptive.

The silken hair, the gentle curves of her body...they disguised a stubborn will.

Under his gaze she drew her eyebrows together and seemed about to issue a warning statement. He headed her off.

"Don't worry," he said. "I'm not going to touch you." He wasn't going to touch her because, if he did, it would be difficult to stop.

"I'm not worried. I just don't think it's a good idea for us to...do what we've been doing."

"Exactly what have we been doing, Dana?" He really wanted to know.

For an answer she only gazed back at him, her expression one of consternation. Her eyes were very dark, a striking contrast to the gold of her hair. But she was a person of seductive contrasts: practicality, stubbornness, optimism, all mixed with an unexpectedly caustic wit...a sunny voice laced with huskiness....

She wrenched her gaze away from his. She was wearing a sleeveless shirt again, the creaminess of her shoulders beginning to turn pink from exposure to the sun. Nick pictured himself running his hands over her shoulders as a prelude to more intimate contact.

Instead he rubbed his neck and tried vainly to bring his imagination back into line. "I won't touch you," he said again, as if these words could have any significance at all.

"You don't *have* to touch me," she burst out. "All you have to do is look at me and..." Her voice trailed off. "I don't understand it," she said finally, in a low voice.

"Understand what, Dana?"

She took a deep, shaky breath. "I don't understand why...why it is that I seem to know you, somehow."

This time when she gazed at him, her expression was troubled, as if she saw more than she wished. Maybe she saw more than *he* wished.

"You don't know me," he said in a warning tone.

"I don't know details, facts. But that's not what I'm talking about. It's something else.... I'm not sure how to describe it." She made a gesture of frustration. "It's as if we knew each other a long time ago."

"Next you'll tell me you believe in reincarnation."

"I don't know *what* to believe." Her tone was grouchy. "I've never felt this way with anyone before. It's very inconvenient. It gets in the way of things, and..." She pressed a hand to her stomach.

"Feeling bad again?"

"Yes, a little. But I shouldn't be. I've adjusted to the climate by now."

An unwelcome thought occurred to Nick. He tried to think of a diplomatic way to phrase it.

"Look, Dana. I realize you broke up with that guy not too long ago. Could it be that you're..." There wasn't any diplomatic way. "Maybe you're pregnant."

She stared at him. "For crying out loud! Just because I was a little queasy that first day and now—I can't believe this. Of course I'm not pregnant."

"It happens," he said.

"Well, not to me. Alan and I were always very careful. But why the heck am I discussing this with you?"

Nick could tell he'd riled her. "You're a member of my crew," he said calmly. "If, for argument's sake, you were pregnant, I'd have to know about it so I could make the proper adjustments."

"Adjustments... You make it sound like I'm a dress and my seams need letting out! But I'm not pregnant!"

Nick leaned back on the temple steps. "No, I guess you're not the kind of person who'd let anything like that happen by accident. You're prepared for everything, aren't you?"

She pushed the hair away from her face impatiently. "Planning ahead isn't a failing, you know."

"Sometimes people are reckless, careless—whatever you want to call it. They end up with a child and their whole lives change."

Dana was silent for a moment, and then she spoke. "Nick," she said reflectively. "Do you have any children?"

He remained in the same relaxed pose, but he could feel his muscles begin to tense. He didn't know how to respond to that question. It was a deceptively simple one, but he had no simple answer.

"No," he said shortly. It wasn't exactly the truth. It wasn't exactly a lie, either.

Dana sipped from her drink. "Well, anyway—the fact is that Alan, in particular, wanted to be careful. He hated the idea of having kids."

"Yet you still wanted to marry this guy?"

"Not everyone needs children," she said.

"Do you need them?"

She gave him an exasperated glance. "Oh, all right. Yes, someday I want to have children. Very much so. And I thought...I thought eventually I could change Alan's mind. I thought it would just be a matter of time."

"You know, Dana—for someone who likes to plan ahead and be prepared, you were being pretty unrealistic."

She gave him another look of exasperation. "Don't you think I figured that out? When I asked Alan to

marry me, and he said no, I definitely figured things
out. But I learn from my mistakes. It won't happen
again." She sighed eloquently. "Alan is one of those
people who seems so dependable and steady at first. So
I assumed from the beginning that he and I would be
something...permanent. Now I know better than to
assume anything."

Nick stood and moved away from the temple steps.
"If you're smart, Dana, you'll leave the island."

"Forget it," she said. "I'm not going anywhere." She
stood briskly, and stepped forward. Then her face went
white and she clutched her stomach again. The bottle of
soda fell from her fingers, and Dana fell, too.

Nick caught her just in time.

CHAPTER SEVEN

WHEN DANA WOKE, she found herself shrouded in darkness. It took her a few moments to realize where she was—in a room at the village hotel. Moonlight flooded in through the window and she recognized the shape of a bureau in the corner. There was another shape in the room, too... the austere form of someone sitting beside her bed. In a heartbeat she knew that it was Nick.

"Hello," she said groggily. Her stomach ached dully and her head pounded with the effort of trying to concentrate. "What happened?"

Nick leaned forward and switched on the small bedside lamp. His features were taut, his eyes shadowed.

"Don't think about it right now," he said. "The doctor just wants you to get some rest."

"The doctor... What happened to me?" she asked again. She struggled to sit up, then sank back. "Nick, tell me!"

He wasn't a demonstrative man, but she could see the concern in his expression as he studied her.

"We don't know exactly what happened," he said. "All we know right now is that Tim and Pat are sick, too, as well as one of the islanders who worked at the site today. They all keeled over not long after you lost consciousness."

"I don't get it," she said, her voice sounding scratchy in her own ears. "What kind of sickness strikes that quickly?"

"It was probably something the four of you ate or drank. The doctor's still trying to figure it out. But it shouldn't have happened in the first place. I shouldn't have let it happen." He seemed angry with himself.

"Are the others—"

"They're fine. Flat on their backs, but fine. You were the most affected. Damn, I shouldn't have let this happen." He kept repeating that, as if he needed to blame himself.

"Stop," Dana said. "Just stop. How could this be your fault?"

"It *is* my fault," he said grimly. "I've suspected someone was playing a game with me. I should have been more careful. And now they've decided to raise the stakes. They've sent another message—one as serious as hell this time."

"You're being very egocentric," Dana murmured. "It happened to the rest of us and you're taking it as a message to *you*." She stopped, amazed she'd had the energy to get out that much. Her thought processes weren't operating up to speed and a sense of unreality engulfed her. During her entire life, she could honestly say that no one had ever attempted to harm her physically. It was difficult to believe that it had happened now.

"There's a boat leaving for the mainland at nine o'clock in the morning," Nick said. "I'm putting you on it."

She glared at him, then winced at a new pain shooting through her head. "Stop being so all-fired dogmatic. You can't control me or anyone else. You're not responsible for every darn thing that happens!''

He continued to regard her with concern, but now she wondered irritably exactly what sort of concern it was. Did he care about her personally—or did he see her only as one more crew member under his charge?

"Don't get worked up," he said now. "Here—drink this." He held a glass of something disgustingly murky next to her lips.

"What on earth is that?"

"An herbal cure the doctor left for you. I'm not sure he knows what he's doing," Nick said in that cynical tone of his. "But...cheers."

She gave Nick a skeptical frown, then tasted the stuff. It was awful, but she managed a few sips. "Just what I need," she grumbled, collapsing back against the pillow.

Nick's face had that shuttered expression she'd come to recognize. It made her wonder if she'd ever know what he was truly thinking. He stood and moved toward the door.

"I want the doctor to have another look at you—"

"Nick, wait. Don't bring him in here just yet."

He glanced back at her and this time there was something different in his gaze—something stormy, something volatile behind his restraint. "You've had a rough time of it, Dana. You're lucky to be all right."

"I realize that. It's just...Don't go yet."

Nick hesitated, but then he came to sit beside her again. "What is it you need to say, Dana?"

He wasn't going to make this easy—she could tell that much. She didn't know how to explain that she simply needed his presence right now. It seemed that no one else would do—it was brusque, domineering Nick Petrie she wanted to be near. What was wrong with her? She would get no tender comfort from the man....

She made a weak attempt at humor. "At least now I'm vindicated," she said. "You can't accuse the others of being pregnant, too."

Nick didn't smile. He leaned forward and clasped his hands together, elbows resting on his knees. "Dana, I wonder if you realize how serious this is. It's not your ordinary case of food poisoning. As far as I'm concerned, someone intentionally tried to—"

"No. Let's not talk about it." That sense of unreality still enveloped her. She couldn't face what had happened just yet. She had to cushion herself against it. "Please, just stay with me, Nick. Talk to me about something else. Anything... I hate lying here like this, feeling out of control. It reminds of me when I was a kid and I had the chicken pox. My parents competed to prove which one of them could take care of me the best...." As she spoke, she watched the doubtful expression on Nick's face. For this moment, at least, she could surmise what he was thinking: he didn't relish the prospect of any personal revelations on her part. And that, perversely, only impelled her to say more.

"My parents had a rather odd relationship—I suppose it was more a power struggle, really, than a marriage, and it seemed to escalate when I was sick. One of them would bring me a bowl of mushroom soup and the other one would point out that a broth would be better. Then they'd argue about whether I needed a dose of the doctor's medicine or just some calamine lotion. They'd both get all these subtle digs in at each other and I'd be sprawled on the bed, feeling lousy."

"All this time, I pictured you having an idyllic childhood," Nick murmured.

"Idyllic...sometimes I think my parents were just too isolated on that farm. They didn't have anything better to do than use me in their little games. I ended up never knowing where I belonged with them."

Maybe this wasn't such a good subject to discuss, after all. Remembering the peculiar loneliness of her childhood, Dana realized that she'd encountered a different sort of loneliness since arriving on this island. She was still looking for her place here, still wondering where she fit in.

Dana gazed at Nick in the shadows of this mysterious night. His expression as he gazed back at her was thoughtful and carefully reserved. All her instincts warned her that it was dangerous to need anything at all from Nick—but here she was, opening up to him, telling him about her self-absorbed parents, attempting to share her memories with him so that he would know who she really was. It was ridiculous.

"I'm sure you're not interested in any of this," she muttered.

He didn't offer a contradiction, but simply went on studying her. At least Dana never had to worry about false platitudes from Nick.

"Well, anyway, it was a relief when I finally moved away from my parents' house. But they're still at it, unfortunately. Still married, still craftily belittling each other. One of them is always calling me up, politely trying to enlist me as an ally against the enemy."

"And you're still trying to walk the middle ground, I take it," Nick remarked.

"Something like that. I suppose I fantasize that one day they'll stop. But perhaps it's hopeless.... Perhaps they don't know any other way of dealing with each other."

Nick continued to gaze at Dana. Once more there was something intent in his regard of her, something that held her. His eyes were a dark, turbulent blue at this hour of the night. She couldn't look away, but it seemed that she didn't have the same power over him. He made as if to rise again.

"You have to rest, Dana."

She despised herself for it, but she still needed him here beside her.

"Please, Nick. Just talk to me some more. Tell me something about *your* life... tell me when you first knew you'd be an archaeologist."

He glanced at her as if in disbelief. "Dana—"

"Please, Nick." She heard the strange urgency in her voice, but she couldn't control it.

Nick gazed at her another moment, and then he complied. "I was ten years old," he said reluctantly. "Living in New Mexico. They wanted to build a new highway through town, but first the county archaeologists had to come out and investigate. The highway was going to cut across part of what had once been a Spanish pueblo and they had to make sure no artifacts would be destroyed. Anyway, every afternoon I'd go down to watch the men at work. After a while, I guess they got to know me, and they took the time to explain things— what they were doing and why. I never missed a chance to be there. I believe that's when I first knew what I wanted to do."

Dana tried to picture Nick at ten years old. Most likely he would have been an intense young boy—enthusiastic, determined. Of course the archaeologists would have taken him under their wing. Dana liked the image—Nick as an enthusiastic kid. She just wondered what had happened to that enthusiasm along the way.

She settled more deeply against the pillow, the ache in her stomach subsiding a bit. "So you had a dream from the time you were ten years old, and you went after it. Not very many people can say that."

Nick looked disgruntled. "Don't try to romanticize it, Dana. Archaeology is just a job. Nothing more, nothing less."

"I don't believe you really feel that way. At least, there had to be a time when you were excited about what you were doing. I saw it in those photographs."

Nick shifted restlessly and glanced toward the door, as if he couldn't wait to leave her. "What photographs?"

"The ones in the books you wrote. I read them, you know. And in the pictures you looked cocky and sure of yourself—and excited to be where you were, doing something you loved."

Was that a flash of regret she saw on his face? It was difficult to tell in the hazy light of the bedside lamp.

"Things change," he said. "I was young and full of myself back then."

Nick Petrie seemed as if he'd known some deep sorrow—a sorrow he'd covered up with that cynicism of his. According to Pat, Nick had undergone a family tragedy....

"Tell me about your ex-wife," Dana said.

Nick straightened, his face taking on that closed expression again. "Forget it, Dana. This isn't a game of Twenty Questions."

"It's common knowledge you were married once. It's no big secret."

For a minute she thought he was going to stand up and leave. Then he gave a shrug that almost seemed weary.

"Meg and I weren't exactly compatible. Not even in the beginning. She was one of my students—not the best way to start any relationship. We got married before we realized how wrong we were for each other. We took too long to get divorced, that's all."

Dana surmised that he was leaving a great deal out of the story. "What happened to your career, Nick?" she asked softly. "That's the part I don't understand."

"You don't need to understand." His voice was steely now.

Dana sensed that she'd pushed too far and she moved her hands over the coverlet. "Okay, I'm turning out to be as nosy as Pat. But I'd damn well rather talk about your past than consider the fact that someone . . . that someone tried to kill me."

Nick captured one of her hands in his, and only then did she realize that she was trembling.

"Steady," he said. "Just keep it steady."

She found the words oddly comforting, even though he delivered them in his usual blunt tone.

"Maybe it *was* just a case of ordinary food poisoning," she argued. "Nothing intentional . . . nothing vicious. . . ."

The glance he gave her was almost pitying. She didn't want Nick's pity. She moved her fingers away from his.

"Very well, it's possible someone is trying to send a message," she said, her voice quite calm now. "But it seems directed at all of us, not just at you. Someone wants us off the island, perhaps."

"I'm in charge, Dana. Whatever happens on the dig is my responsibility."

"There you go again," she protested. "Turning it around to point at you. Maybe you're still full of yourself, after all."

"Maybe." He took her hand once more in both of his. She felt the roughness of his skin against hers—roughness from years of working in the earth—and that carried its own reassurance. Gradually her shakiness stilled. She studied the harsh, strong lines of Nick's face. She knew that he was the type of man who tried to protect those around him. He did it without fanfare and with little demonstration of kindness or sympathy to those he protected. When he didn't succeed, he cursed himself, allowing no excuses for failure. Yes...he was a harsh, strong man.

But Dana had to draw on her own strength—not merely on his. She took her hand away from his again and folded her arms above the coverlet. She stared at Nick.

"There's something you should know," she said. "I don't want to be someone's target in all this. What happened scared me.... I like surviving. But I'm going to stay on this island. And there's nothing you can do to change my mind."

LATE THE NEXT AFTERNOON, Dana still felt a little wobbly. She and Pat were resting in the courtyard of the hotel. It was pleasant here, hardly the sort of place where it seemed possible to imagine life-threatening circumstances. A poinciana tree in the very center of the courtyard showed off its dazzling red flowers, and hibiscus and bougainvillea bloomed among the rich green of the philodendrons. Pat and Dana sat on a low bench where the sweet, humid scent of growing things surrounded them. Pat appeared alternately caught up in the drama of what had happened and horrified that it had happened to *her*.

"I'll admit that Nick works fast. I mean, the way he went through all the food supplies at the camp, practically tearing the place apart, to hear Jarrett tell it.... But what if Nick's wrong about it being the water? Maybe we're still in danger, after all...."

It was clear that Pat needed reassurance, and Dana stifled her usual irritation. They'd been through this a dozen times already, but what was once more?

"It makes sense, Pat. Think about it. Nick said that particular container had a slight odor to it. And the four of us affected are the only ones who drank from it. That water tasted a little off, too, if I remember. Of course, those old water jugs could make champagne taste like plonk...but Nick is sending a sample off to the mainland. He'll get it analyzed and we'll know for sure."

Pat shuddered. "Meanwhile, I'll wonder every time I take a bite of food or a drink of anything...."

"It won't happen again," Dana said with growing conviction. "Whoever was responsible probably didn't mean us any real harm, anyway. They were just trying to frighten us."

"Yeah, frighten us to death...." Pat grabbed hold of Dana's arm in a vigorous grip. "It's awful. To think I could've been a goner. What about Robert?"

Dana gently but decisively pried her arm free. Pat sank into a gloomy silence for a moment, no doubt imagining her own funeral with a distraught Robert hovering at graveside. But it was difficult to picture Robert acting distraught about anything— Maybe that was what depressed Pat.

Dana gazed at a tiny lizard darting along the wall. She had to admit that the whole matter was very puzzling. It didn't seem logical that she, Pat, Tim and that other poor man had been targeted in particular. Anyone might have ended up taking a drink of that water. It was sheer chance that Robert, Jarrett and Nick hadn't taken a drink. Unless one of them was the perpetrator, of course....

Dana couldn't believe that she'd suspected Nick, even for a second. The idea was crazy. Just because sometimes she sensed almost a self-destructive quality in him....

"Nonsense," she muttered out loud. That was a mistake, because it encouraged Pat to start right up again.

"I have to find out about Robert and me. I can't go on this way, you know what I mean? Maybe it would just be better to have him slam me down with the truth, have him tell me he's not even interested...." Pat looked genuinely miserable. There it was—the vulnerability, the insecurity she manifested at unexpected times. She looked even more rumpled than usual today, her collar sticking straight up and her hair parted unevenly.

"Pat, why don't you just come right out and tell Robert how you feel?"

"Get real, Dana! Have you ever done something like that with a man?"

Dana thought this over carefully. A memory came to her that she would have far rather avoided. "As a matter of fact...my last year in college, I fell in love with my roommate's brother. Quite desperately in love, to tell the truth. For a long time I didn't know what to say to him or how to show him I was interested. He treated me almost as if I were another of his sisters. He was affectionate but brotherly."

Pat seemed unusually interested in the tale, considering it didn't involve her. "So what did you do?"

At this point, Dana would have liked to change the subject, but she felt obliged to finish. "One night, I simply couldn't take it anymore. I cornered him and blurted out exactly how I felt about him. I made it very clear...."

"And?"

"And the poor guy got horribly embarrassed and managed to let me know that he wasn't interested in me that way. Our relationship was never the same again." Dana had felt crushed. It had taken her a long while to get over it, because she really *had* been in love. She'd been careful after that...so careful that she hadn't allowed a serious relationship to develop with anyone until she'd met Alan. Safe, dependable Alan...

"You're not exactly convincing me I should be open and aboveboard with Robert," Pat muttered. "In other words, telling a guy how you feel only forces his hand."

"And maybe that's the best thing in the world," Dana said briskly. "You find out sooner rather than later how someone feels and you stop wasting your time. For example, if I had proposed to Alan a few years earlier than I did—"

"Proposed? Wait a minute. This is someone else? You have a habit of doing this kind of thing?"

"I wouldn't call it a habit," Dana retorted. "The point is, after what happened with my roommate's brother, I was too hesitant with men. I didn't put myself on the line. That's why I allowed four years to go by before I ever confronted Alan."

"Four years," Pat said on a note of incredulity. "I'm starting to think my love life's a charmer compared to yours, Dana."

Pat didn't know the half of it. Now Dana had to contend with all her conflicting emotions in regard to

Nick. She tried to marshal those emotions, to subdue them, but so far it was no use. Her feelings seemed to grow more insistent each day: perplexity, uncertainty, longing...

Pat had reverted to her favorite subject—her own personal life. "I don't know what I'm going to do. I mean, if I say something to him I could really regret it. But if I *don't* say something I could really regret that, too."

"Look, just tell the man how you feel and be done with it!"

"What man?" queried Robert. He came wandering into the courtyard, stroking his beard in a reflective manner. He seemed to have his mind on something else and appeared solemn. That was unusual—Robert being serious for once.

Meanwhile, Pat turned a red as bright as the poinciana flowers and scowled furiously at Dana. "No man," she muttered.

"Come, Pat," Robert said, resorting to his usual nonchalance with what seemed to be an effort. "We have enough mystery taking place in our midst. If you are engaged in a love affair, then we must know about it. Don't you agree with me, Dana?"

"I suppose that's up to Pat," Dana said in a neutral tone, then quickly changed the subject. "I take it you've been at the dig all day. Any news?"

Robert was successfully diverted. "We are in uproar, I can assure you. Nick is not happy, not happy at all. If he had his way, he would surround the place with a barbed-wire fence."

Pat recovered some of her own customary aplomb. "You haven't been any help in all this, Robert," she said scathingly. "You have a tendency to stand on the sidelines and smirk, no matter what's happening."

"My dear Pat, no one has ever accused me of smirking."

"Please—I'm not your dear anything. And I've definitely seen you smirk. You do it all the time—"

Dana excused herself and escaped while she still had a chance. She went down one of the narrow corridors of rooms and knocked at Tim's door. In response, she heard someone mumble something so low she couldn't make it out. Tim was probably telling her to go away, but she opened the door and poked her head inside.

"How are you feeling?" she asked. "The doctor said this hit you pretty hard, too."

Tim sat up in his bed, looking uncomfortable. He wore plaid pajamas that took away what little dignity he might have possessed otherwise. Dana had a feeling that Tim was not the kind of person who liked being seen in pajamas.

"I'm fine," he said, although he looked even more sallow faced than usual.

"Glad to hear it. We've all had a scare." She made to close the door again but then stopped herself. "Tim...I suppose Nick has said the same thing to you that he's told me and Pat. He says he'll understand if we decide to leave the island." Actually Nick had been a great deal more explicit than that when he'd discussed the matter with Pat and Dana this morning. He'd practically ordered both of them off the island. And they'd both refused.

"Anyway," Dana went on, "if you decide to leave, Tim, I'll wish you the best of luck."

Tim pulled the sheet clear up to cover his shoulders, and for a second Dana had the impression he wanted to disappear entirely. But then he spoke.

"I'm staying," he said, and now he did have an odd dignity in spite of the fact that he seemed surprised by his own words.

Dana smiled. "Glad to hear it," she said again. She shut the door, leaving him in peace and going to her own room. It cheered her, knowing that both Pat and Tim would be staying on, too. They weren't allowing anyone or anything to intimidate them. Dana wasn't allowing it, either, and that felt very good. At this moment, she was no longer afraid.

Once in her room, she pushed a slope-backed chair over to the window and sat down. From here she could see across the street to a joined row of houses stuccoed in pastel shades: pink, yellow, peach, oyster white. It was like gazing at a sketch done in chalks, soothing to the eyes. Dana leaned back in her chair, realizing this was the first day she hadn't worked since coming to the island. Apparently something drastic had to happen for her to earn a little leisure.

One of the hotel maids came in with a cup of tea and a plate of rolls. She was a woman about Dana's age and she wore the beautiful island clothing—a loose embroidered blouse in soft cotton known as a *hüipil*, and a flowing skirt woven in a bright pattern of colors. Her demeanor, however, wasn't cheerful. She set the food and drink on a small table beside the window, her expression almost contemptuous. She didn't respond to Dana's greeting and left quickly, as if wary of catching some disease. It was just as Nick had said: so many of the islanders wanted nothing more to do with the ar-

chaeological crew. That was especially apparent now
that one of the islanders had become ill along with Tim,
Pat and Dana. Suspicion and distrust abounded.

Dana stared into the cup of tea, for a second wondering if she dared drink it. Could she trust anything...? Deliberately she took a good, long sip,
reminding herself that she would not allow fear to rule
her actions. The tea and a few bites of roll actually
helped to settle her stomach. She rested her head against
the cushioned back of the chair and closed her eyes,
lassitude drifting over her.

Dana didn't know how long she slept. But when she
opened her eyes again, the slant of the sun had changed
and mellowed. And Jarrett Webster had drawn up a
chair beside her and was now peering into her face with
a look of concern. She started a little and sat up
straighter.

"Jarrett—"

He drew back, instantly apologetic. "Sorry. It's just
that you looked so—still. I've been worried about you,
Dana. About Tim and Pat, too, of course." Jarrett
seemed self-conscious. Dana supposed that he had been
working at the dig all day, but clearly he'd showered and
changed his clothes. His hair was still damp, his old-
fashioned band-collar shirt freshly laundered. He'd
brought along a few hibiscus flowers arranged in an
impromptu bouquet, and he presented then to Dana
with a guilty air.

"I stole them from the courtyard," he confessed.
"You could call them a sort of get-well wish."

Dana held the flowers in her lap, not quite sure what
to do with them—or what to do with Jarrett, for that

matter. "It's kind of you," she said. "But I'm feeling much better. It was a scare more than anything else."

Jarrett looked grave. "Someone tried to hurt you."

"Not me specifically," she reminded him. "You could've been sick, too, Jarrett. It was just chance, which of us drank that water."

"It's a damn good thing Nick found it. He's already sent a sample of the water off, and we should hear back from the lab soon. You do realize Nick still thinks it's one of us causing all the damage."

Dana sighed, resting her head against the cushion again. "I hate to say it, but that points the finger at you or Robert...or Nick himself. You're the only ones who weren't sick."

"I wonder what my motive would be," Jarrett said wryly. "Disrupting my own work? I was lucky to get this position in the first place. Actual fieldwork for once, instead of just teaching."

Dana eyed the man closely. Jarrett seemed to be someone hovering on the brink of middle age and doing his very best to resist it. His youthful shaggy hair, his boyish manner... All the signs were apparent. Even his predilection for the Victorian style of clothing contributed to the image. He looked like a nineteenth-century explorer still out and about, refusing to grow old and leave the field to a younger generation.

Dana supposed it didn't make much sense to suspect Jarrett. After all, he'd been the first one harmed on the dig, his head bashed with a rock. Dana shivered a little. She wanted to think about something else.

"So you're a teacher, Jarrett. I didn't realize that."

"I'm on sabbatical right now. I'm with a very respectable, very dull college in Oklahoma, where it's considered perfectly acceptable to talk about life but not really live it."

She almost smiled, and looked at him with more interest. "Do you know something? That's exactly how I felt about my own life in St. Louis. It was just so static. But I don't know if I can complain about that anymore."

Jarrett looked rueful. "I can't complain about it anymore myself. I seem to be getting more than I bargained for with this job. In spite of everything that's happened, though, I wouldn't trade it. Not to be stuck in a classroom all day, staring at apathetic students...that's worth a lot." He sounded earnest, like someone who'd set forth on his first real adventure and didn't want to see it spoiled. He sounded just like Dana herself, she realized. She didn't know what to think about this new camaraderie she felt with Jarrett. Today he seemed to be making an effort to keep a careful distance from her, as if he understood that his attentions had made her uncomfortable in the past. Jarrett was so...accommodating, when it came right down to it. Maybe too accommodating, in some ways.

Now Jarrett stood, as if he sensed how tired Dana felt and didn't want to intrude any further.

"I'm relieved that you're doing so well," he said. "Get some more rest."

"Thanks for stopping by, Jarrett."

"Dana...maybe Nick is right. Maybe you should think about leaving the island."

"I can't turn and run. Not after all the years I spent playing it safe."

He nodded, a look of recognition on his face. "I'm here for the duration, too. I guess once you start taking chances—you just have to keep at it." He let himself out of the room, closing the door behind him with just a whisper of sound.

Dana stared down at the hibiscus flowers in her lap—and wondered why their scent suddenly seemed cloying.

CHAPTER EIGHT

NICK CROUCHED DOWN and once more ran his fingers along the mossy uneven stone midway up the temple steps. Quickly he jotted additional notes on his clipboard, the sense of purpose inside him growing. He knew what he had to do now—exactly what he had to do. The time for speculating and theorizing was past. Nick had the uncanny feeling that he was running out of time on the island. Part of that could be blamed on all the trouble surrounding the dig. But it was something else, too—Nick's conviction that he had to put himself on the line at least one last time with his career. Hell, there might never be another opportunity.

Nick was already organizing the details in his mind. His crew was just about to learn what it really meant to work. He could spare no effort in the project ahead of him—and he could spare no one, not if he wanted any possibility of succeeding.

He hadn't felt like this in a very long while. If Dana were with him right now, she'd want to use words like *enthusiasm* and *excitement*. Nick himself wouldn't go that far, but he had to admit a certain...determination. Yes, that word was acceptable. He felt determined to go ahead, whatever the outcome.

Turning, Nick saw young Daniel waiting silently below, hands tucked into the pockets of his threadbare shorts. Nick had been so absorbed in his own thoughts that he hadn't heard the kid approach. He was glad to see Daniel . . . very glad, in fact. For the past couple of days, Daniel hadn't shown up at all. Nick couldn't help wondering how Daniel spent his time. This claim of his, that he was busy, that he had other things to do—he'd never explained it to Nick's satisfaction. But Nick had suspicions about what kept Daniel so busy elsewhere, suspicions that he was quietly beginning to investigate.

Now, after a nod at Daniel, Nick positioned his level along another one of the temple steps. Daniel climbed up to observe.

"This step's crooked," he remarked after examining the level.

"Yes, just the slightest amount," Nick said. "Water erosion, I'd say." Nick didn't elaborate on what that erosion had suggested to him so far, and Daniel seemed to understand this wasn't the time for questions. With an air of concentration he simply ran his fingers over the mossy stone, in much the same way Nick had done a few moments earlier. Always Daniel had this ability to focus quickly, as if determined to learn as much as possible during the brief times he spent with Nick.

As it was now, Daniel slipped to and from the dig at odd hours, possessing as much access to the place as anyone. Perhaps he could have been the one who'd tainted the water supply.

Nick impatiently dismissed the thought as soon as it came to him. He refused to be so warped by suspicions that he'd start accusing the kid who reminded him of Josh. . . .

Of course, this last thought of Nick's didn't make any sense, either. Josh had been Nick's seven-year-old child—transparent, easygoing, eager to share affection. Daniel was a thirteen-year-old boy too mature for his age, already concerned with survival from one day to the next. He was imaginative but also proud and very protective of his own emotions. There could be no real comparison between Josh and Daniel. None...

Daniel seemed uneasy, as if he regretted coming here at all today. He stood and began climbing down toward the base of the temple.

"Daniel, I need to consult with you," Nick said.

That got his attention. He glanced back at Nick with an expression of cautious inquiry.

"Who's causing all the trouble here? I'd like your opinion."

Daniel considered the question for a moment or two, then spoke. "The people who work for you don't like you, Señor Petrie. I would look there first."

Nick gave the kid points for uncompromising honesty. "My feelings too, actually. But which one?"

Daniel climbed back up a little, a thoughtful expression on his face. He seemed to like having a puzzle set out before him. "I believe it is the Frenchman."

Nick sat down on the temple steps. "Interesting," he said.

Daniel also sat down. "The Frenchman doesn't like what you tell him to do."

Daniel was observant. Nick, too, had surmised that Robert Lambert was a man accustomed to wielding authority—not following it. Robert played the part of a volunteer on the dig with an air of amused detachment, like an actor portraying a role he felt beneath his talents. But why was Robert playing the role in the first place?

"You say no one on the dig likes me," Nick pointed out dryly to Daniel. "That means everyone is a suspect."

"I guess one person likes you," Daniel said in a sour tone. *"La rubia."*

Nick frowned. "You're mistaken there. She disapproves of me heartily."

"You still look at her all the time," Daniel said, his tone disparaging now. "And she looks at you when she thinks no one's watching."

"She does, does she...?" Belatedly Nick realized this was a line of conversation that was best not to pursue. "You know, Daniel, for disliking the woman so much, you bring her up a lot."

Daniel gave one of his dismissive shrugs. "She acts like she wants to be my friend or something. I don't trust that."

"Maybe she wouldn't be such a bad friend to have."

Daniel gave Nick a skeptical glance. "Is that how you feel, Señor Petrie?"

The kid sure knew how to ask difficult questions. "I'm not in the market for friends," Nick said after a moment. Daniel almost looked relieved at this statement.

"I'm not in the market for friends, either," he said. He tried so hard to prove that he was independent, that he didn't need anybody. But just how self-sufficient could a thirteen-year-old kid be?

"Daniel, it's getting pretty dangerous around here. I want you to be more careful. If you have a family—"

Daniel didn't wait for Nick to finish; clearly this was a forbidden topic. He scrambled to his feet, all his pride apparent. "I know how to handle myself." He seemed to ignore the fact that he was skinny and undersize for his age. He stood there in his wrinkled shirt with the two buttons missing, his threadbare shorts, his frayed sandals—and he looked belligerently independent.

This time when Daniel left, Nick couldn't think of a reason to stop him. He watched the boy go, feeling a deeper frustration than ever. He wanted to keep Daniel safe—hell, it was his responsibility to keep everyone safe. But he didn't get a lot of cooperation in the matter, not from Daniel and certainly not from his crew. Dana, *la rubia,* was the most stubborn of all. She refused to see just how much danger she'd been in.

Nick stood restlessly, clipboard tucked under his arm. That water sample wasn't back yet from the lab on the mainland, but Nick was pretty sure that the results of the test would be ominous. He'd asked Anton and Elena to keep a strict watch on the camp food supply and on the rest of the drinking water...even though danger would most probably strike from a new direction next time. The person causing this trouble obviously liked changing tactics, doing everything possible to keep Nick off-balance. Well, it was time for Nick to change tactics, himself.

THE WHOLE CREW WAS in turmoil, the responses to Nick's project ranging anywhere from excitement to skepticism. Jarrett's reaction, however, wasn't easy to read. He confronted Nick in the field hut, only a short while after Nick had announced his plans to the crew.

"Well, Petrie, you know how to cause a stir—I'll give you that much. You've disrupted what little stability we had left." Jarrett paced in front of the shelves, where artifacts had been labeled and stored in trays and boxes. He seemed possessed of an odd restlessness, almost an agitation.

Nick remained in his own deceptively relaxed pose, sitting back in his chair, resting his feet on the desk in

front of him. "If you have something to say, Jarrett—
say it."

Jarrett refused to be rushed. He took a notebook
from one of the shelves and flipped through it ran-
domly. Now a pleased, rather secretive smile hovered on
his face. "Most of the others think it's a mistake—the
fact that you're asking us to abandon all the work we've
done up until now."

"Not abandon. We're only setting it aside for a
time."

Jarrett tossed the notebook down carelessly. Usually
he was meticulous and orderly when it came to everything he did, but today he seemed to be experimenting
with a deliberate recklessness.

"I'll admit it's a surprise," he said to Nick. "I didn't
know you had it in you—actually discovering where the
entrance to the temple crypt is hidden."

Nick studied Jarrett astutely. "You sound as if you're
certain I'm correct—that there is a tomb beneath those
steps. But as I explained to everyone, it's only speculation."

Jarrett came to the other side of the desk. "Speculation," he remarked. "What is this, Petrie—false mod-
esty? Any archaeologist worth his salt can read the
signs. The new erosion, the drainage around those particular stones of the temple.... It's all there, if your eye
is trained well enough. It has to lead to a chamber of
some kind. And it's not a wild guess. The last team that
explored this island believed the temple was more than
a shrine. They believed it held a crypt, but either they
weren't smart enough to locate it or the conditions on
the site have changed— It *was* nearly four decades ago.
Well, I've located it...and it seems you have, too, even

though I've been taking you for nothing more than a burned-out drunk."

Jarrett delivered this last comment in a particularly condescending tone, as if to incite Nick. But Nick only gazed across the desk with calm restraint. He'd long ago learned to control his emotions. He might have a reputation for being ill-tempered—but not for losing his temper. There was a difference, and Nick always observed it.

"All right, Jarrett. You're trying to inform me that you've been conducting your own investigation of the temple. Fine. Why didn't you tell me about it?"

Jarrett leaned his hands against the rickety desk and stared at Nick. Again he conveyed a reckless air, as if he found it invigorating to challenge Nick.

"Hell, Petrie. Why didn't you say anything until now?"

Nick studied Jarrett with a scientific sort of interest. He'd never seen the man like this before. Usually Jarrett conveyed a buttoned-down image: the proper college teacher maintaining a civilized attitude even on a remote island.

"The way you tell it, you've known about the temple for some time," Jarrett persisted. "Why keep it to yourself? Again—why did you wait until now?"

Nick had reasons he didn't want to share, the main one being that he hadn't wanted to give a damn about his career until now.

"It should be pretty obvious," he told Jarrett. "With all the trouble going on, I have to start excavating the temple before it's too late. You and I both know we could be pulled out of here at any moment. The Institute frowns on complications like sabotage and attempted murder. But I'm asking the same question— If you knew about the tomb entrance, why didn't you say anything?"

Jarrett's gaze shifted a little. "The timing wasn't right," he muttered. "But you've changed that, Petrie. You're grandstanding and taking all the credit for the discovery."

Nick wondered if Jarrett had, indeed, located the tomb entrance on his own. Maybe he was just trying to get in on the action after the fact.

"We'll all get credit, if there really is a tomb," Nick pointed out.

Jarrett continued leaning on the desk. Light filtered in through the slatted walls of the hut, making his eyes glitter for a moment. "You'll take full responsibility for the find, Petrie, given the chance. You know what discovering a tomb could mean. The Maya weren't exactly paltry when it came to burying their dead. They knew how to do the job up right."

Nick did realize exactly what it would mean to find a previously undiscovered tomb. It was the kind of thing that archaeologists dreamed about. Lord, everyone fantasized about another find like the great Mayan funerary crypt uncovered at Palenque in the 1950s. Even the discovery of a lesser tomb would be a professional coup....

"Jarrett, you can rest easy. We'll all get the credit we deserve."

At last Jarrett straightened up, but he didn't seem to take Nick's words into account. "There's still a big question, isn't there?" he said. "Which one of us discovered the entranceway first...? That could be an important factor. Very important."

"Let it go."

"Like hell," Jarrett muttered, and then he left the hut abruptly. Nick could picture what Jarrett would do next—smooth the perturbation from his face, slide back into his well-bred demeanor and then go talk to Dana, no doubt. Jarrett was always talking to Dana.

Nick uttered a descriptive oath and stood. He'd really have to watch Jarrett from now on. The guy was starting to sound paranoid. He had to understand that he'd get whatever credit he deserved. *If* he deserved any....

Nick went to the door of the hut and gazed out at the dig. He grimaced. It was just as he'd predicted. Jarrett stood off to one side, deep in conversation with Dana. Dana held her arms crossed against her body, not a welcoming stance, but she seemed to be listening to Jarrett with a great deal of attention. She nodded once or twice as he spoke, as if taking in his words with special care.

After a moment Dana seemed to sense Nick's gaze, and she glanced toward him. She kept her expression devoid of emotion, as if she were merely looking at a stranger. Then she glanced back at Jarrett.

Nick wondered what the hell they were talking about...and what Dana was thinking. It struck him how much she'd changed in the short time she'd been on the island. She'd arrived full of idealistic hope about her new adventure, every emotion visible on her open, expressive face. But now she seemed much better at disguising what she felt. Often she wore a guarded look beneath the floppy brim of her canvas hat. Nick couldn't help missing her frank optimism. Why wouldn't she just leave the island, before it changed her even further?

She'd undergone other transformations, too. Under the relentless tropical sun, the creamy skin of her arms and legs was turning a golden brown. And after all the work she'd done on the dig her body seemed subtly stronger, her womanly grace all the more defined....

Nick turned from the doorway. He couldn't give in to his need for her. Not now. Not ever....

EVERYONE AGREED THAT Nick was being impossible. For the past few days, he'd driven the crew mercilessly. He seemed focused only on opening up the temple as soon as possible, and he expected the others to share his obsession. As far as Dana was concerned, that was exactly what it was—an obsession. If there really *was* a tomb hidden inside the temple, it had waited there for centuries. It could afford to wait a little longer, if need be. Dana had started to forget what it felt like to sit down for a meal, take a shower on a regular basis, get a full night's sleep. This morning her eyes were bleary, her clothes and skin grime streaked, her hair hanging in limp strands down her back, and she hadn't yet stopped for breakfast.

"Dana...slow down, please. You almost covered *me* up that time," Robert protested mildly.

"Sorry," she replied. She and Robert were in the process of covering the excavation pits with tarps. The pits had to be protected, because it was clear no one would be working in them for some time. Nick had curtailed all study of Mayan farming. The temple was everything.

Dana wrestled with another tarp, anchoring it to the ground with stakes. To be completely truthful, she understood the fascination that the temple held for Nick. The idea of a hidden tomb was certainly an intriguing one, and Dana herself wondered how it would pan out. But Nick seemed to have forgotten that his crew consisted of actual human beings, not automatons in service to him....

"Damn," Dana mumbled to herself.

"What's wrong?" Robert asked, without any real show of curiosity. He spread out a tarp as if it were a linen tablecloth and he was about to set it with the family silver. Robert always gave the unspoken impression of coming from great wealth. That might be intentional, or simply a natural part of his character. With Robert, who knew anything?

"Nothing's wrong," Dana grumbled. "Except that everything's wrong...." She sat down with a thump, allowing herself an unauthorized break. Deep down, she knew what was really bothering her, but it wasn't something she cared to share with Robert. The bottom line for her wasn't how Nick treated the rest of the crew.... It was how he treated *her*. He seemed to have completely forgotten Dana's existence as a woman these past few days. He seemed to view her as simply one more worker... one more cog in the wheel....

The worst of it was the fact that she minded so much. She ought to be relieved that Nick no longer seemed interested in her in any way. She ought to be relieved that the almighty temple took all his attention and concentration.

Instead she kept thinking about Nick, pondering the few moments of closeness she'd shared with him. He'd held her in his arms... he'd kissed her... he'd provided her with his matter-of-fact strength. He'd done all those things at one time or another, but now he seemed to have retreated from her and she couldn't stop wondering why....

Somehow she had to gain control of her thoughts. The whole point of this new life was to stand on her own, to find happiness without a man. It was the only logical choice, after all. Being with Alan hadn't given her happiness. And gruff, dictatorial Nick Petrie certainly wasn't a man who brought cheeriness to mind! Dana would be much better off if she dampened her attraction to him right now. So she had to stop thinking about him. She had to stop dwelling on him.

Dana spread out another tarp, purposely centering her thoughts on the work before her. She almost began to feel better, almost began to feel in control...but then, completely against her will, a memory seared her mind. It was the memory of Nick's lips against hers....

"Damn," she said again, more loudly this time.

Robert glanced over at her. "You are in a foul mood," he commented.

It was an observation that required no great abilities of deduction. Dana sighed, and took a sip from her can of lukewarm papaya juice.

"We're all in a foul mood lately," she said. "Even you, Robert." She looked him over. It was true that Robert had lost some of his usual self-possession. His khaki trousers were wrinkled and smudged with dirt, his russet beard no longer trimmed quite so neatly. It gave him a rakish appearance, yet there was something more that seemed to have changed in him. Dana could see small cracks in Robert's facade of indifference. At least a few times this morning she had caught glimpses of a new expression on his face. She would glance up and see him staring off into the distance at no object in particular, a disturbing intensity marring his handsome features.

Dana took another sip of juice. She listened to the rasp of a saw from a short distance away, where Tim was cutting lengths of wood. Tim was his usual sullen self; Dana had never realized someone could saw wood despondently. Nonetheless, Tim was helping to fashion the winch-and-pulley system necessary to move the large stones of the temple. Meanwhile, the others were busy at the temple itself, engaged in the preliminaries of excavation: clearing the site, mapping the site, testing the site. In archaeology, it seemed that preliminaries were always the most important part of the job.

Dana smoothed out yet another tarp and glanced at Robert. He was doing it again, frowning off into space with a mixture of perplexity and profound concentration.

"All right—what's up?" she asked, unnerved by him. "Something's obviously on your mind."

He hesitated before he spoke. "I am imagining myself at the café in the village, Dana, with a very cold drink in hand. Nothing more, nothing less."

She ought to have known better than to expect a direct answer from him. "Pat's right about you," she said grouchily. "You're deliberately mysterious, Robert. You never tell us anything real about yourself. Why? Do you have something to hide, after all?"

Robert shrugged. "Perhaps the problem is that I have nothing to hide. Perhaps I am concerned that Pat—and the rest of you—would find my life mundane and monotonous, were you to know the truth of it." He spoke lightly, putting her off with what could only be termed a non-answer. But Dana wasn't in the mood to be put off.

"I don't buy it," she said. "I'm starting to think you really *do* come from a wealthy background. If the rest of us knew about your life, we'd probably envy you."

Robert gave a half smile. "Suppose that I am, indeed, born of privilege. But perhaps I find little pleasure in my good fortune. Perhaps it fatigues me with its very familiarity. Perhaps I am like a king who possesses so much gold that he longs instead for tin and copper." Robert's voice held mockery, and it was impossible to know if he was actually talking about himself. Maybe this was simply more evasion.

He leaned back on his elbow, legs stretched out and crossed at the ankle. He looked as if he ought to be garbed in a silk lounging robe—a world-weary aristocrat at repose. "Perhaps I need more of a challenge," he commented. "Danger, for instance. That is a challenge. Perhaps I need to seek danger...or to create it myself. What do you think, Dana?"

"I think you're intentionally trying to sound sinister, instead of coming right out and telling me to mind my own business." Dana went back to work, but she was conscious of Robert's lingering gaze. A small chill traveled down her spine in spite of the oppressive heat. Maybe Robert had merely been fabricating nonsense about himself...or maybe he'd been confessing something real.

The rasping noise of the saw had stopped. Tim gathered up his cuts of wood, obviously preparing to return to the temple. Dana rose to her feet.

"I'm going back with Tim," she said. "Are you coming?"

"No. I will remain here and finish this job," Robert said. "It will allow me an opportunity for solitude. We have each had so little of that."

Dana got the message. He'd had enough of her...just as she'd had enough of him this morning. She hurried to catch up with Tim—quite happy to leave Robert to his solitude.

CHAPTER NINE

THAT EVENING DANA ALMOST began to feel human again. Nick drove into the village to consult with Inspector Maciel, grudgingly allowing Pat and Dana to hitch a ride with him as far as the hotel. After he dropped them off, Dana took a long, luxurious shower. Then she went to the café, grateful that Pat had conked out for a nap and wouldn't be accompanying her. Dana would have at least a little time for herself. She settled at one of the outdoor tables and ordered a plate of what had become her favorite island meal, *pollo pibyl*—chicken in banana leaves. She was hungry and tired. She did her food justice and then leaned back in her chair, gazing toward the plaza.

A shadow fell across her table and she glanced up to see Nick standing over her. Nick Petrie, the man who too easily threatened to dominate her senses, her thoughts, her very emotions. She straightened and observed him with a frown.

"No," she said. "I won't give you a chance to ruin my evening. Don't tell me that I shouldn't be out here alone—just don't. You can't shackle the lot of us together, Nick. We all need our privacy and—"

"I haven't even said anything yet," he remarked. He pulled out a chair and sat beside her. His features were as sternly molded as ever, his eyes an austere slate blue in the encroaching night. But he seemed to be fighting his own tiredness, new lines etched across his forehead. "Dana...I didn't come here to lecture you. I have some information you should know about." He stared out at the plaza for a moment, then turned back to her almost with reluctance. "Today Inspector Maciel received the lab report on that sample. It turns out the water was laced with an antidepressant medication, quite a sophisticated drug. In large enough doses, it can kill."

Dana tightened her fingers around her beer glass. The past few days, she'd managed to push the incident to the back of her mind. But now she had to acknowledge that it had been more than an incident...much more.

"Who would have access to such a drug?" she asked, dismayed to find that her voice shook a little.

"Not one of the islanders, I can tell you that. It's not available here. It's a powerful prescription tranquilizer, used for patients undergoing severe depression. You do realize what this could mean, Dana. Possibly a stranger brought the drug onto the island...or one of us—"

"Stop it!" she said. "Please...just stop." Dana pushed her glass away and stood. "I don't want to hear any more about it. I just need...I just need to walk."

Without waiting for a response she left him and crossed the street. She didn't have any illusions about Nick letting her go on her own. She certainly didn't need to glance back to know that he was following her. Without a word she led the way down to the beach. This time she didn't bother to take off her shoes. She simply strode forward in the damp sand. Nick fell into step beside her.

"It's all right to admit that you're afraid," he said.

"I'm not afraid." She stopped and gazed out at the Caribbean. The sunset tonight was gentle, the sky a pearled gray and rose, the waters shimmering with the last fading light. "I hate being afraid," Dana said at last in a low voice. "It makes me feel so...craven. I wanted to start a new life, not long for the old one."

"Is that what you're doing right now—longing for your old life?" Nick's voice held an unexpected gentleness.

"Yes," she admitted reluctantly after another moment. "All of a sudden I'm picturing myself back in Saint Louis, with my apartment and my job, knowing exactly what's going to happen every morning and every night. I think about the fact that I purposely built that type of existence for myself. Safe, predictable... And I wonder if I really have what it takes to change."

"Dana, this isn't a test of character. It's a matter of survival."

She took a deep breath. The breeze sifted through her hair and she bent to pick up a small shell. She ran her fingers over its delicate fluted edges. Seashells on the sand... This ordinary beauty seemed to calm her a bit. Surely this island held more than danger for her.

She waited, however, for Nick to elaborate on the danger, to tell her that she should give in to her own fears and leave. But he surprised her.

"Come with me," he said tersely. Now he was the one who led the way along the beachfront. Dana lengthened her stride to match his. He moved with a sense of purpose, not saying any more, and she went along with him in silence.

She glanced at him as they walked, but the intractable lines of his profile revealed nothing to her. What was he thinking—what was he feeling? Did he truly wish her presence or did he merely tolerate it? But harder questions than these plagued Dana. She couldn't fathom her *own* emotions, let alone Nick's. She wanted to be with him, she wanted to resist him....

Nick led her far along the curve of shoreline until they came to a small secluded bay. Pure white sands sloped down to the water's edge and reefs of black limestone jutted in silhouette against the rose-tinted sky. Nick stopped and gazed out at the horizon.

"This is my favorite place on the island," he said, his tone abrupt, as if he disliked sharing such private information. "Not very many people come here. It's a good place to... just a good place to get away."

So Nick, too, felt the need for escape at times. This isolated stretch of beach, the craggy, jagged outline of the reefs, seemed appropriate to him—all rough, uncompromising edges.

She sat down and at last slipped off her shoes, burying her toes in the warm sand. "I'm glad you brought me here," she murmured. "It's a wonderful place. Wild but romantic at the same time.... I don't mean romantic in the usual sense," she hastened to amend. "Because I'm not a romantic. Not by any means."

Nick laughed—a low, easy laugh. It struck Dana that she had never heard him laugh before. He sat down beside her in the sand.

"You're a romantic, all right. You even asked a guy to marry you... with mood music and a candlelit dinner—"

"Alan was definitely a mistake," she said quickly. "I know that now. But there wasn't any way to see that in the beginning. He was so attentive and considerate at first... so courtly, if you want to call it that. As a matter of fact, he behaved a lot like Jarrett."

Nick seemed to tense at her mention of Jarrett's name. "Some people put on a good act," he said cryptically, and she wondered whether he was talking about Alan or Jarrett.

"I don't think it was an act with Alan," Dana said. "I think he really did want to please me...at first, anyway. Then he just got too comfortable. I accommodated him too well, for too long a time—and that's not conducive to romance." She sighed. "It's a no-win situation, really. You accommodate a man, you lose your self-respect. You demand what you want from him and he declines to marry you. I've really had enough of the whole thing."

As she said the words, she wanted to believe them. Surely it was necessary that she believe them, for the sake of her own tranquillity. But Nick Petrie, it seemed, would never allow her to be tranquil.

"So now you're a cynic about love?" he asked. "I don't think so...." He rose, then grasped her hand and pulled her up beside him. They stood very close to each other, and once again Dana was aware of Nick's lean strength. Achingly aware...

She was afraid he would kiss her. No, if she was to be completely honest...she wanted him to kiss her. Dana held her arms tightly against her body, struggling with this unbidden desire. She wouldn't ask for a kiss. She refused to ask—

"A swim might be a good idea," Nick suggested, his voice taut, as if he, too, battled some unspoken need.

"A swim...I didn't bring a suit," she said automatically.

"What happened to being prepared?"

"There wasn't any way I could know you'd suggest a swim, dammit...." She felt foolish, uncertain, especially as Nick began to unbutton his shirt. She turned away a little.

"Sometimes you just have to improvise," he said, his tone ironic.

Dana envied the unselfconscious way he shrugged out of his shirt. Now an even greater awareness of him pervaded her. She glanced at him, and found that in the deepening twilight he looked just as she had imagined he would: the muscles of his shoulders and chest molded in understated power. Nothing too blatantly emphasized...that was Nick. Even the swirl of dark hair across his chest wasn't excessive. It only made him seem all the more powerful. He didn't need to announce his strength, his masculinity. These qualities existed in him of a quiet surety. And Nick's sureness commanded a troubling warmth inside her.

He discarded his boots next, then unzipped his jeans and pulled them off with that same lack of self-consciousness. Even his underwear suited him—navy blue, a subdued and unaffected choice that made his masculinity all the more apparent. Dana's pulse throbbed uncomfortably as she watched him reach down to remove the underwear as well.... Then he stopped himself, issuing one of his more ironic smiles. He turned, and she watched him stride out into the water, the first moonlight silvering the outline of his body. He didn't look back at her, but she knew that he was waiting for her to join him.

She wished that she could be carefree about this, but she didn't know how. Her fingers trembled on the buttons of her own shirt. It wasn't prudishness that made her hesitate. It was the knowledge that she was about to reveal her own practicality in its most basic form: pragmatic white cotton bra, modest white cotton underpants. Nothing lacy, nothing imaginative—nothing seductive.

But she didn't want to seduce Nick Petrie. She just wanted to take a confounded swim. Grumbling to herself, she tossed her shirt on the ground, slid off her shorts and then stalked into the water until it was waist high. The waves lapped against her, buoying her. Nick still hadn't looked at her, and he began to swim out into the bay. He made no concessions, allowing her to decide on her own whether or not she would keep up with him. It made Dana realize how essentially separate Nick kept himself from others . . . how separate he kept himself from her.

At first she swam after him, employing her own competent breaststroke. But then she stopped and rode the waves lazily. The limestone and coral reefs jutted up around her, like the backbones of mysterious sea creatures. She felt she could remain floating here forever, allowing the waves to caress and soothe her. She'd longed for just such a swim since the moment she'd arrived on the island, and she knew that she ought to enjoy it while she could. Nick allowed so little time for leisure. Why he was allowing it now, she couldn't fathom.

She could no longer see him in the glimmering darkness of the waters, but she wasn't concerned. She knew he could take care of himself. And eventually he swam back toward her, coming to her on the gentle crest of a wave.

"If we had time, we could do some scuba diving here," he said. "There's a lot to experience among these reefs. Angelfish, devilfish—whatever you want to find."

Scuba diving sounded like Nick's type of activity. Exploration with a hint of danger. . . .

"We don't have the time," she said. "I doubt we ever will. Especially not now, when you're so concentrated on excavating the temple."

"You disapprove." He said it as a statement, not a question, although Dana couldn't read his expression.

"Somehow I can't help feeling a little reluctant to disturb the past. If there is a tomb under there, it was meant to remain hidden . . . secret . . . safe."

"Archaeology is a type of desecration," Nick said. "You can't get around that."

"But you'll go ahead with the excavation anyway."

"Yes."

Nick Petrie made no excuses for himself, that much was certain. Dana turned and headed back to the shore. Water skimming off her, she walked onto the sand, intent only on reaching her clothes. She picked up her shirt.

"Dana," Nick said behind her. "What are you ashamed of?"

She flushed in the darkness. "Nothing."

She felt his hand on her shoulder and he turned her to face him.

"You're beautiful," he said. He delivered these words in an unvarnished tone, once again simply making a statement.

She stared at him. "Please, Nick—" She didn't know what she was asking. He seemed to know, however. He cupped her face in both of his hands and bent his head to kiss her.

Now the breeze was cool against Dana's wet skin. Nick's lips were cool at first, too. But then heat sparked between him and Dana, ignited by their kiss. Dana lost her grip on her shirt and it fell unheeded to the ground. She brought her hands up to Nick's shoulders, learning the texture of his skin. Her heart pounded wildly, but she didn't know how to control it. She didn't know how to control anything with Nick.

She did know this kiss was a prelude to something more. His embrace compelled her to acknowledge her own desire. How quickly, how irrevocably the desire fanned inside her. But all during the past weeks she had been waiting for this night, moving toward it in spite of her doubts and fears. From the first moment she'd seen Nick, she had been waiting for him to hold her in just this way....

She gave a small sigh of surrender against Nick's mouth as she molded herself to him, showing her need without coyness or denial. They were still kissing as they sank down onto the sand. They knelt together and Nick moved his hands over her, tantalizing with his touch. Now her heart truly pounded. She was swept up by her own desire, her own need—and by something else she could not even put a name to. A yearning so intense, so poignant, it threatened to engulf her....

Nick traced a finger gently over her collarbone, lingering just above the swell of her breasts. She gave a soft moan of acquiescence and kissed him once more. Slowly he reached behind her to undo the fastening of her bra. He wasn't entirely successful.

"Have I forgotten how these things work?" he murmured, his voice thick. "It's been a while for me, Dana."

Somehow his confession emboldened her. She reached behind her back and unfastened the bra herself. But it was Nick who slid it away from her, trailing the straps down her arms. Now she could do nothing to hide from him . . . and she did not want to hide.

"You're beautiful," he repeated huskily. He touched her breast and she moaned again, arching toward him. Intense emotion mingled with the physical sensations he evoked in her. She had known a strange, inexplicable connection to him the first moment she'd seen him, and she knew it now.

He lowered her onto the sand, holding himself over her. She needed the feel of his hands on her, needed even the roughness of his skin. He seemed to understand. He caressed her, gentle and masterful at once, encouraging her own caresses. She moved her fingers over his chest, over the taut line of his hips, no longer thinking, no longer heeding danger. She was filled only with her yearning for him, allowing it to course through her unfettered. She would think later . . . much later. . . .

Nick gave a low groan of his own, his hands more urgent upon her, and she exalted in her power with him. She helped him to slide away the last remaining scraps of cloth between them and he crushed her body against his. Now she exulted in his maleness, the hard contours and muscles so different from her own softness. Already the ancient rhythm had begun between them, the movement of their bodies that would lead to exquisite intimacy. Dana opened her legs, aching to receive him. Then she hesitated.

"Nick," she said. "Oh, Nick, I don't have . . . I'm not . . . I want children, but not just yet. . . ."

Somehow this garbled message got through to him, and he raised himself just a fraction of an inch.

"So much for being prepared," he murmured. "I'm not prepared, either." He kissed her again, and it was a sweet torment. "We'll improvise," he said.

Nick trailed kisses along the hollow between her breasts and then traced a path down to her stomach. He used his mouth to caress her, lightly, gently, maddeningly.... He lingered, tantalizing her, and then his lips moved lower, between her legs....

She'd never experienced this type of intimacy before, and she gasped at the sharp pleasure of it. "Nick...please..." Again she didn't know what she was asking. Part of her wanted to pull back, to stop this overwhelming spiral of sensation. It was happening too fast. But Nick obviously knew what he was doing. With his mouth, his tongue, he commanded the most intimate response from her. She tried to clutch at him—to hold on to him—but the swirl of her own arousal captured her, took her with it. It was like falling into a vortex, whirling through a pleasure so profound that she sobbed with it. Her whole body shuddered, and only gradually did the ripples of sensation release her.

As reason came drifting back to Dana's mind, she realized in dismay her awkward position: her legs tangled around Nick, his cheek now resting against the sensitive skin of her stomach. There was no way to extricate herself with any grace. Never had she felt more exposed, more vulnerable. What had she done?

Nick seemed to understand. He held her against him, running his hands over her sweat-dampened skin. "It's okay," he said. "It's okay."

She closed her eyes, clinging to him. "No...it's not okay," she said, her voice shaking. "I've never been so...so damn self-indulgent...."

"Isn't that what sex is?" Nick asked. "It requires a healthy dose of self-indulgence, at least, or it isn't successful."

She couldn't talk about it any more. Somehow she managed to untangle herself from him. She grabbed her shirt and struggled into it, wondering why she felt no less exposed than before. Quickly she donned her shorts. That didn't help either, especially when she had to stuff her bra and underpants unceremoniously into her pockets.

Nick, too, dressed with quiet efficiency. Afterward they stayed seated side by side on the sand. But to Dana the distance between them suddenly felt immeasurable. She could scarcely believe that only a few moments earlier she had lain naked with the man.

"Nick..."

"There's something about myself that I have to tell you, Dana." The words were ominous, and she didn't like them.

"You don't have to tell me anything."

"Yes. I believe that I do." He stared out at the sea, not looking toward her at all. When next he spoke, his voice was oddly expressionless. "I'm an alcoholic, Dana. I'm a damn drunk."

She wanted to reach out a hand to him. She did reach out, but stayed herself before she touched him. He held himself rigidly, his very posture forbidding contact. "Nick, I don't get it. I've never even seen you take a drink."

He laughed—without humor this time. "I'm experimenting with sobriety. So far the results aren't in."

"Your career... Is that what happened to your career?"

His response was silence.

"At least you've stopped drinking. That's the important thing."

"You really don't get it, do you, Dana? I'm an alcoholic...whether or not I ever take another drink. I'll be one the rest of my life."

As usual, Nick made no excuses for himself. And she suspected he wasn't in the habit of forgiving himself, either. Dana felt a heaviness deep inside.

"What are you really trying to tell me, Nick?" Her own voice was quiet. "I know you well enough by now—you wouldn't share such a confidence with me for no reason. Certainly you don't want my sympathy."

"No. I sure as hell don't want your sympathy." He stood restlessly, jamming his hands into his pockets. "I'm telling you to stay away from me," he said.

"I didn't ask for tonight...." Even as she said the words, she realized they weren't true. She'd asked, all right. With every glance, every unspoken longing these past weeks, she'd called Nick to her. She didn't know how to stop herself from wanting him.

"I'm no good at relationships," he said with a warning note. "My wife left me at last and it was the only choice she could make."

Dana felt an inexplicable anger, and she scrambled to her feet. "Our little encounter hardly qualifies as a...a *relationship*. But I'll tell you something, Nick. If your wife left you, I'm sure you wanted her to go. I'm sure you pushed her away purposely. Just as you're pushing me away now."

They stared at each other in the darkness. There was just enough moonlight for Dana to see the grim, forbidding expression on Nick's face. In spite of the intimacy they'd just shared, he seemed a stranger to her at this moment. Nothing remained to be said.

The waves surged against the shore, the warm, fragrant breeze of the Caribbean drifted over them...and still nothing remained to be said.

CHAPTER TEN

RAIN STREAMED DOWN the sides of the field hut, making a curtain of water in the doorway. It rained almost every day now. The air would turn heavy and humid until the moisture was almost palpable against the skin—then the deluge would start.

Nick finished his solitary lunch of black-bean stew and pushed the bowl away. He spread out his diagrams of the temple, trying to concentrate, but all he could think about was Dana. Since the night on the beach, he'd been thinking about her a lot.

Nick swore and rubbed both hands through his hair. He found it hard to believe there'd ever been a time in his life when he'd actually taken sex for granted. But there *had* been such a time, long ago. Sex had been a need fulfilled, an activity enjoyed on a regular basis . . . a natural part of his life. Eventually his drinking had changed that, of course. He'd grown accustomed to performing in a fog of alcohol, but that hadn't been satisfactory for his ex-wife. Later, when he'd met Kathryn, it hadn't been satisfactory for her, either. Both women had ended up leaving him. Hell, he didn't blame them. No one could live with a drunk.

But now he was sober. And now he knew Dana Morgan. Now he'd seen every sensual inch of her body by moonlight. . . .

Nick cursed again. He pushed his chair back and paced the hut restlessly. No, sex wasn't something he could take for granted anymore. With Dana, it was a need that had to remain unfulfilled. No matter that the need gripped him until he could think of nothing else. As far as he was concerned, Dana Morgan would remain forbidden territory. He'd assumed correctly that her experience was limited. She'd demonstrated a capacity for passion, for pleasure, that had seemed to take her by surprise.

Apparently good old Alan hadn't introduced her to some of the finer points. But it wasn't up to Nick to fill in the gaps. Something warned him that Dana couldn't take any sexual encounter lightly. The past few days she'd avoided him even more diligently than usual. Hell, wasn't that exactly as he'd intended? Yet she seemed determined not even to meet his glance—as if, by refusing to look at him, she could make him disappear. He couldn't oblige her on that count, but he damn well wouldn't touch her again.

"Nick, I have to talk to you." Pat strode into the hut, raindrops splattering from the plastic poncho she wore. She stared at him, a defiant expression on her face. He didn't welcome her intrusion. Pat had a tendency to dramatize, and she seemed to be doing so now. He wondered what problem she'd blown out of proportion this time. Without enthusiasm, he motioned toward one of the camp chairs.

"Have a seat."

She plunked herself down, splattering more raindrops. But, for once, she seemed at a loss for words. Nick studied her more carefully now. He'd never seen her look so strained. He'd never seen her look as if she didn't want to talk.

He sat down on the opposite side of the desk from her. "Tell me what's on your mind, Pat."

It seemed that she still couldn't speak. But she reached into her pocket, pulled out a bottle and thrust it at him.

He took the bottle and silently read the label. It was a prescription made out to Pat, by a pharmacy in Tucson, Arizona. The name of the drug was very familiar to Nick by now. A potent antidepressant...

"It will be easier if you just explain it to me, Pat." He set the bottle down on the desk and leaned back in his chair. As customary, his relaxed pose was deceptive.

She still looked defiant. "Yesterday, when you told us exactly how the water had been contaminated...I just couldn't believe it. I checked my prescription right away—and I found the bottle empty. So I knew it had to be true. Someone stole my medication and put it in that water."

"Why didn't you notice this before?" He kept his voice neutral, devoid of accusation, but Pat grew defensive anyway.

"I haven't needed to take this stuff for quite some time. I hadn't even opened the bottle since I came to the island. I only brought it with me because—" She stopped, pressing her lips into a thin line, as if to prevent more words from escaping.

Nick waited for her to continue, watching her all the while. Pat often tried to put on a veneer of flippant sophistication, and she was doing so now. It only made her seem younger than her years. At the moment, sitting across from Nick, she reminded him of the students who had come to speak with him during his teaching days. Freshmen and sophomores trying too hard to explain why they had done so badly on a test or why they wouldn't be able to complete their term papers on time. Pat could pass for one of those students...except that the matter under discussion was attempted murder.

At last she went on, speaking quickly. "The point is, someone stole my medication and put it in the water. It was no doubt an attempt to implicate me."

Nick picked up the bottle in front of him and turned it around in his fingers. It looked harmless enough, but this prescription had been meant for someone in despair—and someone had almost killed with it.

"It was yesterday morning when I made the announcement about the lab report. That means you waited over twenty-four hours to come speak to me about it, Pat. Why?"

"You can't possibly think *I'm* guilty." Her voice sounded brittle. "You can't possibly think I'd use those pills to—of course not. After all, I drank from the water myself. I got sick, too—" She broke off and made a bitter grimace. "It should be perfectly obvious why I waited. You can't blame me if my first impulse was not to say anything to anyone. I knew I'd look guilty. But then I realized I couldn't let someone get away with using me like this."

Now Pat stood. "I've told you everything I can, Nick. I've been as straightforward as possible. I don't know what else you can expect of me." With that she turned and strode back into the rain, yellow poncho billowing out behind her.

Nick stayed where he was, considering what had remained unsaid. From what he had observed of Pat over the past few months, she liked portraying herself as someone thoroughly in control of her own life. Perhaps she talked incessantly about herself, but she also put herself in the best possible light. She'd never before revealed a problem with depression. Surely she wouldn't have revealed it now, unless circumstances had forced her to do so. . . .

Nick wished he had a drink—a strong one, undiluted—but at the moment he felt completely unmoved by Pat's self-professed innocence. Maybe she was guilty and she'd come forward only as a ploy to make herself seem innocent. It would be a clever tactic on her part, if she was the culprit. Or perhaps the culprit was Robert or Jarrett—or even Tim. As for Dana . . .

Nick was back to Dana again. But, hell, he couldn't suspect her of anything. He couldn't suspect her of anything except destroying his last vestige of peace of mind.

DANA'S TEMPER FRAYED just a little more as she rummaged through her knapsack and pulled out her insect repellent. She spritzed herself, but it did nothing to discourage the small swarm of gnats that had pursued her everywhere this morning. She spritzed the darn gnats, but even that didn't do the trick. Grumbling to herself, she brought out her sunscreen and slapped on some of that. Not that it would do her any good; she'd already achieved a burn on her arms. No matter what ointments, creams, lotions and sprays Dana used, the island assaulted her with too many bugs, too much sun, too much of everything. For crying out loud, now she suspected she had athlete's foot to cope with on top of all the rest of it: hair limp and dirty from too few showers, skin itching in the humidity, muscles sore from straining at the winches and pulleys with the rest of the crew. So far the massive stones of the temple refused to budge—and that didn't contribute favorably to Dana's morale, either.

She tossed aside her knapsack in disgust and sat back on her heels. She felt keyed up, trapped by an irksome feeling of suspense. But did she really have anyone to blame besides herself? She'd come looking for adventure—and she'd found it, all right. She'd found it in all its buggy, sticky, humid splendor. She was in the middle of a search for a hidden tomb—a search that made the islanders whisper more than ever of curses and dire retribution. Plus, she'd almost been poisoned to death. Plus, she'd given herself with a most embarrassing abandon to Dr. Nicholas Petrie, that night on the beach.

Dana's skin heated at the memory. Against her will, she glanced over to where Nick and the others worked at the pulley system, still trying to move one of the temple stones. Nick seemed completely absorbed in the task. Patches of sweat stained his shirt and dampened his dark hair, and it seemed that he hadn't stopped working in hours. But now he returned Dana's gaze for a moment, his expression grim and unyielding. Could it have been only a few nights earlier that he had lain with her on the beach, his harsh features transformed as he made love to her...?

Heart thudding, she bent her head and pulled down the brim of her canvas hat, as if that would shield her from her own desires. First of all, she didn't know if—speaking in a strict technical sense—they'd actually made love on the beach. Nick had taken her to a fulfillment she'd never quite experienced before, but still...

It had always been so different with Alan. Alan had never put her pleasure before his own. She had never questioned that until now—

Dana's skin heated all the more, and she pressed both hands to her cheeks as she sat cross-legged in the dirt. What was happening to her? New sensations stirred inside her and she found herself aching for the fervor of Nick's touch. But it was more than a purely physical longing—he'd awakened a tempestuous center of emotion in her that she hadn't known existed.

Of course, Nick had told her bluntly that he wanted nothing more to do with her. He'd kissed her, held her, taken her to a passion that had shaken her... and then he'd turned from her. If she was wise, she would forget all about him.

But that was the biggest question of all, wasn't it? *How* did she forget? Things had already progressed too far with Nick. She wanted to turn back, but she was like a traveler lost in uncharted territory. She hadn't expected this when she'd started her new life. She hadn't expected it at all.

Everything had been so clear before she'd met Nick. She'd formulated her plans and proceeded, confident that she'd be able to adapt to any contingency on this island. She'd prepared herself to confront hard work, rough-and-ready living accommodations and—yes— bugs. But, she hadn't counted on such a contingency as Dr. Nicholas Petrie. No plan of action, no measure of adaptability could have prepared her for the powerful, tumultuous reactions he evoked in her. She might as well have headed into a hurricane on nothing but a raft....

Dana tried to distract herself by watching the crew at the pulley system, but of course that meant watching Nick again. Young Daniel worked side by side with him, carefully and intently copying all of Nick's movements. A pull on the ropes here, a tug there.... Nick and

Daniel were obviously a team apart from the rest of the crew.

The two of them were alike in more ways than Dana cared to count. Both Nick and Daniel seemed to harbor an intensity that they kept restrained behind a certain aloofness. You could never tell what either one of them was really thinking or feeling. And in spite of the companionship they shared, each of them seemed essentially separate. It almost appeared to be a point of pride with them to maintain that separateness. They were both incredibly stubborn, that much was for sure. Take Daniel, for instance. All Dana's efforts to befriend him had so far been to no avail. It was as if the boy possessed a code of honor that decreed friendship as superfluous. Apparently Daniel allowed himself only that constrained camaraderie with Nick.

The group working to remove the stone shifted and regrouped. The few islanders still willing to come near the dig now joined Nick, Daniel, Robert and Jarrett in their efforts. Pat, of course, made certain she was in the thick of things. However, this regrouping seemed to leave Tim without a place. Looking vaguely dissatisfied, he hovered next to the others for a few moments and then wandered over to where Dana sat. Tim reminded Dana of a somnolent moth drifting about without direction. The fact that he had settled next to her seemed only an accident.

"How's it going, Tim?" she asked.

"Fine," he muttered. He sat down a few feet away from her, bony knees jutting up awkwardly.

Dana nodded toward the group straining at the winch and pulley. "We don't seem to be making much progress at this. It gives me the feeling that those stones aren't meant to be moved. If there is a tomb, it isn't meant to be disturbed.''

Tim made a sound something akin to "humph." It made for a one-sided conversation, but Dana wasn't about to give up. She needed *some* sort of success at socialization. Whereas young Daniel remained intently aloof at her efforts, Tim seemed merely apathetic—a much easier proposition. Dana clasped her arms around her own knees and leaned back a little.

"All those stories about a curse..." she murmured. "I'm not particularly superstitious, but I'm starting to think more and more that we shouldn't be intruding here." She glanced over at Tim. "I suppose I'm showing that I'm not really an archaeologist at heart," she said ruefully. "What about you—have you decided this is the career you want?"

She was rewarded with silence. Dana didn't feel discouraged. It was always a challenge to get anything at all out of Tim.

"Of course, the way I understand it, you'll be going back to the States when the summer's over," she went on. "You'll be getting ready for another semester at school." She waited, then went on again. "You're lucky. If you decide archaeology isn't for you, you'll have all your choices in front of you."

At last this inspired a response. Tim scowled at her. "What choices?"

Tim had posed this question with such rancor it made Dana stop and consider her own life. There'd been a time when she hadn't seen very many choices, either. It had taken her far too long to realize all the options available to her. Options such as working on an archaeological dig, surrounded by gnats. . . .

"You know, Tim, you're young and you have everything ahead of you. You can do anything you want."

"Are you supposed to be an advice columnist or something?" Tim muttered.

That was a good sign—Tim showing enough gumption to be sarcastic. Dana soldiered on.

"Maybe I should go into the advice business," she remarked. "It's a whole lot easier to solve other people's problems than your own."

Tim took off one of his shoes and shook out the dirt. "My mom was forty-two years old when I was born. My dad was forty-six. They figured it was time to produce an heir. They figured everything." Tim hesitated, but after a moment he added, "Except what to do about a son who didn't measure up. Nothing I ever did was right. It still isn't right."

It seemed that Tim, indeed, carried a heavy burden. It sounded as if his mother and father had never accepted him simply as he was.

"Look, I know firsthand how difficult some parents can be. But, Tim—what do *you* want to do with your life?" Dana asked. "Forget your parents, forget everything else.... What do you want?"

This question, perhaps, had been too direct. Tim jammed his shoe back onto his foot and yanked the laces tight. But it seemed that he still needed to talk.

"I don't know what I want," he said. "If I knew, everything would be different. I could finally be somebody."

"You already are somebody," Dana pointed out. "You don't have to prove anything—you just have to find what makes you happy."

"Yeah, right," Tim muttered, sarcastic again. "It's supposed to be that easy."

He got to his feet. "Save it," he said. "You don't know anything about me. My dad died two years ago. He had a heart attack. My mom just kind of faded away after that.... Never once did they approve of me."

"I'm sure they'd approve of you now, if they had the chance."

Tim shrugged. "People don't change just because they're dead. They're even worse then."

What an odd thing to say. Tim made it sound as if his parents were still observing him from some other dimension—still finding him lacking in some way. Dana supposed there were many different types of ghosts that could haunt a person.

Tim appeared to regret having said anything at all. He walked away, going to stand at the very edge of the forest. Dana had already noted that Tim had a habit of doing that: creeping up to the very edge of the jungle and then hovering there, as if he couldn't decide what to do next. That Tim was troubled, there could be no doubt. What he really needed to do was stand up to his parents and declare his independence from them. But the fact that both his parents were dead complicated matters quite a bit. Perhaps it wasn't so simple to stand up to ghosts.

Dana rummaged through her knapsack again, but found nothing in it that could be of use to her at the moment. She probably ought to go take another turn at the ropes and pulleys, but she couldn't shake her conversation with Tim from her mind. She'd told him just to believe in himself and to find what made him happy. But was she capable of following her own advice? Ever since she'd arrived on the island, all her own beliefs about herself had been tested. Was she truly as courageous and adventurous as she longed to be? Could she really start a new life and avoid repeating the mistakes of the old? In her old life, she'd believed that she needed to love a man in order to be happy. She'd therefore convinced herself that she was in love with Alan and that it was only a matter of time before they would be husband and wife. It had all turned out to be an illusion....

She had no place for illusions in this new life. But even so, her gaze strayed once again to Nick as he worked among the others. By now he'd taken off his shirt and tossed it aside, sweat glistening on the muscles of his back as he hauled on the ropes. He gave the task all his concentration, all his focus. And then he gave a shout—a sound of pure triumph and exhilaration.

"It's moving!" he called. "The stone...it's moving."

CHAPTER ELEVEN

"A TOAST, DANA. To Dr. Nicholas Petrie, the finest archaeologist on the island." Jarrett raised his glass of pallid white wine, then took a long sip from it. If he was trying to sound enthusiastic, he didn't succeed. Instead, he sounded bitter.

Dana sipped from her own glass. The wine tasted as flat and uninspired as the toast. She set her glass down and leaned back in her chair at the village café. It had been an exhausting afternoon. Working together for hours, the crew had finally managed to removed that one massive block of the temple foundation—and uncovered the first few steps of a narrow stairway leading down into the unknown.

Of course, this was only the beginning. The stairway was blocked with stones and sand that would take days to clear—perhaps weeks. Apparently the ancient Maya had been determined to make it difficult for anyone to unearth their secrets. But a passageway *did* exist—Nick's theory had proven correct.

Dana's muscles were sore even after a bath at the village hotel; she'd put in her fair share of work this afternoon. And her emotions about the whole endeavor were mixed. She'd shared the others' excitement when they'd uncovered the opening of the passageway. Her natural curiosity demanded to know what waited at the end of those narrow stairs. But she also regretted that soon the temple secrets would be secrets no longer. In some ways, it might be better only to imagine what had remained hidden all these centuries.

Jarrett set his own glass down with a thump. This evening he wore one of his old-fashioned vests, and Dana caught the scent of his after-shave—something minty that was old-fashioned in its own way. She didn't like the scent, although she couldn't say why. Maybe it was simply the fact that Jarrett had used a tad too much of the stuff. He didn't look quite so boyish tonight; his face almost seemed to have sagged, revealing the slackening of muscle tone that could accompany middle age. It occurred to Dana that Jarrett was probably older than she'd originally thought. Older and more discontented.

"Good for Petrie," he muttered now. "Just grand for Petrie. He thinks he's going to manage it, after all. He thinks he's going to pull his career out of the toilet."

Dana wasn't in the mood for Jarrett tonight. She'd come to the café hoping for a respite, only to have Jarrett invite himself to her table a few moments later. He'd ordered the wine and settled in. Strangely keyed up, he had abandoned the cautious deference he'd shown Dana these past few days.

"Jarrett, I really am tired," she said. "I'd just like to sit here and—"

"You'd just like to sit here and be alone," he finished for her. "Right, Dana. Right. But somebody has to know the truth." He propped his elbows on the table and leaned toward her. "The truth is—I'm the one who realized there had to be a crypt in that damn temple. I'm the expert on Mayan burial practices—not Petrie. But he stole the idea from me. He's taking all the credit for it. Hell, he said we'd both get credit. He agreed to that much, at least. But do you see it happening?''

Dana stiffened. ''Nick isn't the type of person who'd take credit for someone else's idea.''

''Do you know him so well, Dana? Ask yourself that.''

Dana was beginning to find the atmosphere of the café oppressive. She'd been forced to sit inside because of the drizzling rain. The light was sallow, and the air carried a stale odor of fried fish. The concrete floor had been painted an unappetizing shade of brown and the oilcloth table covers were beginning to tatter. But it was Jarrett's presence that oppressed her most of all—Jarrett and his insinuations.

''Look, if you have some complaint about Nick, handle it with him—not me!''

Jarrett took his glass and swirled the wine in it. ''Maybe you haven't noticed yet, but Petrie isn't into friendly communication. He's too busy just trying to stay sober.'' Jarrett's tone took on a vindictiveness. Then he paused, studying Dana with an appraising air. ''Well...I see you already know about Petrie's little problem. He's a drunk, and it's not a surprise to you.''

''I don't want to talk about Nick.''

''So that's how it is,'' Jarrett murmured.

''I don't know what you're hinting at,'' Dana said firmly. ''Just find a better topic or—''

''I'm not hinting at anything. It's fairly obvious how you feel about Petrie. I'm not the only one who's noticed it.''

Dana curled her fingers around her napkin. ''Why don't you get to the point, Jarrett? I don't think you joined me just so that you could complain about Nick.''

A little of the fight seemed to go out of Jarrett. He slumped back in his chair. "Maybe I just wanted to warn you about Petrie. You'll tell me it's none of my business and you're probably right. But I don't want to see you get hurt, Dana. He's hurt people before. Ask him about Kathryn Ames."

Now Dana was the one who studied Jarrett. What game was he playing at? His tone, no longer bitter, seemed to convey only a regretful solicitude . . . as if he disliked warning Dana about Nick but felt obliged to do so anyway.

She pushed back her chair and stood. "You're right about one thing, Jarrett—none of this is any of your business."

"I guess I've touched a nerve," he remarked, and now he sounded truly regretful. He raised his wineglass in another mock salute that did not come off successfully.

Dana refused to say anything more. She went out into the rain. The drops of water felt warm against her skin, a welcome sensation after the stifling air of the café. But her brief exchange with Jarrett had put her into an unwelcome state of turmoil once again and she walked quickly along, wishing she could outdistance her thoughts. She hated the fact that she was actually considering Jarrett's nasty little tidbits of information. She'd already sensed a disturbing potential for self-destructiveness in Nick Petrie. Did that mean he was also capable of hurting others . . . ?

Dana walked faster. The rain blurred the gentle hues of twilight, the rose and amethyst and violet of the sky washed like streaks of watercolor on an alabaster canvas.

Huddled between the jungle and the sea, the village consisted of only a few meandering streets that converged on the plaza as if knowing of nowhere else to go. Stucco houses hunched shoulder to shoulder along the sidewalks, while any beauty remained hidden behind the walls in private courtyards. It occurred to Dana that this village was a place closed in on itself. Few of its inhabitants ventured into the jungle or across to the mainland. Contact with the outside world came mostly through the tourists who visited here—but even that contact was transitory. Rarely did the tourists stay for more than a few hours. Such insularity did not welcome more intrusive outsiders—particularly outsiders who probed for ancient secrets. As Dana walked along, one or two villagers brushed past her without even acknowledging her nod of greeting.

She circled the plaza and came to the old mission church built under the supervision of Franciscan priests some three centuries earlier. Entering, she found herself in a sudden quiet where not even the sound of the rain intruded; the missionaries had made certain that their stone walls were built thick and strong. Votive candles flickered from the dim recesses where the statues of saints presided, but no one worshiped here at the moment. Dana slid onto one of the benches at the back of the nave, gazing through the dusky light toward the simple rough-hewn altar.

This should have been a soothing atmosphere: the sweet, pungent scent of incense smoking the air, the walls scalloped from innumerable coats of whitewash, the dark wooden ceiling beams rising protectively overhead. Nonetheless, the calm Dana sought eluded her. It dismayed her to realize that her confused feelings for

Nick could be so apparent. Jarrett had noticed them, and—if he was to be believed—so had the others.

Dana was convinced that Jarrett had intentionally set out to disturb her this evening. He hadn't just been venting steam about his own dissatisfactions. No... there'd been something calculated in everything he'd said. Was he jealous because of her too-obvious preference for Nick? Did it just come down to that, in the end? If only he knew the irony of the matter— She and Nick scarcely constituted an item.

"I thought I'd find you somewhere like this. I knew you'd probably wandered off by yourself again." It was Nick's disapproving voice. He stood over her—as if she had called him to her and he had come unwillingly. Dana gazed at him, but here in the dusky light of the church his face was thrown into shadow. Nick Petrie... a man of shadows, indeed. He was an enigma to Dana. He seemed to follow his own inflexible principles of conduct—among them a determination never to let anyone get too close. So why was he seeking her out today? Did he wish to torment her still further? Could he have any idea of his unwelcome power over her emotions? Apparently everyone else knew how she reacted to Nick. Why shouldn't Nick himself know about it!

She folded her arms tightly against her body. "Go away, Nick. For once I'm going to find some actual solitude on this island."

He sat beside her. "Solitude isn't a luxury you can afford. I'm convinced it's still dangerous for you or anyone else on the crew to be alone."

"Nothing's happened lately. Our troublemaker seems to be taking a vacation. I'd like to do the same." She knew it was an inadequate argument. Like the rest of the crew, she was constantly on edge these days, waiting for the next threat. But she did need a respite from everyone—especially from Nick.

"Go away," she said again.

He didn't budge. He just sat there with her and now his profile was all decisive lines. Dana glanced at him from the corner of her eye and she couldn't help comparing him to Jarrett. Nick wore jeans and a plain cotton shirt in faded blue; no Victorian affectations for him. And Nick wasn't the type of man who'd use too much after-shave. He wasn't the type of man who'd use after-shave at all, no doubt considering it unnecessary, unessential. Dana would have to agree with him on that.

"You should be at the temple," she said. "It was quite a coup for you today, uncovering that entrance. I'm surprised you're not still working to clear it."

"I'll be heading back in a little while. And I probably will work some more tonight. Tim and Robert are ready to put in a few hours with me. So is Anton."

"I'll bet," Dana said skeptically. She knew that Robert and Tim had remained behind to guard the temple site, along with Anton Montano. She seriously questioned whether any of them wished to continue toiling with Nick until midnight or beyond. "You ought to stop pushing people so hard," she said. "Jarrett's turning downright unpleasant, and even Pat hardly talks anymore. She's holed up in her room at the hotel right now, even though she usually loves to be surrounded by an audience."

"Pat's fine," Nick said brusquely. "And my guess is that Jarrett's only showing his true colors for once."

"Wonderful. We're all starting to unravel and show our true selves. We've been isolated together too long." Dana glanced at Nick again and had to admit that *he* wasn't unraveling. The discovery today had only seemed to fill him with renewed energy. She sensed the vigor in him, barely contained as he now shifted position restlessly.

"Don't let me keep you," she said.

"You've been making a great effort to avoid me, Dana."

She couldn't deny that. She'd done her very best to avoid him, ever since the night on the beach. Even now her face burned at the memory. She'd made herself so vulnerable to him that night, and she still felt vulnerable. It was as if she'd given a part of herself away and didn't know how to get it back. She wanted it back, quite desperately. . . .

"In case you've forgotten, you were the one who told me to stay away," she said acidly.

"I didn't mean for you to take it so literally."

Now she turned on the bench and stared straight at him. "Exactly *how* was I supposed to take it, Nick—if not literally?"

"I simply wanted you to realize that I'm not looking for involvement with any woman." His voice was calm, dispassionate almost, in spite of the tension she perceived in him.

"I suppose I should feel better that you've excluded all the rest of the female gender, too. But it seems that every time we end up together . . . you're the one who's instigated it. You came looking for me tonight—remember?"

Apparently he couldn't deny that. He leaned forward and rested his arms on the pew in front of him. "I don't know why I'm here," he said. "I just don't know."

The hushed atmosphere of the church descended upon them. Neither said anything for a long while, but Dana felt it all over again—that inexplicable sense of connection to Nick. It was a persistent impression that somehow, underneath all their differences, a deep similarity united them. But what could that similarity be? They were really two such different people. Nick seemed convinced that he had to punish himself for his past— for being an alcoholic. Dana believed firmly in new beginnings. Nonetheless, a warmth imbued her simply because of his nearness, and that stubborn sense of connection remained. . . .

"Who's Kathryn Ames?" Dana asked abruptly.

The gathering darkness cloaked Nick's reaction. "How do you know about Kathryn?"

"Jarrett told me her name. He said I should ask you about her."

"And so you obliged him."

Dana expected Nick to stand and walk away from her—just as she had walked away from Jarrett a short while earlier. But he stayed, and after a moment he spoke.

"I don't know how Jarrett learned about Kathryn, but there isn't much to tell. She and I were . . . involved. It was some time ago. Kathryn decided she could change me. Sometimes I think our entire relationship was based on that—Kathryn's determination to make me into the kind of person she needed me to be. After a while she wisely gave up."

"Maybe she didn't give up. Maybe you sent her away."

"Maybe I did," Nick conceded. "But the end result is the same."

Nick's tone had a finality to it, as if he'd offered all the information he intended. But somehow Dana couldn't let the subject go.

"What did Kathryn want from you? What was it that you couldn't give her?"

Again he waited a moment before answering. "What she wanted was reasonable enough. Sobriety, a long-term commitment, the hope that we'd start a family someday. I couldn't offer her any of those."

"But you're sober now."

"Sober... right. I don't have the best track record, Dana. For Kathryn's sake, I quit drinking for a time. But I found out it's not the kind of thing you can do for anyone else—even for the woman you love. I started getting drunk again. Things deteriorated after that."

It was certainly an unembellished account. As usual, Nick offered no excuses for himself. But he made it sound as if he had loved this woman—this Kathryn. A new emotion took over Dana now, one she despised. It was nothing but jealousy—jealousy toward the woman who had apparently broken down Nick's defenses at one time. That was something Dana herself hadn't been able to do.

Dana hated her fascination with the story, but still she felt compelled to know more.

"Jarrett says you hurt Kathryn...."

"Jarrett's a real fountain of information, isn't he?" Nick remarked. "I'll have to find out just why he knows so much. But it's true—I did hurt Kathryn. I hurt her by trying to be what she wanted at first. I gave her hope and then I crushed it. It actually seemed possible for a while... going the whole route again. Marriage, a family somewhere down the line. Except that I figured out I couldn't do it again. Never again."

Now Dana heard the bleakness in his voice, a starkness she didn't understand. "Nick, you told me once that you didn't have any children."

"Hell, Dana. Why don't you ask Jarrett about that, too? He probably knows all about it."

Dana glimpsed a raw pain in Nick, and knew she could probe no further. She sat beside him, her hands clasped tightly together as if to prevent herself from reaching out futilely once more to him. Incense drifted through the air and candles guttered their silent supplication before the statues of the saints. Nick bowed his head, but she didn't think he was praying. Nick did not seem like a man who believed in prayer. She could only wonder what he did believe in.

ONE WEEK LATER, Pat was up to no good.

"Pat, are you out of your mind?" Dana whispered. "This is crazy. It's stupid. It's—"

"Haven't you done anything sneaky your entire life?" Pat asked. "Loosen up. Live a little. And come with me—it'll give me the creeps if I do this on my own." With that, Pat grabbed Dana's arm and pulled her the rest of the way into Robert's room at the hotel. She clicked the door shut and leaned against it.

"There," Pat said, glancing around with an air of purpose. "We're in. I don't think anyone saw us. Now all we have to do is find what we're looking for."

"I'm not looking for anything," Dana said in exasperation. "Robert could appear any minute—how will you explain yourself? And what on earth do you think you're going to find in here?"

"Something—anything," Pat muttered, crossing the room and going to lift the coverlet so she could peer under the bed. She rummaged around down there, eventually pulling out an expensive-looking leather suitcase and plopping it on top of the mattress. "Just listen at the door, will you? Robert and Jarrett should be at the café a while longer, but we don't want to take any chances."

With an effort, Dana stifled some of the more imaginative curses she'd learned on this island. A few moments earlier she'd been in her own room, actually trying to listen to some music for once, when Pat had burst in and demanded her help snooping through Robert's belongings. What had brought on this sudden urge, Dana still hadn't been able to learn. She knew that what she ought to do was get out of here and leave Pat to her own nefarious activities.

Dana put her hand on the doorknob but found she couldn't leave, after all. She watched Pat, who unbuckled Robert's suitcase and flung it open with single-minded zeal. Pat had been behaving in an odd manner of late. She'd swing between withdrawn moods and the rather frenetic energy she was demonstrating now. Dana had begun to worry about her a little and it didn't seem right simply to abandon her here.

"Pat . . . are you okay?"

"I'm fine. Just fine and dandy." Pat stared into the suitcase, frowning as she poked through a few sweaters and jackets. "This doesn't help," she said. "It doesn't help at all."

"What on earth *are* you looking for? On second thought, let's just get out of here before Robert finds us!"

At last Pat turned and actually focused on Dana. "If you want to know the truth—this is really all your fault."

Dana stared at her. "My fault—"

"Yesterday I did what you suggested. I cornered Robert...and I told him exactly how I feel about him." Pat sank down onto the bed, looking suddenly crestfallen. "It was awful, Dana. You know how Robert never loses his cool.... Well, he lost it with me. Not that he got angry or anything. He just got horribly quiet, as if he couldn't possibly think of anything worse than me declaring myself to him."

Dana shook her head in consternation. "Pat, I never intended something like this—"

"And then you should have heard Robert." Pat went on relentlessly, with a sort of morbid relish. "You know how it is when someone wants to reject you, but they're determined to be polite about it at the same time? That's how it was. For the first time ever, Robert was *polite* to me. He told me how flattered he was, but he explained that he had certain commitments that prevented him from reciprocating. Those were his exact words. Certain commitments prevented him from reciprocating."

The scene did sound as if it had been awful and Dana fully commiserated with Pat. That didn't change the fact that she had to get Pat out of here.

"Look, we'll go somewhere and talk about it some more. Somewhere else— That's all I ask." Dana grimaced to herself, realizing what she'd just done. She'd offered to serve as a sounding board to Pat, who was no doubt capable of discussing Robert all night.

Pat, however, remained seated on the bed, glancing around speculatively once more. "There has to be some type of clue in here," she said. "He refused to tell me what he meant by 'certain commitments,' but I have to know. If I could just find a photograph of a wife...or maybe a Wanted poster from the Foreign Legion!"

"You're being a little dramatic—even for you, Pat."

"Well, there has to be something concrete, something tangible I can get my hands on." Pat sprang up and hurried over to the bureau, where she pulled out the top drawer and began rummaging through it. "Everyone has photos, traces of their life lying about. Why not Robert? There has to be something *tangible,*" she repeated almost fiercely. "Because surely he wasn't just making excuses. It can't just be me he's rejecting." Pat glanced over at Dana, as if seeking reassurance on this point. Unfortunately, Dana could offer no comfort at all. Robert had made himself so mysterious that it would be impossible to tell whether or not he was making excuses. And this room didn't seem as if it would offer any insight. Robert was a very neat and organized person, it appeared. He hadn't left traces of himself lying around. The plain wooden bedstead, the rickety bureau, the bare walls—they belonged to a cheap hotel clinging to the edge of respectability. Certainly they revealed nothing about the occupant.

Pat shut one bureau drawer and pulled open another, grumbling when all she found was an orderly stack of the khaki shirts Robert favored. Dana opened the door a crack, peering outside. The corridor was empty, but who knew how long that would last.

"Just hurry it up—"

"Has Nick said anything to anyone about me?" Pat asked abruptly. "Just go ahead and tell me if he has."

It was an odd question. "I don't know what you're talking about," Dana said. "Nick's never seemed the type to gossip, if that's what you mean. Besides, what could he possibly have to say about you?"

"Forget it. Nothing." But Pat looked strangely relieved as she continued her snooping.

By now Dana was thoroughly annoyed. She'd had enough of Pat's erratic behavior—and she really wished Pat hadn't brought up Nick. Dana didn't want to think about him any more than she had to....

Who was she kidding? She thought about Nick all the time. She thought about him in spite of the fact that once again he'd categorically pushed her away. After their conversation in the church, he'd seemed more determined than ever to keep a distance between them. That she helped contribute to the distance, there could be no denying. She spoke to Nick only when absolutely necessary. But it was a method of self-preservation on her part, a response to Nick Petrie's indomitable reserve. She feared what would happen if she were actually to reach out to him, if she were actually to make herself even more vulnerable to him....

At the moment, all Nick's efforts and all his concentration seemed directed solely on the temple, as he supervised the laborious clearing of that secret passageway. Perhaps he found it easy to dismiss any woman from his life. Obviously he was growing adept at the practice. So why couldn't Dana just dismiss *him?*

If she didn't watch out, pretty soon she'd be as pathetic as Pat, searching for clues to the man who had rejected her. Deep down, she understood Pat's frantic grasping at any explanation for her romantic predicament. Deep down, Dana herself longed to know more about why Nick needed to turn from her.

Dana expressed a few more imaginative oaths to herself. She opened the door another crack. "All right, that's it," she said. "We're leaving. Trust me, the worst thing you can do is humiliate yourself over a man like this—"

"My God!"

Pat's small cry of dismay interrupted Dana and she twisted around. She saw Pat kneeling before the final bureau drawer, holding a small, exquisitely formed pottery jar adorned in faded colors. Dana recognized the jar immediately. It was one of the artifacts that had been stolen from the site.

CHAPTER TWELVE

NICK SUPPOSED THAT as jail cells went, this one qualified as habitable. Some twelve feet by eight, it allowed
sufficient room for a narrow cot and a straight-backed
chair. The cot was spread with a ratty blanket, but the
concrete floor had been swept clean. If the air smelled
dank and unused, maybe that couldn't be helped. Isla
Calamar didn't have all that much experience in hous-
ing prisoners. According to Police Inspector Maciel,
Robert Lambert was the first to occupy this cell in over
a year.

At the moment Robert sat in the straight-backed
chair, trying to achieve a pose of leisurely indifference.
Only the slight twitching of one foot betrayed any
nervousness. Nick sat on the other side of the thick steel
bars.

"Nick," Robert remarked, "you must consider the
absurdity of this situation. Someone planted those artifacts in my room. Someone who wishes to implicate
me."

Pat had used almost those exact words to defend
herself when she'd told Nick about the missing medication. Someone, indeed, was playing havoc with Nick's
crew, but he hadn't ruled out either Pat or Robert.

Nick shifted in his own chair. "Anything's possible," he said. "Although I'd hate to think you were

stupid enough to steal the artifacts and then hide them
in such an obvious place.''

''My point exactly,'' said Robert, stroking his beard
in a judicious manner. ''Especially with someone like
Pat around, who is capable of almost anything, it
seems.'' Robert's voice held a note of acrimony. He
couldn't be blamed for that. Yesterday Pat had made
such a dramatic public revelation of the artifacts that
Inspector Maciel had felt obliged to clap Robert in jail
immediately. In fact, Robert had spent the night in this
cell.

''Nick, has it occurred to you that Pat herself may
have planted those things in my bureau drawer? It is
highly suspicious that she chose to search my room in
the first place.''

Nick had to agree with that. The way he understood
it, both Pat and Dana had been rummaging around in
Robert's possessions. Dana, of all people . . .

''Right now I'm still considering the possibility that
you stole the artifacts yourself,'' Nick said.

''What could be my motive?'' Robert protested. ''Let
us be reasonable about this, please.''

''Okay, then cut the bull. Tell me what you're really
doing on this island.''

Robert looked mildly peeved. ''I assure you that I am
hiding nothing about myself. I am on this island because I wish to take a . . . a leave of absence from my
ordinary life. That is it—a salutary leave of absence.
Surely you can understand that.''

Nick understood, all right. At the moment he wanted
to take a leave of absence from his whole damn crew.
Pat and Robert could well be the worst of the lot. Pat
had gone nosing around and had then caused a ruckus
about something that should have been handled in a

calm, rational manner. Robert himself wouldn't drop the blasé attitude, even after a night in jail. Nick had had enough of both of them.

He stood. "You should be out of here in about half an hour. There isn't enough evidence to hold you. Like you said—anyone could have planted those things in your room."

Robert stirred. "Only moments ago you led me to believe I would be enjoying these accommodations indefinitely. Now you tell me I will be released. Are you trying to test my fortitude, Nick?"

It appeared, despite the posturing, that Robert hadn't enjoyed his incarceration. He seemed unable to conceal the relief that overtook his usual pose of unconcern.

The outer door opened, but it wasn't the inspector come to release Robert. Instead, it was Tim. He walked into the jail anteroom with an air of reluctance, hands stuffed into the pockets of his baggy pants, and stopped cold when he saw Nick.

"I'll come back later," he said, already turning to go.

"Stick around," Nick said.

Tim glanced over to where Robert remained behind bars. "Uh...Pat asked me to deliver a message. But it's supposed to be private." Tim wore an expression that conveyed his wish to be somewhere else at the moment—anywhere else. He took another step toward the door.

"Spit it out, Tim," Nick instructed. "We're all friends here."

"Quite—we're all good friends," said Robert, his tone only slightly ironic. "Go ahead, Tim. Let Nick hear what you have to say."

Tim projected all the enthusiasm of someone who had stepped into a mess and was now trying to figure a way to clean his shoes. "Pat says to tell you she's sorry. She lost her head and acted...rashly. That's it."

Knowing Pat, Nick suspected that the original message was somewhat more rambling; no doubt Tim had condensed it down to manageable proportions. But how had Pat induced the normally uncooperative Tim to come here today in the first place?

"Charming," Robert commented. "First Pat rifles through my belongings. Then she rushes around, making accusations. She lands me in jail...and then she decides to apologize. Through an intermediary, no less. Why did she not come herself?"

"She didn't think you'd put out the welcoming mat," Tim said. He seemed to be relaxing just a little. Now he glanced around. "Jail," he said. "I've never been in a jail before." He made it sound as if he'd welcome the experience of getting behind bars himself. Tim was a strange bird, always skulking around listlessly, reluctant to exert himself. Except when it came to Dana, of course. Nick had observed that lately Tim seemed to be seeking Dana out to engage in short, almost animated conversations with her. Nick wondered what the two of them found in common, but Dana seemed to treat Tim with the casual regard of an older sister. Easygoing affection seemed to come naturally to her....

"I've been on digs where the lodgings weren't much better than this," Nick said.

"Yeah?" Tim studied him speculatively. "You ever been in jail before, Nick?" Tim clearly appeared fascinated by the subject of incarceration.

"Twice," Nick said. "Once when I was in college, they locked me up overnight for too many unpaid parking tickets—over fifty, if I recall."

Tim seemed disappointed by the mundaneness of this incident, and Robert contributed a bit of sarcasm.

"Captivating story," he said. "No pun intended, however. Perhaps we could discuss something else—such as my own impending release."

Tim would not be dissuaded. "You said twice," he told Nick. "What was the other time?"

Nick hesitated a second or two before answering. "The other time was also in college—except that I was a teacher instead of a student. Drunk and disorderly, I think they called it."

Now Tim gave him a look almost of respect, and Nick felt a flash of pure irritation.

"It wasn't a good experience," he said sternly. "I wish to hell it had taught me a lot more than it did. Otherwise I might not have wasted so many years afterward—" He stopped, aware now that both Tim and Robert were observing him with interest. The last thing he needed to do was share his life story with these two—Tim no doubt trying to think of ways to get himself locked up and Robert just thinking about getting himself let out.

But Nick couldn't evade his own words, and they plagued him even after he had lapsed into silence. He'd spoken of all the years he had wasted, and he couldn't deny that waste. He couldn't ignore it or forget it. He couldn't get around it, either.

He'd thrown away too damn much of his life, and he didn't know where to go from that painful knowledge.

THE NEXT AFTERNOON, Nick and Daniel worked together at clearing more rubble from the inner stairway of the temple. There wasn't much room in this dark, narrow space, but the two of them had settled into an efficient rhythm, carefully removing stones from the barricade and piling them into baskets they would later cart outside. Without the need to speak to each other, they proceeded in this manner for some time. Then, still without the need for speaking, they took a short break. Nick handed Daniel a lime soda and began drinking one himself. Ancient dust clotted the air and seemed to have settled in Nick's throat. No matter how tepid the soda, it went down well. Meanwhile, Daniel played his flashlight over the walls of the stairway, studying the Mayan glyphs painted there so many centuries ago. Thrown into relief were vivid images of kneeling gods, necks bowed under the weight of their elaborate, symbolic headdresses, faces contorted forever into grimaces at once ominous and regal.

But it was Daniel's face that Nick watched in the wavering illumination thrown out by the flashlight beam. Daniel's expression, normally reticent, at this moment revealed an intensity as he studied the glyphs. Nick recognized that look. It was the expression of someone enthralled by the secrets of the past. Nick himself had no doubt worn the same look years earlier, when he'd been starting out in the field. Maybe he'd lost it somewhere along the way, but he still recognized it in Daniel....

"You could be an archaeologist someday," Nick said. "You'd be a damn good one, too, from what I've seen so far."

Daniel gave him a quick glance, as if not trusting what he'd heard. Maybe that was understandable. Nick didn't make a habit of handing out compliments to anyone, so Daniel probably didn't know what to do with this one. No matter; Nick had meant what he'd said. He wouldn't repeat his praise anytime soon, letting the words stand on their own—and letting Daniel decide what to do with them.

Daniel leaned back and swigged some of his soda. It was quite a few moments before he spoke. "I'm too busy to be an archaeologist," he said at last. "I have other things to do."

Always Daniel needed to assert his independence, his self-reliance. Nick thoughtfully considered what he should say next, knowing that he had to exercise caution.

"Daniel . . . I have an idea about what keeps you so busy—"

"What idea, Señor Petrie?" Already Daniel had gone on alert, as if Nick had attacked him somehow. He straightened, setting down his soda while it was only half-finished.

"Maybe I'm wrong about it," Nick said in a mild tone. "Maybe not."

The kid was still intently wary. "Did you check up on me, Señor Petrie?"

Nick cursed himself. This wasn't going well, but he'd known that he'd have to broach the subject sooner or later. He'd been putting it off, as it was.

"Look, Daniel, I'm . . . concerned about you. And I think maybe I can help—"

"I don't need help." Daniel scrambled to his feet, although the confined space forced him to stay hunched over. "What I do is my own business."

"Daniel, listen—"

"Goodbye, Señor Petrie." Daniel sounded very distant and formal. He turned and made his way quickly up the stairway, disappearing outside.

Nick cursed again. Stooped over, he made his own way outside, emerging just in time to see Daniel reach the base of the temple and head straight for the jungle.

"Daniel," Nick called peremptorily. The kid didn't spare him even a backward glance, and now he headed right into the trees. He was gone.

Nick had botched it with Daniel, all right, but he wondered what choice he'd had. After what he knew about Daniel's activities, he suspected the kid could be in as great a danger as anyone. All Nick wanted was to help him. But help, ironically, was the last thing Daniel wanted from Nick.

THE REST OF THE DAY didn't go well, either. Later the same afternoon, Nick spent a frustrating half hour on the phone to the director of the Mesoamerica Institute in Saint Louis. The Institute was getting too damn close to pulling the plug on the Isla Calamar project, frowning as it did on the poisoning of crew members and the theft of artifacts. Nick had finally convinced the director that it would only be a few days, a week at the most, before the inner stairway of the temple would be totally cleared. This was Nick's grace period—one week in which to show results. He'd do it, whatever it took. He'd find what waited at the end of that stairway.

Now he climbed into the Rover, put it in gear and drove out of the village. Dana sat beside him. She'd asked to come into town with him today in order to make a phone call of her own. Nick couldn't help wondering whom she'd been so anxious to speak with. One of her troublesome parents? Maybe even Alan, the ex-boyfriend. Maybe the guy was starting to look good to Dana after her time on the island—who knew?

All Nick could say for sure was that Dana distracted him. Today she'd plaited her hair into one long golden braid that dangled over her shoulder. She wore a white shirt that offset the honeyed tan of her arms and her snug jeans did justice to her curves. She radiated sensual good health and strength. Nick cursed himself for even noticing.

As they bounced along over the pockmarked road, Dana seemed determined to keep their conversation impersonal.

"It really does appear as if someone planted those artifacts in Robert's room," she said. "I don't think he's guilty. And at least now we have the artifacts in our possession again—every single one of them."

He noted how she used the pronoun *we* without even seeming aware of it. Was she referring to the entire crew—or to herself and Nick? Maybe she was getting personal, whether she knew it or not.

"Listen, Dana—forget about Robert and the rest of them right now."

"I can hardly forget, after everything we've been through in the past few days."

He pulled the Rover to the side of the road. From here they overlooked the sea, waves crashing against limestone cliffs. At times it seemed as if the turbulent waters would overtake this small island, engulf it somehow. Nick drummed his fingers restlessly against the steering wheel. He didn't know what he intended to say to Dana—but then the words came, without any preamble, without any warning.

"I had a son once. My marriage wasn't going all that well, but we decided to have a child anyway. We named him Josh." Nick stopped there. He hadn't spoken to anyone about his son in a very long while. Saying the words out loud made Josh's image in Nick's mind seem more real and vivid than ever. Josh, shoelaces always coming untied as he sprinted along, his hair flopping over his forehead, his freckled face breaking into a grin.

"He was a funny kid," Nick went on. "Light-hearted, a little clumsy, an explorer at heart. . . ."

"I was starting to suspect you'd had a child," Dana murmured. "Just from a few things you'd said." She spoke cautiously, as if feeling her way step-by-step with Nick. He was feeling his own way step-by-step.

"He would've been fifteen this year," Nick said, and then he felt as if he'd taken one step too far. Because that was something else that tormented him in his new sobriety—his ability to picture Josh at different stages. Josh at three . . . Josh at five . . . Josh at seven. . . .

He didn't look at Dana, and she didn't speak to him. She didn't need to speak; already he felt the unwelcome weight of her caring, her sympathy.

Gradually Nick realized that he was gripping the steering wheel so hard his knuckles had turned white. He didn't know why he was telling any of this to Dana, but he had to continue.

"When Josh was seven, he was killed. He was on his bike and a truck— Well, maybe the details don't matter. I've gone over the details hundreds of times and they still add up to a stupid, senseless death."

At last Dana did speak. "I'm sorry," she said, her voice soft. "It's terrible, Nick. I can't imagine what I would do—how I'd handle such a thing."

"Meg handled it by blaming me," he said. "I blamed myself, too. Hell, Meg and I finally agreed on something."

"But the accident couldn't have been your fault, surely—"

"Logic doesn't have anything to do with it," Nick said roughly. "I was out of town when it happened—I blamed myself for that as much as anything. I told myself if I'd just been around more, instead of trying to build my damn career, or instead of spending too many nights at my favorite bar... I had dozens of reasons to blame myself. So did Meg. After the accident I started drinking more, Meg and I started sleeping apart more.... The divorce didn't take long in coming."

Dana touched his arm. "It's understandable things would go a little haywire. Even your drinking, Nick."

He felt the same flash of irritation and frustration he'd experienced yesterday with Tim. People sometimes built up distorted views of someone else's drinking. It became an activity to be admired, if you were an unsure person like Tim. Or it brought out understanding and pity, in the case of a warm, giving woman like Dana.

"You don't get it," Nick said harshly. "I'd had a drinking problem for a long time before Josh died. I just thought I knew how to control it. And I knew all the rationalizations—I'd had a bad day, my career wasn't all it was cracked up to be, I'd had another fight with Meg. So I'd take a drink and go from there. The rationalizations can be endless, Dana. The fact that I started drinking more after Josh died—I was just using his death as one more excuse. He deserved better than that.... My son deserved better."

Dana's eyes were a rich, deep brown as she gazed at him, and he still sensed in her the compassion he didn't want.

"Let yourself off the hook, Nick. Doesn't it count, the fact that you're not drinking now?"

A too-familiar weariness seeped over him. "I don't know what counts anymore. It takes everything I have just to make it through each day without a damn drink. I don't have room for anything else."

Again, Dana didn't answer for a long moment. When she finally did speak, her tone was curiously flat. "What you really mean to say is that you don't have any room for me. You're afraid you haven't made it perfectly clear yet that you want nothing more to do with me. Damn you, Nick. You'd already got it through quite well. You didn't need to make another attempt."

He could tell she was starting to get angry, and that was good. He preferred her anger to her compassion.

"There were a few points I hadn't cleared up," he said. "For example, I know you want children someday. I guess I wanted to explain why I don't intend to have another kid myself."

She was definitely getting angry. She yanked her seat belt free, and for a minute Nick thought she was going to jump out of the vehicle. Instead she just smacked the dashboard.

"I don't believe this. You assume that I could fall so hard for you I'd want to—I'd want to start a family! Even worse, you use your own son as an excuse to push me away. All this time, Nick, I've thought you were the kind of person who didn't hide behind excuses. But I was wrong. You're using your son's death to keep yourself apart from everyone else."

He couldn't deny the truth in her words. Josh's death had changed him irrevocably. He didn't know how to move beyond it. He'd stopped drinking, but that hadn't done the job. In many ways, it had only made things worse. Sobriety was supposed to give you a whole new life, but for the past eight months Nick had only been retracing his old life with uncompromising clarity.

Dana was still worked up. "It really bugs me, the way you think I want a permanent relationship with you."

"Not with me, then. But you want one with somebody, Dana. You're looking for a man who'll give you permanence, a family—all of it."

She stared at him. "You're wrong, Nick. I've learned that I can't wait around for a man to *give* me anything. If I want a family, someday I'll create one for myself. I won't count on you or any other man—trust me." She sounded defiant, disillusioned and very determined. Again Nick was reminded just how strong and stubborn Dana could be. But she had a few weaknesses, too.

"Think about it," he said quietly. "Maybe you're doing the exact same thing I am. I'm retreating behind Josh.... You're retreating behind that failed marriage proposal of yours."

She drew her eyebrows together. "It's not the same thing at all."

"Maybe it is, Dana. Maybe it is."

She didn't seem to have any further response. She yanked her seat belt back into place, and Nick started the Rover again. He followed the road as it twisted along the shoreline and then began to turn into the jungle. Branches splayed overhead to blot out the sun. Everywhere vines crept, intent on smothering the forest floor and climbing the immense trunks of the mahogany and cypress trees. A potent silence descended between Nick and Dana, along with the shadows of the jungle.

But then the silence ended, as a bullet shattered the windshield of the Rover.

CHAPTER THIRTEEN

Two MORE SHOTS SOUNDED in rapid succession. One hit the side of the Rover, and the other struck a nearby tree. Nick twisted the steering wheel, plunging off the road and into the forest. The Rover came to a shuddering halt, but even before the engine died Nick had popped Dana's seat belt, wrenched her from the vehicle and pulled her behind a fallen tree. It was the best cover he could find. He crouched beside Dana.

"Are you all right?" he asked in a low voice, quickly checking her over. Her eyes had widened and she was very pale, but otherwise she seemed fine.

"Nick—who could it be—"

"Your guess is as good as mine. Stay down. Stay quiet."

The cries of startled birds had faded and an eerie silence enveloped the forest once more. Nick, however, had no doubt that their stalker still waited for a chance to fire another volley. Swiftly he considered different options. If they left the fragile protection of this log, they would all too easily become a target for their attacker. If they remained here, they would only be engaged in a perverse waiting game, hampered by their own immobility.

Nick brought his arm around Dana, pressing her lower to the vine-cushioned ground. All his senses strained to hear any sound that would betray their attacker. He listened for the snap of a twig, the whisper of a footfall. But no sound came—no clue, no help.

Minutes passed. Nick kept his arm around Dana, holding her close. A chill went through him as he realized how easily she could have been harmed by one of those bullets. Lord, she could have been killed....

He turned his head toward her. They stared at each other silently. Nick saw the fear and longing mingled in Dana's expression. She lifted her hand and with trembling fingers touched his face. He cupped his own hand over hers. He knew what she was thinking.... How close they'd both come to losing their lives—to losing each other....

Dana wasn't Nick's to have, but at this moment he made his claim on her anyway. He kissed the palm of her hand and then he molded her yet closer to him. It was a gesture of protectiveness, an acknowledgment of fierce tenderness. He would allow nothing to happen to her—nothing.

He didn't know how long he stayed like this, using his body to shield Dana. Time seemed to have lost any significance, but Nick did know that they could not go on waiting indefinitely. They were too vulnerable. Their attacker, obviously clever, could even now be circling, finding another vantage point.

The air had a heavy, expectant feel. Raindrops began to pelt down, finding their way through the canopy of branches overhead. Damn—the noise of the rain would give excellent camouflage to any sounds their stalker might make. Nick no longer had any choice. He and Dana were targets—but they'd have a better chance as moving targets.

Slowly he lifted himself up, creeping gradually to the right, sweeping his gaze across the forest. The dense foliage gave nothing back to him, concealing its secrets too well. He moved another fraction to the right, still doing his best to shield Dana.

This time the gunshot sounded like a crack of thunder.

"Nick!" Dana screamed, reaching out to him. It was then he saw the blood splattered on her hands, her face, blood that was already smearing in the rain.

NICK'S SHOULDER HURT like hell, but the doctor had told him he'd live. The bullet had passed right through, fortunately. And fortunately the sound of gunfire had brought the Montanos thrashing through the forest. The final shot had directed them to Nick and Dana's location—and in all the ensuing commotion the mysterious attacker had simply disappeared. Thank God the blood marring Dana had been Nick's and not her own.

Now Nick lay in a bed at the hotel, his shoulder trussed up with an elaborate bandage. He was in a lousy mood. All he wanted to do was get out of here, find out who the hell had been taking those potshots at him and Dana, and then get back to work at the temple. The doctor, however, had given Nick one of his noxious herbal cures—something dark green and glutinous— and Nick felt so woozy that the evening shadows seemed to dissolve and change shape around him.

The door opened quietly and young Daniel slipped into the room. This was a surprise, indeed. After their confrontation in the temple stairway, Nick had been worried that he'd scared the kid off—but here Daniel was, skinny arms held close to his sides. He hovered beside Nick's bed, frowning down at him without a word.

"Well, Daniel. Still ticked at me?"

The kid seemed to think this question unworthy of an answer. He just went on frowning at Nick.

"You shouldn't be here, Señor Petrie," he said after a moment.

Nick almost managed a grin. Daniel, at least, seemed to understand the reality of the situation.

"You're right. I shouldn't be here. I should be out getting to the bottom of this mess."

"Can I see the hole in your shoulder?"

This time Nick actually did grin, although even that effort seemed to hurt. So often Daniel seemed older than his years, but right now he sounded just like a kid.

"Afraid not," Nick said. "The doctor's proud of his bandage job. I wouldn't want to upset him by fooling with it."

Daniel seemed restless. He shifted from one foot to the other and nodded toward the door. "I can tell you what's happening out there. Inspector Maciel is questioning everyone. He's angry that someone brought a gun to the island, and he's searching for it."

"He won't find anything. Our culprit is a smart one, Daniel. He—or she—leaves no trace behind."

"You think it could be a woman?" Daniel asked skeptically.

"Why not? But whoever it is, he or she is growing more bold—more reckless." That was the understatement of the year. Nick winced as he tried to shift his position a little.

Daniel didn't say anything for a while. He just stood there, head lowered as if deep in thought, occasionally scuffing one of his sandals over the floor. Nick waited. He sensed that the kid had something to tell him, but this time he knew better than to press for information. He didn't want Daniel running away from him again.

At last Daniel glanced at Nick, his dark eyes somber. "I don't know anyone who'd use a gun, Señor Petrie."

"Can you be so sure of that?" Nick asked quietly. "All it takes is one person who goes a little too far...."

Nick wished he could get out of this damn bed, but every time he tried to move, the evening shadows seemed to shift around him all over again. What the heck *had* the doctor given him?

"I have to go now," Daniel said abruptly.

"Where to? It's almost nightfall."

"I have to go," Daniel repeated, his voice stiff.

"Stick around a—"

"I only came to tell you what's happening." Daniel spoke quickly now. "Your workers are all talking at once. They all have ideas—and they all say they're innocent."

Nick could picture his unruly crew, led no doubt by Pat in eloquent protestations of innocence.

"Thanks for the report, Daniel. But I want you to be careful—"

"You should talk, Señor Petrie." With that, Daniel headed for the door.

"Dammit, stay and—"

But the kid was already gone. Nick tried to struggle up to a sitting position, felt the room spin and sank back again. He considered bellowing some of his frustration but knew that wouldn't do him any good. How the hell could he get the kid to really listen to him for once? Before it was too late. . . .

Daniel's visit this evening had been a peculiar one. For a moment there, Nick could've sworn he'd detected worry on the kid's face. It almost seemed as if

Daniel had come to reassure himself that Nick was all right—still alive and kicking.

Nick shifted again in the bed, ignoring the pain that sliced through his shoulder. He was admitting the possibility that Daniel—in spite of his semblance of aloofness—was growing attached to him in a personal way. But that was the last thing the kid needed. Hell...it was the last thing Nick himself needed.

There was something else, too. Tonight, Daniel had seemed wound up, tense. Maybe he knew more than he was telling. Maybe he was frightened about something and just didn't know how to say it.

That was all Nick had to go on right now—a whole lot of maybes. It could have been anyone who'd fired those shots today. More than ever, Nick wanted to get up and start figuring out exactly who it had been. But the doctor had dosed him with something genuinely potent, and Nick couldn't stop himself from sinking into an uneasy, fitful sleep. In his restless dreams he saw blood streaked on Dana's face, and this time it was her own....

He awakened slowly as the door to his room opened. It was dark by now, but a sliver of light from the corridor briefly outlined the slender form of a woman. Nick fought his grogginess, struggling to be alert. It seemed he still had some adrenaline left over from this afternoon, his muscles coiling for action. His new visitor closed the door and came toward him in the night. She leaned over to switch on the bedside lamp and he caught her scent—feminine, musky, with a hint of mildly perfumed soap. It belonged unmistakably to Dana. As the light from the lamp spilled over her, he studied her face, making damn sure that she *was* intact. She looked good—more than good. Now her hair hung loose down her back, falling in silken ripples after being plaited all day. She'd changed into one of her sleeveless blouses and she wore a colorful island skirt that swirled gracefully around her legs. She was barefoot, and that was the detail that did Nick in. Dana, feet sensuously bare, gliding into his room at night....

She sat on a corner of the mattress and studied him. "The doctor says you're going to be fine, but he's fed up with me constantly asking questions about you. At the very least, I'm sure he'd like to see my Spanish improve."

"I need to find out who was gun happy this afternoon," Nick said. He made to sit up, but Dana prodded him down to the pillow again with a hand to his good shoulder.

"You and I both know that isn't going to be easy," she said. "Pat swears that this afternoon both Robert and Jarrett went off for a while by themselves. Tim claims he took a nap in one of the field huts, but no one can really seem to verify that, either. The Montanos vouch for each other, of course, and—"

Nick swore. "You'd think all of you could just follow instructions for once. You're supposed to stay together! Is that too damn much to ask?"

"I was with you," Dana reminded him. "I have the perfect alibi."

"Right...and I almost got you killed." His gaze strayed over her. He needed to keep affirming that she was, indeed, safe and well.

"You truly are arrogant, Nick, if you think you're responsible for that. We're dealing with someone who's very clever as well as ruthless. Actually, there could be more than one person involved, and that would make the whole situation all the more difficult. But just for tonight... let yourself off the hook. About everything."

Nick didn't see much chance of that happening. Meanwhile, he could tell that Dana seemed tense and wrought up in her own way. There was a new tightness to her features and he wished he knew how to smooth it from her.

"You should be getting some rest yourself," he said gruffly.

"I'm not the one who got shot. I'm perfectly fine." Now she sounded strangely irritable. With a quick motion she left the bed and went to the door. Nick felt disappointed. He hadn't expected her to leave quite so readily.

It turned out, however, that Dana wasn't leaving. She locked the door with a decisive gesture, then turned back to Nick. He recognized the determined expression on her face. It meant that she was set on a particular course of action and would not be dissuaded from it. But she looked just a little uncertain, too. It was a puzzling combination: determination and uncertainty at the same time.

She came to stand beside the bed. Staring at Nick almost defiantly, she began to undo the buttons of her blouse, starting at the top and working her way downward. As the blouse came open, he saw the soft camisole she wore underneath, the cloth shaping itself to her breasts.

"Dana..." His voice sounded thick to his own ears.

"Don't try to stop me, Nick," she said. But she had it wrong. He hadn't been in mind to stop her at all.

She slipped the blouse from her shoulders, no longer looking at him. He wondered if she knew how beautiful she was, with her hair cascading over her arms and a flush tinting her cheeks and throat. She pulled off her skirt, revealing a thin slip underneath. It was enough to drive him wild: this peeling off of clothes, only to divulge another skimpier layer underneath.

"I'm no good at this, Nick," she said, pausing after tossing her skirt to the end of the bed. "Seducing a man and all . . . I just haven't had a lot of practice at it." Uncertainty had won out over determination, it seemed.

"I'd say you're doing a great job," he murmured. "But maybe I can help." Maneuvering wasn't all that easy for him at the moment, but he managed to lift aside the sheet in a welcoming gesture. Dana hesitated, but then she crawled into bed with him. He cradled her with his good arm, reveling in the feel of her next to him. Lowering his head, he kissed her, brushing his lips lightly against hers.

It was Dana who deepened the pressure of the kiss, tangling her hands in his hair, running her fingers over his face. "If only you knew," she said, her voice shaking now. "When that bullet hit you today and I thought . . . I thought you could be dying—"

"I know. I do know." He kissed her again.

"I realized then that I couldn't bear it," she whispered. "If something happened to you—"

"I'm here. I'm with you. It's all over."

"But it's not over. I was so scared, and I'm still scared. . . ." She didn't say exactly what frightened her at this moment, but Nick did his best to take away her fear. He kissed her again and again, demanding her passion and then giving it back to her in full measure.

He was at a distinct disadvantage, however, his wounded shoulder immobilizing him far too much. He fumbled with the straps of Dana's camisole, caressing the silken skin of her shoulders. How to proceed from there was the real question.

"Dana," he murmured, and she seemed to understand his predicament. She drew the camisole up over her head, tossing it aside and then leaning over him with provocative daring. Maybe immobility wasn't so bad, after all. As Dana bent over him in this awkward but most tempting position, he raised his head just a fraction and managed to kiss the rosy tips of her breasts. He was rewarded by her gentle moan of response. Then she bumped against his bad shoulder, and his own moan expressed more than a little pain.

"Oh—I'm sorry," she said breathlessly. "Do you want me to stop?"

"Hell, no," he said.

Urgency swept over both of them, but it was up to Dana to tug off the clothing that still separated their bodies—her lacy slip, her underpants, Nick's own shorts and underwear. In her haste, Dana snagged the zipper of Nick's shorts on a bit of cloth, but that was only a temporary impediment. At last they lay together, skin against skin, the sheet tangling around them. Nick's shoulder hurt worse than ever, but the rest of him felt better than it had in a long while... a very long while.

"Dana," he groaned as he cupped her hips with his one free hand. "That small matter of being prepared..."

"I took care of it." She sounded embarrassed, but she sat up and groped for her skirt, poking her hand into one of the pockets. Nick traced his own fingers down her spine, gazing at the ivory skin of her back, a lovely subtle contrast to the golden brown tan of her arms. Then Dana found what she was looking for and she lay beside Nick again. She tore open the small packet she held and self-consciously produced a condom.

"Don't even ask," she warned. "You can't imagine what it's like, going into the village store when you hardly know Spanish and trying to procure a—just don't ask."

He smiled as he kissed her again. Dana was a resourceful woman. Due to his restricted range of motion in the bed, she had to go on proving herself resourceful. With some fumblings that proved exquisitely pleasurable, Dana managed to get the condom on Nick and they went from there. She opened herself to him, offered herself with the passionate generosity of her nature. But he wanted her to take as well as give, and he was happy when eventually she arched over him, lost in her own sweet pleasure. He loved watching her as she moved against him with greater and greater abandon, her eyes closed, her features contracted as she rushed with him toward reckless fulfillment. Nick watched Dana even as she gasped in climax, lamplight showing the flush that suffused her. She opened her eyes almost in a daze of wonder and held on to him as his own powerful fulfillment came.

Afterward they lay wrapped closely together still, limbs tangled in the sheet. Gradually Nick's breathing quieted down. His pleasure had been far more than a physical release—although he wasn't complaining about that part of it. But the way Dana made him feel when she was close to him like this...

He stroked her hair gently. "Lord, Dana, that was nice," he muttered. "It was also the first time I've made love sober in a very long while."

She ran her fingers over his chest. "I hope it wasn't just the lack of alcohol. I hope I contributed something to the experience."

"You shouldn't even have to ask. You're very sexy."

She moved her legs uneasily. "I've wondered a lot if I was...sexy. It's not one of those things you know right off the bat."

"Let me tell you—your ex-boyfriend was a damn fool if he didn't let you know just how fantastic you were."

She sighed, and the sound was one of quiet contentment. "You were pretty nice yourself. Of course, I always suspected you would be."

He smiled again. "You've been speculating on the matter?"

"No—of course not! I mean... Oh, what's the point of pretending? I've wanted to be like this with you ever since the first time I saw you."

"I've wanted it, too," he said. "I just knew it was wrong to give in."

She raised herself up on one elbow and gazed at him earnestly. "Why does it have to be wrong, Nick? I can't explain it very well, but it feels...right. What we just did feels right."

"I think you want it to be that way. You're not the kind of woman who can take something like this lightly—"

She drew her eyebrows together. "Yes, I do take making love seriously. What's your point, Nick?"

He stirred reluctantly. "You and I don't belong together. That's my point."

She sat up, the sheet falling away from her bare shoulders. She didn't seem to notice. In anger, as in passion, all self-consciousness seemed to leave her. "Nick—both of us could have died today! Doesn't that make you reconsider your life a little? Doesn't it make you question a few things?''

"It makes me question a lot, Dana. You came to me tonight because you were badly shaken by what happened. An impulse brought you here. Believe me, it's an impulse I understand. I felt it myself today. The need to hold you, the need to prove that we both *are* alive. . . ."

"It's more than an impulse. You know it is." She spoke with an odd dignity, considering that she sat there naked before him. A thread of huskiness laced her words. He gazed at her, at the soft fullness of her breasts, the gently rounded slope of her stomach. She was a woman of beguiling curves, and Nick felt a new impulse. He wanted to take her into his arms and make love to her again. All over again . . .

"I can't give you what you need," he said, his voice strained.

"Maybe you don't know what I need, Nick Petrie. Maybe you don't even have a clue." She stood and began yanking her clothes back on, concealing herself from him once more. When she had finished, she stared at him for a moment. "You keep pushing people away often enough, Nick, and maybe they'll stop even trying to reach you. Is that what you really want?"

With that, she simply walked out of the room, closing the door behind her. She hadn't waited for an answer—not that he had any answer to give. Nick was all out of answers.

CHAPTER FOURTEEN

THE INNER STAIRWAY of the temple was a narrow shaft leading from daylight into darkness. Dana took a few deep breaths, trying not to feel claustrophobic as she went down one step after another. The walls seemed to press in on her, swallowing the light from her lantern with their centuries of darkness. Early-morning dew beaded on the walls like a cold sweat. By now a great deal of the stairwell had been cleared, but more rubble still remained. Dana crouched down, painstakingly working to remove yet more stones blocking the way.

The passage was so cramped that only one or two people could squeeze in here at a time, and Dana was taking her turn at the job. She glanced up at the designs looming above her, marveling yet again at the Mayan glyphs so vividly preserved on these ancient walls. Each symbol was a small, intricate work of art, rendered in bold and graceful lines. Nick said that many of the glyphs seemed to deal with astronomical data, but he had also pointed out the pictographs representing Mayan deities. Now Dana's gaze was continually drawn to Ixchel, the goddess of medicine and fertility: a woman crouched down with a feline grimace, her hands and feet curled into claws. Dana continued working, although she didn't relish the thought of the goddess frowning upon her as she disturbed this shrine. Nick was impatient to have the passageway cleared as soon as possible. Nick was impatient about everything lately. He was perpetually in a foul mood, chafing at the restrictions his gunshot wound had placed upon him. It had only been a few days since the attack, but he was driving himself and his crew more relentlessly than ever.

Dana was in a foul mood herself, for that matter. She couldn't believe she'd done it again. She'd practically thrown herself at a man, and he'd turned her down. There could be no other way to describe her encounter with Nick two evenings earlier. Very well, they'd actually made love. They'd got that far...but then Nick had rejected her. He'd told her, in so many words, that what they'd done had been wrong—a mistake driven merely by impulse.

Dana poked her fingers into a crevice and placed another stone into her small tote basket. She had to admit that no logical thought had impelled her to Nick's bed that night. She'd simply been caught up by her own irresistible yearnings. What she'd told Nick was true: being shot at like that, coming so close to death, had shaken her. It had made her desperate to seize any moment she could with Nick. And so, not stopping to reason with herself, she'd gone to him. She'd lain in his arms and experienced a passion like none she could have imagined. Theirs had been an exquisite give and take, and Dana had known a commingling of intense pleasure and even more intense emotion. Her body heated with just the memory of it....

She dislodged yet another stone, but she worked automatically now, hardly paying attention to what she was doing. Making love to Nick...touching him... embracing him—it had only deepened her confusion and given her more troubling questions that seemed to have no answers. How, for example, could Nick have

offered her so much of his own passion, so much unexpected tenderness—and then have turned from her
more irrevocably than before? Was it easy for him to
dismiss her? Or might he possibly lie awake at night
himself and remember what they'd shared in each other's arms? How could she reach him again... and,
dammit, *why* did she want to reach him so badly?

The sound of footsteps disturbed her chaotic
thoughts and she realized that Jarrett was climbing
down toward her.

"How's it going?" he asked, his voice echoing
weirdly in this narrow channel.

"Just fine," Dana answered, bending to her task.
The last thing she wanted this early in the morning was
Jarrett's company. As usual, he was overly officious.

"You shouldn't be doing this work. You shouldn't
even be on the island, after what happened."

"Believe me, Nick has tried to make me leave." Dana
pulled a little too quickly at one of the rocks and now
several of them came tumbling downward. She had to
be more careful. That was Nick's rule—in spite of his
impatience, he required the work to be done with great
care.

Jarrett squeezed in next to Dana, kneeling to work
beside her. "If it were up to me, I'd handle everything
much differently than Petrie. I'd ship the whole crew
back to the mainland—it's the only way to guarantee
everyone's safety."

"Not one of us wants to leave. We're all determined
to see this through to the end." Dana knew that Jarrett's proximity couldn't be helped in this confined
space, but it made her uncomfortable. The batteries in
her lantern were wearing down and the light flickered
eerily over Jarrett's face as he glanced at her.

"Dana, one of those bullets could have struck *you*. Every time I think about that..."

"I'm fine," she said firmly.

"For now, you are. But we don't know what's going to happen next." He sounded distressed. "Anything could happen. Whoever's doing this is blindsiding us. We don't even know how much time we have left before he strikes again."

"Let's not be morbid about it, for goodness' sake."

He placed his hand on her arm. "Dana, I'm not doing this very well. But I'm trying to tell you that—I do care about you. Under other circumstances, I might even be more forward in—in expressing my regard for you. But surely you've had to notice all along how sincere my affection is...."

This was dreadful. Jarrett seemed to be searching anxiously for just the right words. She drew away from him.

"Jarrett, I'm sorry. I simply don't feel that way about you."

"It's Petrie, isn't it?" A different note came into Jarrett's voice, almost a sadness. "You keep trying to deny it, but I suppose it's been Petrie all along. He's bad news, Dana—can't you understand that? He's trashed his own life and he'll trash yours if you give him a chance." If Jarrett was trying to sound noble, he didn't succeed.

"Just leave Nick out of it," she said.

"Dana... for what it's worth, I really do care about you." Shadows consumed Jarrett's face, and now his tone was expressionless. Dana felt the need to get away from him, that was all she knew. Carrying a load of stones in her basket, she turned and went up the steps, the ceiling so low above her that she had to keep her shoulders stooped in order to proceed. She emerged gratefully into the sunshine, began scrambling down the outer steps of the temple—and bumped smack into Nick.

His right shoulder was still thickly bandaged, his arm bound in a sling, but he steadied her with his free hand. How different his touch was from Jarrett's—reassuring and matter-of-fact rather than cloying. Not that the look on Nick's face did anything to reassure her. He scowled at her.

"Your instructions were to work with Pat this morning. Now I find you were down there with Jarrett."

"Believe me, I can handle Jarrett," she said testily. She couldn't prevent Nick from escorting her down the rest of the steps, but at the bottom she pulled away from him and deposited her load of rubble onto the ground. Unwillingly her gaze strayed back to Nick. Since making love to him, that inconvenient sense of connection between them was stronger than ever. It seemed as if, by learning the responses of Nick's body, she'd attained some deeper knowledge about him that could not yet be translated into words. But what good did any of the knowing do her? It didn't tell her how to handle the fact that Nick was pushing her away.

She turned from him and walked toward the edge of the jungle. She was beginning to understand why Tim so often stood here and stared among the trees as if seeking escape. She wouldn't mind a little escape herself, especially with Nick dogging her footsteps.

"I don't want you alone with Jarrett," he said.

She glanced over to where Tim, Robert and Pat were sorting through the growing piles of stones already removed from the temple's interior, making certain that no important archaeological data had been missed.

"Everyone else was nearby," she said. "Besides, why are you suddenly so concerned about Jarrett and me?"

Nick made a restless gesture as he gazed back toward the temple. "Let's just say Jarrett and I have been having a few not-so-friendly chats. Evidently he feels bitter, resentful. He thinks he should be in charge of this project, not me. I'm starting to think he's one of those people who feels he never gets what he deserves."

Dana considered her own recent *chats* with Jarrett. "I think he's jealous of you, Nick, that's all. But that doesn't make him a criminal. I really don't think he's the one behind all our problems."

Nick studied Dana intently now. "What makes you say that? You sound very convinced."

She gave a shrug. "Just a feeling I have."

"It's more than that. Out with it, Dana. I need every piece of information I can get." Nick stared at her in that unyielding way of his. It amazed her that even with his arm in a sling, he could exude such force of personality. And his was a relentless force, showing in the cool slate blue of his eyes, the hard lines of his features....

"It's ridiculous even having to mention this. But Jarrett has made it clear that he...likes me. And that leads me to conclude that he wouldn't purposely try to harm me. That gunfire...it targeted me as much as it did you, Nick. So I just don't think Jarrett was involved."

Nick was observing her with an expression that she found quite annoying. "What's wrong?" she asked caustically. "Is it so difficult for you to believe another man could be interested in me? Dammit, Nick, just because *you're* determined to keep me at a distance—"

"It's easy to believe any man would find you desirable." Nick's voice was low, his eyes smoky now as his gaze lingered on her face. "I'm just considering all the possibilities. If Jarrett were to feel that you didn't return his sentiments, he might resent you as he appears to resent me."

Dana stared into the vine-tangled forest. "That doesn't make any sense. Jarrett doesn't seem vindictive toward me. Instead, he's . . . persistent. Even when I try to discourage him, he seems to think it'll only be a matter of time before I stop pining after you and—" Dana realized what she'd just said and wanted to kick herself. She moved away from Nick, tempted simply to plunge into the forest, after all. But Nick stayed right by her side, allowing her no retreat.

"Dana," he said, his voice surprisingly gentle. "I wish it could be different—"

"Don't," she said rigidly. "This is going to end up sounding too much like the speech I just gave Jarrett. Skip it, Nick."

He swore under his breath. "I'm not going to make another failed attempt at a relationship, a family. For your sake, for my own sake, I'm not going to do it."

Dana looked at him, studying the lines etched across his brow, the inflexible set of his features. "I wish you could forgive yourself," she said, her voice softened. "I wish you knew how to do at least that much."

"It's not so simple. No one can live with a drunk, Dana. Not even you."

Dana stifled her first automatic response and remained silent for a long moment. Even this early in the morning, the tropical air gathered its heat around her. A hummingbird flickered past, its wings a vivid blur of turquoise and scarlet and gold. From somewhere in the jungle came the strident call of a macaw and the more musical chatter of other birds. And at last Dana had an answer as honest as she could make it.

"You're right. I couldn't live with someone who drinks all the time," she said slowly, almost reluctantly. "I'm not a martyr and I have a lot of self-respect. But I can picture myself living with someone who's doing his best *not* to drink. I'd give that person the benefit of the doubt."

Nick shook his head. "You're too damn naive, Dana. You don't realize how easy it would be for me to slip into my old way of life. I've done it before."

"Right, Nick. You've used alcohol as one more barrier between you and someone who could actually love you. That's exactly what you've done."

IT RAINED THAT AFTERNOON, the rain pelting down in huge drops through the jungle canopy. But it was a quick storm, as if the sky had spent its fury in one frantic burst. When it had passed, leaves shone wetly and the earth was moist and fragrant. Dana paused in her work to sit at the base of the temple. She scooped up a handful of rich soil, letting it sift through her fingers as she gazed at it contemplatively. Then she glanced up and saw young Daniel observing her with his usual disapproving frown. Daniel had just carted another basket of stones from the inner stairway and now turned to go back again.

"You know," Dana said, almost as if speaking to herself, "dirt is an amazing thing. It's full of all sorts of fascinating life—earthworms, larvae, protozoa you can't even see going about their own business." She allowed more damp soil to trickle through her fingers. Daniel only gazed at her with an expression of incredulity. Maybe he couldn't believe she'd actually try to involve him in a conversation about dirt. But she'd tried talking to him about everything else. Nothing seemed to work; maybe it was time for the direct approach.

"You don't like me much, do you, Daniel?" she remarked.

Now he looked distrustful, as if he thought Dana was setting some type of trap for him. But at least she had his attention. Daniel stayed where he was, watching her scoop up another clump of earth.

"I have a few theories about *why* you don't like me," she went on. "You seem to think that if you're the least bit friendly to me, you'll compromise yourself somehow. Then again...maybe you think I pay too much attention to Dr. Petrie. Maybe you think he has only so much attention to give in return."

Daniel's features seemed to tense. "I work with Señor Petrie. That's all."

For crying out loud, Daniel wouldn't even admit that Nick meant something to him. How did you reach a boy who was so determined to stand alone?

"Well, whatever the reason, Daniel...I don't want to be a threat to you. I'd rather be your friend."

For a moment she thought she saw some new emotion flicker across Daniel's face—almost a wistfulness, perhaps. But it was gone too quickly for her to be sure, replaced by his usual guarded demeanor. Without another word, he climbed back up and disappeared inside the narrow opening of the temple stairwell, leaving Dana with nothing but that clump of damp earth in her hand. Slowly she let it crumble to the ground.

She knew that Nick harbored deep pain behind his own reserve. Could it be that Daniel, too, had learned to hide pain? If so, he was doing it well...too well.

Dammit... he really was just like Nick—and Dana didn't know what to do about either one of them.

TWO DAYS LATER, Dana stood in front of a structure that was little more than a jumble of plywood scraps, pieces of cardboard and sheets of tin. Inside this hovel, from what little she'd been able to see, were a dingy sleeping bag, several stacks of Spiderman comic books, a Frisbee and a small crate supporting a shiny new radio and a can of peaches. The shack was huddled in a dirt alleyway and its fragile walls looked as if they might come tumbling down at any minute. This was a hopeless, dreary place, without even the slightest hint of beauty. There was not a single flower, not a single patch of grass—only the parched dirt and the stained walls of this meager shelter. Dana was appalled. She'd grown up surrounded by well-tended gardens, gracious shade trees, luxuriant lawns. She couldn't imagine living without at least a little such beauty.

Nick stood a short distance down the way, talking in Spanish to a woman who peered from the back door of a more substantial house. The woman stared at Nick suspiciously, answering him only in short, curt sentences. Dana struggled to understand the conversation, but she caught barely a word or two.

She and Nick had come here today searching for Daniel. The boy hadn't appeared at the archaeological site these past few days and Nick was concerned about him. Of course, Nick hadn't said he was concerned in so many words; he'd simply gone into action, making inquiries in the village as to Daniel's whereabouts.

At last Nick came back over to Dana. "This is the place, all right," he said, motioning toward the shack. "This is where Daniel has been living."

"Alone?" Dana asked.

"It appears that way. The woman says that he keeps to himself as much as possible. She knows hardly anything about him. He seems to have no parents, no brothers or sisters . . . no relatives at all."

Dana felt more oppressed than ever by this cheerless place. It was horrible to picture a thirteen-year-old boy struggling to survive here on his own.

"Has Daniel been around recently?" she asked. "Has anyone seen him?"

"Yes—he was here only this morning. If he's staying away from the site, it's by choice, nothing else." Nick looked discontented. "There's something about Daniel that no one else knows . . . something that no one else *should* know. I believe he's involved in the black-market trade on the island."

Dana looked at him in dismay. "He's just a kid," she protested.

"So you've said before . . . and this time I happen to agree. I know Daniel's had to do whatever he can to survive, but now he could be in danger. There's a possibility someone in the black market is causing all our trouble, resentful because we've staked out our own turf here. If that someone were to decide that Daniel knows too much . . . or is just too involved with our activities . . ." Nick looked more than discontented now; he looked downright worried.

"What can a thirteen-year-old boy have to do with the black market?" Dana asked.

"Plenty," Nick said. "Daniel knows how to find artifacts. He's good at finding them—damn good. From what I've learned, he scavenges on his own and tries to sell whatever he can come up with. I gather that sometimes he sells to other traders and sometimes he goes directly to the tourists. It could be risky for him, either way, depending on who the hell he's involved with.''

The implications of what Nick said were disturbing. After all, Nick hadn't mentioned one possibility: that Daniel himself might have caused some of the trouble on the dig....

Dana shook her head. She wouldn't go down that route—not yet, anyway.

"Have you tried talking to Daniel? Surely he would confide in you, if no one else—''

Nick seemed to shrug aside this remark. "No luck there. Believe me, I've tried to get him to open up, to talk about it.''

Dana dragged her foot across the barren dirt. "I wish there were some way we could get through to him,'' she murmured.

"It's my responsibility,'' Nick said. "Not yours, Dana.''

She gazed at him, wondering why he couldn't truly let her into his confidence. They were both concerned about Daniel—shouldn't that count for something? Couldn't they share at least this much?

But Nick's expression grew closed to her. His dark hair was swept back from his forehead, emphasizing more than ever the bold, arrogant lines of his face. There *was* arrogance in his belief that he didn't need other people. He seemed to think he could solve all problems on his own, including this one.

"Maybe you should just admit that you miss Daniel when he's not around,'' Dana said. "Maybe that would get you farther than anything else.''

Nick frowned. "You want to prove that I'm sentimental, after all—is that it, Dana?''

"It's actually possible you *are* sentimental, underneath. Why else would you try so hard to disguise your feelings?" Dana turned and walked down the alley, eager to be somewhere else. Nick came along beside her. In a short while they reached the more pleasant area where they'd left the Rover. Here the street was paved with cobblestones and red jasmine bloomed along a wall of limestone bricks.

"He's just a kid," Dana said again. "He needs a family, a real home."

"I sure as hell don't like him living where he is." Nick began climbing into the driver's seat of the Rover.

"Aren't you forgetting something?" Dana remarked. "I'm the driver now."

Nick glanced down at his sling as if prepared to rip it off. Dana knew that he'd only allowed her to come with him today as a matter of logistics. With his right arm out of commission, he simply couldn't drive himself.

Looking disgusted, he swung around to the passenger seat. Dana settled herself in front of the steering wheel, gazing at the bullet hole that had shattered the windshield. Her nerves tightened as she remembered precisely how dangerous the island had become. She didn't start the engine, reluctant to begin the journey back toward the temple. Nick, surprisingly, didn't protest the fact that they just went on sitting here. He seemed lost in his own thoughts. When eventually he spoke, he almost seemed to be talking to himself.

"Daniel isn't the type of person who'd ever accept a handout. He's so damn stubborn, so determined that he's going to do things on his own."

"What do you know—sounds just like you, Nick Petrie."

He glanced at her briefly. "I think you'll admit a few differences. You've already pointed out that Daniel's just a kid. He needs someone's help, whether or not he'll admit it." Nick pushed his free hand through his hair, looking more frustrated than ever. "I have a good idea why Daniel's been staying away. Unless I miss my guess, he's starting to feel he's made too much of an emotional investment where I'm concerned. When I was laid up with this damn gunshot wound and he came to see me...I could tell he was worried about whether or not I was all right. He didn't like being worried—I could tell that much, too. He's probably trying to decide how to pull away before it's too late."

"As I said...sounds just like you, Nick."

He studied her. "I've already explained why nothing more can happen between us, Dana. If you don't understand by now—"

"I understand, all right." She clenched her hands together. The last thing she wanted to do was get into this. With Nick, her emotions were too close to the surface, threatening to overwhelm her. It would be foolhardy to stir them up even more. But *he* was the one who'd brought up personal matters again, and that made her reckless against all her better judgment.

"You're not afraid of botching another relationship," she told him. "What you're afraid of is needing someone again. It would require too much—too much of an emotional investment from you!" When he didn't respond to that, she took a deep breath and plowed ahead.

"I suppose I might as well tell you something. Today, when I picked up my mail at the hotel...there was a letter from Alan waiting for me."

This evoked at least a minimal response. "The ex-boyfriend," Nick murmured.

"Exactly. I was quite surprised to hear from him—but he's had a change of heart, it seems. He's decided to accept my proposal of marriage."

Apparently Nick had to think this over at some length. He stared broodingly out through the shattered windshield. Dana did some thinking herself about the letter. She knew that perhaps she was quibbling about small details, but it annoyed her that the letter had been typed rather than handwritten. She could picture Alan tapping away at his computer keyboard—but a love letter, as such, should have been dashed off fervently in ink.

She hadn't been either happy or relieved to have received this message from Alan. She hadn't been gratified, either... or even flattered. The letter had seemed a nuisance, as much as anything else. She'd grown accustomed to seeing her life as pre-Alan and post-Alan, a sharp division. Leaving Alan, after all, symbolized her ability to change, to break free of stifling routine. Hearing from him now was just... untidy. It didn't fit anywhere.

So why had she told Nick about Alan's letter? She didn't have any illusions about trying to make Nick jealous. She was too straightforward to use such coy tactics, and she knew they would have had no effect on him in any case. Why, then, was she tormenting herself like this? It was simply one more question she didn't know how to answer.

"I'm glad for you," Nick said at last. "Maybe the guy's a little late in coming around... but he *is* coming around. You got what you wanted from him."

Dana almost laughed. "You're unbelievable, Nick."

He attempted a shrug, in spite of his bandaged shoulder. "For a long time you thought this Alan was right for you. Give him a chance—maybe he's still right."

Now Dana clenched the steering wheel, although she managed a caustic tone. "You haven't asked me what I want, Nick. You haven't even asked me if I love Alan anymore. Don't you think that might be of some importance? Or maybe you're just relieved at the thought of me going back to Alan and leaving you in peace."

"The last thing you'll ever allow me is peace of mind," he said, his voice rough.

"Of course," Dana said mockingly. She jammed the key into the ignition. She wanted to yell at Nick, for all the good it would do her—and she wanted so much for him to take her into his arms at least one more time.

Dana cranked the ignition and the Rover sputtered into life. She yanked the unwieldy gearshift into first, then pressed her foot to the accelerator, taking the vehicle bouncing over the cobblestones and out of the village. Perhaps she traveled toward new danger, perhaps not—but she couldn't seem to escape the danger in her own heart.

CHAPTER FIFTEEN

PAT YELPED, AND FELL back against the cot in the field hut. "I feel like I've been boiled alive," she said dramatically. "I just want to lie here and suffer."

"It's only a sunburn," Dana said with forced patience. "You'll be fine. Elena left this salve for you, and it ought to do the trick. It's made from cactus, I believe." Dana opened the small pot of cream that Elena Montano had prepared. By now the Montanos were almost the only islanders still willing to come near the archaeological site—the attempted shooting of Nick and Dana had seen to that. With fewer workers, the clearing of the temple stairway proceeded much too slowly for Nick's liking. It seemed, in fact, that nothing proceeded to Nick's liking. He certainly didn't act happy to have Dana still around. What did he expect—that she was going to jump at the chance to marry Alan and leave on the first available boat? Did he feel even the least disquiet over the fact that another man wanted her? Dammit, what *did* he feel?

Dana thrust the pot of cream unceremoniously at Pat, who took it and began spreading it on her reddened arms. "Sunburn is an occupational hazard, I suppose," Pat intoned. "But who knows if I even *have* an occupation. No decent university has offered me a job yet. I can't possibly accept a position at that junior college...."

Dana sighed: here Pat went again with the interminable discussion of her career prospects.

"What's wrong with working at a junior college? They've given you a firm job offer—take it, for goodness' sake!"

Pat gave her a condescending glance. "Get real, Dana. You start out at a little place like that and you're stuck for life. No prestigious university will even *look* at you after that. I'll admit it's a sign of deplorable narrow-mindedness, but still—"

"You're the one who's narrow-minded, Pat. Loosen up. Broaden your horizons."

Pat seemed offended. "Dana, you don't understand a thing about the academic world. I only applied at that junior college as a lark—sometimes your ego needs the boost of an acceptance. I'm not desperate enough to take the job...."

Just then Robert poked his head into the hut. He had allowed his beard to grow even longer, and it gave him a decidedly roguish appearance. He frowned at Pat.

"Are you still making a scene?" he asked. "You've attempted to put the entire camp in an uproar over a mild case of the sun."

Pat glared back at him. "It's a severe burn, thank you very much. The only reason you're carping at me is because you can't forgive me for...for investigating your room. You refuse to acknowledge that if it weren't for me, those artifacts would still be—"

"If it weren't for you, my life would still be thoroughly enjoyable," Robert said crabbily. Apparently, he'd lost his ability to project a detached air of amusement. "You are a bane, Pat. A veritable bane." With that, his head disappeared from view.

"Well," Pat said in a self-righteous tone. "He's certainly out of sorts. You'd think he'd be grateful to me, in the long run. I really don't see—"

"Hurry it up, will you?" Dana said. "Let's just get back to work."

"Robert isn't the only one out of sorts," Pat observed, patting cream on the end of her nose. "What's been eating you lately?"

"Nothing." Dana stuck her hand into the pocket of her shorts and encountered the crumpled sheet of paper that was the letter from Alan—his acceptance of her proposal....

The previous night she'd been about to toss the letter into the trash, but something had made her hold on to it. She couldn't explain what. As far as she was concerned, Alan's answer was too little, too late. He wrote that he loved her, but the neatly typed words didn't move her. To Alan, love was a carefully measured emotion, given out in acceptable portions. He seemed to have decided on the portion he would allot to her— and it included room for marriage, after all. But there was nothing unrestrained about Alan's love, nothing extravagant. Dana needed extravagance in her new life. So why didn't she just toss Alan's letter away?

Pat rambled on. "I swear, you're getting as cranky as Nick. Of course, being shot at is enough to make anyone ill-tempered, I suppose. I wonder how it would be if *I'd* been the one shot at." Pat almost sounded sorry that she'd missed being in on the excitement.

Robert popped his head back into the hut. "Are you ever going to be finished?" he demanded. "Tim and I are waiting to escort you and Dana back to the temple. We all have work to do."

"Leave me alone, Robert," Pat snapped. "I have enough on my mind right now."

He uttered something disdainful in French, and his head disappeared again. Dana shook her own head.

"Can't the two of you reach some kind of truce? You're only making things more nerve-racking than they already are in this place."

Pat stared despondently into her pot of cactus cream. "Truce...sure. I'm madly in love with the man, and he hates me worse than ever."

"He hardly hates you. He can't seem to stay away from you. He follows you around so that the two of you can constantly argue."

"I'm supposed to see that as an encouraging sign?" Pat scoffed.

Dana took off her hat and wiped the perspiration from her forehead. The air in here was stifling. Rain threatened to fall at any moment, and she wished it would just hurry up and get on with it.

"Both you and Robert should stop all your nonsense and resolve your differences. Then the rest of us can tend to our own lives."

"You've forgotten the small matter of Robert's 'prior commitments.' He still won't tell me what they are, you know. It's not like I haven't *asked.* . . ."

"Well, ask him again," Dana said impatiently. "Tell him to stop being so damn mysterious. Sometimes Robert acts as if he'd like all of us to believe he's our attacker."

"I can't decide which would be worse—discovering he's behind all our trouble or finding out he has a wife stashed away somewhere." Pat lapsed into an uncustomary silence, then slowly glanced at Dana again. "Look, it's true that Robert's mysterious in the most aggravating way,'' she said. ''But there are things about me that *he* doesn't know. Things I'd hesitate to tell him ... and I wonder what's best. Letting Robert know all the pathetic details about me or just keeping them to myself.''

Pat seemed to be waiting for an opinion on the matter, but at the moment Dana didn't feel like the best adviser on romantic troubles.

''You're the only one who can make that decision,'' she said.

''That's a cop-out if I ever heard one. Come on, Dana. What you really want to tell me is to be honest with Robert. You want to tell me that no relationship can survive without total trust between the two people involved. Not that what I have with Robert even qualifies as a relationship, per se ...''

Dana couldn't take any more. ''Use the rest of that cream and then get your tail out of here, Pat!'' She exited the hut and found that Robert was pacing restlessly in front of the shrouded excavation pits, while Tim wandered aimlessly about. Purplish clouds gathered overhead, bloated with moisture. The clouds reminded Dana of water balloons. She wished she could reach up and puncture them.

Robert gave her a sour glance. ''I imagine you and Pat have been discussing me, as usual.''

''Believe it or not, there are other topics of conversation.'' Dana's comeback, unfortunately, lacked the proper conviction. Pat discussed only two topics of significance: her career and Robert.

''I have always admired you for your discretion,'' Robert said sardonically. ''However, it is rather too late for diplomacy. Pat seems determined to prove that I am the culprit. She has insinuated her belief that I am the one who shot Nick. She actually believes me capable of attempted murder." Robert was trying to sound affronted, perhaps, but in actuality he seemed intrigued with the idea of himself as a dangerous sort. By now Dana's patience was wearing very thin with both Robert and Pat.

"Robert, open your eyes and see what's really going on for once. Pat's far more interested in your marital status than whether or not you used Nick for target practice."

Robert stroked his beard. "I see. You have been discussing me."

"For crying out loud—just put Pat out of her misery. Tell her if you have a wife and three kids, and be done with it. Meanwhile, Tim and I will go back to the temple. You can argue with Pat on your own for a while."

"You must wait—the four of us will go together. Nick's orders."

"Safety in numbers and all that," Dana said tiredly.

"Nick will come looking for you any minute, I suspect. He does not like to let you out of his sight."

She flushed. "Nick is trying to protect everyone's safety, not just mine."

"Open *your* eyes, Dana, and see what's really going on," Robert said with not-so-subtle mockery.

She turned away from him. Robert had it all wrong. The truth was that Nick seemed determined *not* to show any special regard for her.

At last Pat emerged from the hut and the four of them began their trek back to the temple. A disturbing silence charged the air between Pat and Robert, threatening just like the rain clouds to break into a storm.

Dana wondered how she could get the two of them to make peace with each other. Meanwhile, Tim moved along despondently, as if each step he took required more energy than he was willing to give, and Dana wondered how to get *him* to buck up a little. Then, all of a sudden, it struck Dana exactly what she was trying to do: she was trying to be the conciliator, trying to run interference for those around her. She was doing the same thing with Daniel and even with Nick, trying to get them to be less rigidly self-sufficient. Well, she ought to leave the lot of them to their own devices! Right now, Dana wanted to wash her hands of *everyone*.

She was glad when they reached the temple site. Daniel hadn't shown up again, and apparently Nick and Jarrett were still hard at the job of clearing the inner passage. Dana had the perfect opportunity to devote herself to her *own* business, sorting through a pile of rubble carted out of the temple.

Unfortunately, however, it seemed that old habits died hard. Dana found herself watching as Tim climbed up to the entrance of the inner stairway and picked up a drawing pad. He hunched over it, holding a pencil as if not quite sure what to do next. The day before, Tim had shown an usual hint of initiative: he'd volunteered to sketch the panels of glyphs that marked the stair-well. Recording the Mayan symbols on paper was an important job. Nick had seemed skeptical about Tim undertaking it, but with his shortage of helpers he didn't have much choice. Now Dana was curious to see how Tim was getting along.

She hesitated for a moment, telling herself firmly to stay put. No more interfering, no more trying to solve other people's problems....

It wasn't any use. Grumbling under her breath, Dana climbed up and sat beside Tim.

He immediately angled his sketch pad away from her. "These aren't ready yet," he said.

She craned her neck and peered at his drawings anyway. Then she took a closer look, impressed by what she saw. Tim had captured the Mayan artistry with a talent all his own. He'd reproduced in fine detail some of the intricate calendar symbols, as well as the panel that depicted the taking of two enemies in battle: the Mayan warriors standing proudly with their elaborate headdresses, plumed spears and armor of tooled leather; the humbled captives bowing down before them. But far more than just the detail, Tim had managed to portray the spirit of the Maya—a devout, warlike people, obsessed with recording their own history and in measuring the passage of time.

"Tim...you're really good at this. I don't know how you've managed it—combining accuracy with your own wonderful style."

Tim shrugged away her compliment. "It's nothing," he muttered.

"Don't be ridiculous. I mean it—you really are good at this. You're a natural artist. If I were you, it's something I'd pursue."

"It's not important." Tim sharpened one of his pencils with a small knife.

"Nothing's more important than pursuing a talent," Dana argued. "You can't just dismiss this, Tim."

She wondered if she was getting through to him at all. He moved away from her, bending over his sketch pad once more. But then he spoke again, without looking up.

"I don't want to be mediocre. I'd rather be nothing than be mediocre."

"You don't have to be perfect, Tim. No one has to be. Just have a little faith in yourself for once."

It was all very well to say that to him, but she couldn't *make* Tim believe in himself. He stared at his pad as if he despised what he'd done. By now Dana knew Tim's patterns. He'd grown up with parents who had set impossible standards for him. Late in life, they'd produced their only son, their only heir, and they had wanted him to be nothing less than brilliant. In spite of the fact that his parents were gone now, Tim still measured himself by those impossible standards.

Dana lifted her gaze to the sky, again realizing the absurdity of trying to solve someone else's problems. She couldn't do it with Tim...and she certainly couldn't do it with Nick.

She clenched her hands. She'd come to this island looking for adventure—thinking that would solve the problems in her own life. But along with adventure she'd found Nick Petrie, and longings both familiar and unfamiliar had stirred in her. Now her own need, her own longing, consumed her.

Against all her better judgment, she needed a man who was harshly determined to remain alone.

IT WASN'T ALL THAT difficult for Nick to find Daniel. Maybe the kid hadn't shown up at the dig in a while, but he wasn't exactly hiding out, either. This afternoon Daniel was hanging around the boat landing at the village, several wares spread out before him on a scrap of blue plastic: a few strings of wooden beads of indifferent value, a small clay idol of great value, and two chips of engraved obsidian that interested Nick most of all.

Daniel stared at Nick. "Why are you here, Señor Petrie?"

It was a good question. The last thing Nick could afford to do was take time away from the temple. He was working his crew in shifts virtually around the clock, and he worked right along with them—one armed and all. Nonetheless, today Nick had allowed a trip into the village so that Dana and Pat could clean up at the hotel while he himself sought out Daniel.

Nick sat down on the splintered wood of the landing. When he dangled his legs over the edge, his feet almost skimmed the water. Daniel wasn't doing much trade at the moment, and after a hesitation he sat down some distance away. He dangled his own skinny legs above the water's edge. He waited, as if knowing that Nick would speak eventually... speak, perhaps, of something he didn't want to hear. But at least he wasn't running away.

"I understand if you don't want to come near the temple any more," Nick said now. "In fact, it's probably better that way. Safer."

"I'm not afraid," Daniel said.

"Sometimes it's good to be afraid. It keeps you on your guard."

"What do you want, Señor Petrie?" Daniel glanced around with an air of purpose, as if he had a whole slew of customers waiting in line and Nick was keeping him from them.

"Look, Daniel... by now you know that I've found out where you live, and that you don't have any parents."

"I never had a father," Daniel said, with an odd note of pride. "And my mother died a long time ago. I don't even remember what she looked like."

Nick rubbed the bandage that confined his shoulder. Lord, the kid just hadn't had a break. But Nick realized that the last thing Daniel would tolerate was sympathy.

"Okay, so you've made it on your own," Nick acknowledged. "But these artifacts, Daniel...there's got to be a better way to do things. When you take them from the places they belong and sell them, then something very important is lost. Not just the context of how or where they were found, but something else. A respect for the past..." Nick listened to himself and realized how paltry his words sounded when compared to the need for economic survival of one thirteen-year-old boy.

"Look, Daniel," Nick went on after a moment. "I'm not trying to make you feel bad about what you're doing. But you're a smart kid. You can do better." Nick stopped again. He knew he was handling this badly; he could tell that just from the defensive jut of Daniel's chin.

Daniel brought up one knee and wrapped his arms around it. "What *do* you want, Señor Petrie?"

"Look, I'll tell you the truth, Daniel. I thought you and I were becoming friends as well as business associates." If Dana were here, she'd probably approve of what he'd just said. But Daniel himself didn't seem particularly thrilled.

"We're not friends," he said conclusively.

"Okay, even if that's true—I thought perhaps you and I could still have...a business arrangement. You could be a real archaeologist someday. If you work with me, you can keep learning..."

"I don't need any handouts."

"I'm not offering you a handout," Nick said. "It's not charity. You're a good worker—you'd earn everything I'd pay you."

Daniel seemed unconvinced. He glanced over at his scrap of blue plastic with its arrangement of wares, subtly conveying the message that he already had his own livelihood. How could Nick get through to the kid? Daniel's pride stood in the way.

"There aren't any strings attached to my offer," Nick said quietly. "It's a job, that's all."

The breeze rumpled Daniel's already tousled hair. His dark eyes seemed to take Nick's measure. "Yes . . . it's only a job. Why don't you go away, Señor Petrie? You have work to do—I have work."

"Daniel . . ." But Nick realized he'd already failed somehow with the kid. He couldn't explain it, couldn't define exactly what that failure was. But the conviction gnawed at him and it wouldn't go away. He'd failed. . . .

CHAPTER SIXTEEN

"THE INSTITUTE IS shutting us down," Nick announced late the next day, his voice carefully devoid of expression. "Effective immediately... this project is closed."

He stood in front of his crew at the field huts. The reactions that confronted him were varied. Jarrett was worked up, pacing restlessly back and forth. Robert looked only mildly perturbed, as if he'd just been informed that his favorite restaurant had closed and he was obliged to find another. Pat blustered for a moment, then fell into a dejected silence. Tim simply looked wary. And Dana...

Dana stared at Nick in an accusing manner, as if he'd let her down personally. Maybe he *had* let her down personally, but that was another matter. He allowed his gaze to linger on her just a moment too long. She'd pinned up her hair beneath the silly canvas hat she always wore. The hat was starting to look battered—its floppy brim, however, couldn't disguise the depths of Dana's rich brown eyes, depths in which a man could lose himself all too well....

Pat regained some of her bluster. "It isn't fair!" she protested. "They can't do this to us. We've already worked too hard and risked too much to stop now."

"You all knew the end was coming sooner or later," Nick said. "I couldn't keep the news about the gunshots from the Institute any longer, and that was the deciding factor."

Pat was nothing if not persistent. "We can't just give up like this. We just can't. I mean, we could be on the brink of a major discovery here. We have to clear that stairway until we find out where it leads."

"I agree completely," commented Robert.

Pat stared suspiciously at Robert. "You never agree with anything I say. So why start now?"

"Because—"

"Enough!" Nick gave Pat and Robert his most quelling look, and then swept his gaze over the rest of his crew. "We have nothing more to discuss," he said. "You can start packing tonight. We'll finish up in the morning and then we're out of here." He turned and went inside the larger of the huts.

Nick sat down behind the rickety wooden desk. Jarrett came striding in after him.

"I don't believe it, Petrie," he said in a tone of disgust. "You actually got us shut down. If I'd been in charge, this never would've happened."

Nick's shoulder ached. The doctor had changed the bandage today and pronounced the wound to be healing nicely, but Nick hated still having his arm confined in a sling. He gazed unenthusiastically at Jarrett.

"Don't flatter yourself," he said. "You couldn't keep this project going—it's all up to the Institute."

"I could get my way around the Institute," Jarrett said contemptuously. "You blew it, Petrie. That's all there is to it."

"It's over. Just accept it."

Jarrett smacked a hand down on the desk. "It's not over," he said. "You get that? It's not over yet." He stared at Nick, then turned and strode out of the hut again.

Nick leaned back in his chair, waiting to see if any of the others would come in to argue. He could hear the sound of their excited, distressed murmurs outside, and he could tell that Pat, as usual, was leading the discussion. But no one else came in to speak with Nick. Obviously he'd convinced them there was no recourse.

Well...so now the die was cast, and all Nick could do was go on waiting. He had a feeling it was going to be a very long night, and the all-too-familiar weariness seeped over him, the desire to allow himself a drink, and just be done with it.

Lord, it would just be so easy to give in...especially tonight.

LATE THAT NIGHT, a crashing sound brought Dana out of a fitful sleep. She struggled to a sitting position in the tent she shared with Pat, fighting the mosquito netting around her. The crashing noise came again, and now Pat sat up, too.

"What was that?" she asked groggily.

"I intend to find out," Dana said, crawling from her sleeping bag to the doorway of the tent. After Nick's announcement that the project was shutting down, the entire crew had been in turmoil. Dana herself had been in turmoil, and she found it amazing that she'd managed to get any sleep at all.

She was upset, of course, about her new job suddenly being wrenched away from her. But the cause of her unhappiness was more than that...so much more. In a few short hours she'd be gone from this island. She would no longer see Nick Petrie, no longer be near him.

It would be over that quickly, that ruthlessly. All connection severed . . .

Part of her protested wildly that it couldn't be done, that she would always be connected to Nick on some deep, elemental level. The other part of her knew that it was best to leave, so she could try to forget Nick. He, after all, seemed to feel he could forget *her*. His cold, impassive gaze today had told her as much.

But now another sound came, a sort of clattering noise, and Dana had no time for her own fevered preoccupations.

Both she and Pat clambered out of the tent, Dana bringing along her lantern. Jarrett, Robert and Tim had been awakened, too, appearing from their own tents. Jarrett was the one who took charge, sweeping the area with his flashlight until he found the source of the mysterious sounds: Nick himself. Apparently Nick had been prowling about in the dark and had tripped over some tools near the excavation pits. He lay oddly sprawled on the ground, and Dana hurried over to him.

"Is he all right?" she asked, her heartbeat quickened with foreboding.

Jarrett leaned over Nick. "He's fine—for being drunk," he pronounced in a disdainful tone. "I always knew this would happen sooner or later. Once a drunk, always a drunk."

Dana froze. "It can't be true. I don't believe it. . . ."

Pat crouched beside Nick and poked him with her finger. He stirred, muttering something under his breath.

"It's true, all right," Pat said dolefully. "He's plastered." She gestured at the shovels and trowels strewn beside Nick. "Looks like he got some crazy idea about coming out here and working, even in the state he's in."

Dana couldn't seem to move, her heart pounding in dismay and outrage. Very well, it had to have been a terrible blow to Nick, learning that the Institute was closing him down. But to react like this—to get drunk—

"Let's haul him back to the hut," Jarrett said, efficiently taking command again. "He'll have to sleep it off. Robert, you get his other side. Tim, stop standing there and goggling. We could use your help—"

It was Pat who intervened, assisting the two men as they lifted Nick and half walked, half dragged him into the hut. Dana forced herself to move at last, following the others and watching as they deposited Nick on the cot. Suddenly impatient, she pushed her way next to him, glancing at the near empty bottle of scotch on the floor.

"Damn you, Nick Petrie," she said fiercely, her voice shaking all the while. "How could you do this?"

Nick opened his eyes and gazed at her, the stench of alcohol wafting from him. "Leave me alone." He spoke with a clear, precise enunciation, as if determined to prove how well he could function even while drunk.

Dana couldn't leave. She continued to stand over him, holding her lantern against the dark shadows of night. Nick's eyelids started to drift shut again, but she wouldn't allow him to escape her so easily. She leaned closer and pushed at his good shoulder.

"Why did you do it?" she said in a low, angry voice. "You've been sober for months and now this—damn you!" She didn't care if the others heard her. She was furious and heartsick all at once.

Nick's eyelids flickered. "Get out of here, Dana. Just get out."

Dana wanted to pummel him. Instead all she could do was reach down and grab the bottle of scotch. She turned it upside down, the few remaining drops spilling onto the dirt floor of the hut, soaking into it.

"Do you really think that'll make a difference?" Nick asked, his voice still clear, his enunciation still just a little too perfect. Dana stared at him as if seeing a stranger. She looked at the dark hair that swept back from his forehead, at the strong, spare lines of his face. She wondered at the fact that he could appear forceful, even as he lay sprawled on that cot. She wondered if she knew this man at all. An acrid taste filled her mouth, as if she herself had been the one drinking. She dropped the bottle and turned away from Nick.

Jarrett took hold of her arm in his unctuous manner. "I'm sorry, Dana, but maybe it's best for you to see what Petrie's really like, after all. Why hang on to any illusions—"

She pulled away from him. "Go to hell, Jarrett," she said, her own voice very distinct and clear. Then she went back to her tent and crawled inside her bed. Although the tropical night was warm, she trembled deep within herself. It was a trembling that didn't stop for a very long time.

NICK HAD NEVER BEEN more sober in his life. It didn't surprise him how easy it was to feign drunkenness. Years of the real thing meant that he was conversant with all the symptoms. He knew enough not to overdo things. Apparently he'd played it just right—everyone had seemed convinced, particularly Dana. She'd stormed out of here a few minutes ago in obvious disgust. That was good. That was fine. The others had followed her soon after.

Nick shifted position on the cot. He was running on sheer willpower tonight. When he'd opened that bottle of scotch and splashed some of it onto his face, he'd almost given in to his own craving. He'd almost taken a drink. He didn't know what had stopped him, and the craving still hadn't abated. It surged over him in waves that receded only momentarily. He'd disposed of the scotch in order to make it appear that he'd drunk the entire bottle. That had been particularly difficult, throwing away good scotch, but he'd managed it. Now the empty bottle lay harmlessly beside him, the last few drops taken care of by Dana.

He shifted again, knowing he had to stay completely alert. He'd already slipped off his sling and he flexed his arm again, testing it. He still didn't have the mobility he desired, and his shoulder hurt like hell. Nonetheless, he had to make do with what he had. He wondered if his plan would bring any results. So far all it had done was set Dana off. That hadn't been part of the scheme of things, but maybe it had enlightened her to see what a drunk could be like. Jarrett was right about that much.

Nick waited on through the night. He didn't know how much time passed—maybe an hour, two hours, maybe more. He remained vigilant, straining to hear every sound. All that came to him was the thrum of nocturnal insects, the whisper of a breeze through the trees of the jungle. Still, he waited.

And then, at last, a figure crept stealthily into the hut. It was someone who needed this secretive darkness— someone who moved with deadly precision. Nick waited as long as he dared, then he rolled off the cot just as a machete blade flashed above him, visible in the moonlight that filtered into the hut.

His attacker uttered a curse that was cut off abruptly as Nick took the offensive and lunged forward. He grappled with his assailant for several moments, and at last the machete clattered to the floor. Nick's shoulder felt as if it were being ripped apart as he aimed first one and then another fist—the blows striking nothing but the night air. With his third punch, however, Nick was rewarded with the satisfying smack of knuckles against his assailant's jaw. Now Nick knew he had the bastard—

Then all hell broke loose. Dana came darting into the hut, swinging her lantern as if about to brain someone with it. Pat came careening in after her, yelling at the top of her lungs. The light revealed Nick's attacker: Jarrett, crouched down, wild-eyed like a cornered animal. The confusion was all Jarrett needed. He hurtled out the door, knocking Dana to one side as he went. Nick raced after him. He could hear Jarrett thrashing through the undergrowth of the jungle and he followed the sounds. But then the thrashing stopped. Jarrett was very clever, indeed; obviously he knew that if he stayed hidden and unmoving in the darkness, under the impenetrable cover of the jungle, Nick would never find him.

Nick himself stood motionless under the trees, his breath coming raggedly. "Enough, Jarrett," he called. "Enough skulking around!"

His taunt brought no results. Nick began circling slowly, heading toward where he'd last heard Jarrett. Surrounded by impervious night, however, his sense of direction tricked him. Thrashing sounds came from far to his left this time, where he hadn't expected them. The noise faded away into the distance; now Jarrett had genuinely escaped into the jungle.

Uttering his own curses, Nick managed to find his way back to the camp. Robert was striding about with a flashlight, while Tim trailed uncertainly after him. But it was Pat and Dana who drew Nick's attention. He scowled at them.

"What the hell did you think you were doing?" he demanded. "I had everything under control. If the two of you hadn't interfered I'd have Jarrett tied up in ropes by now, ready to ship off to the police."

"What were we supposed to do?" Dana exclaimed. "You were drunk, Nick, and someone was attacking you. Not exactly a fair fight!"

"You're lucky we were awake to help," Pat added self-righteously.

"All right... all right... over here," Nick commanded, waving Robert and Tim toward the huts. "Listen up, and I'll tell you exactly what's going on and what's expected of you next."

The four of them gathered around him. He disliked explaining himself, and he intended to keep it short. "Here's the way it stands. The Institute hasn't actually shut us down yet, and I wasn't drunk. I was merely trying to force our troublemaker's hand—"

"You weren't drunk?" Dana said, her tone indignant. "That was all part of some act you were putting on?"

Nick found himself in a peculiar situation. Often enough in the past, women had been ticked off at him for being drunk. Only a short while ago, Dana had been angry for precisely that reason. But now it appeared that she was angry because he *wasn't* drunk. It was a novel experience for Nick, but he didn't have time to ponder it.

"You get the idea," he said. "I was pursuing the probability that the troublemaker was one of our crew—not an outsider. Going under that assumption, I wanted our attacker to think we'd been shut down—

anything to upset him, put him off-balance. I also figured that he might try to take me out if I appeared vulnerable... drunk, in other words."

Robert made a gesture that sent his flashlight beam traveling in an arc. "A clever plan, Nick," he said somewhat snidely. "However, you failed to include the rest of us in your confidence."

"He certainly couldn't take *you* into his confidence," Pat objected. "You've been the prime suspect all along, Robert. Frankly, I still don't know if you're exonerated. Just because Jarrett decided to take a whack at Nick doesn't mean you're not guilty of *something—*"

"Give it a rest," Dana said. Her voice had gone cool and quiet, and she glanced at Nick dispassionately now. "I think it's safe to assume that Jarrett's our culprit. I suppose that courtly attitude of his was just a pose all along"

Tim spoke up for the first time. "What about the person who knocked Jarrett over the head that day?"

"*That* could have been Robert," Pat said belligerently.

"Thanks for the vote of confidence," Robert said in a dry tone.

Nick intervened. "Just now Jarrett tried to decapitate me with a machete. He's our man, all right. He must have knocked himself over the head with that damn rock to divert suspicion from himself. But the rest of it doesn't matter right now. He's on the loose, and remember he's still got that gun—so he's dangerous. Very dangerous. My guess is that he'll attempt either to harm one of us or to sabotage the temple. We have to be ready for him. I want all of you dressed in the next five minutes and prepared to follow my orders exactly."

Nick went back inside the hut. He knew without turning around that Dana had followed him. She set her lantern on the desk and confronted him.

"I can't believe you put me through that," she said, her voice still cool, as if she were discussing someone else. "You let me think the worst—you let me think you were drunk."

He rubbed his shoulder. It felt raw, as if he'd opened up the wound all over again. "I had to make the whole thing as realistic as possible," he said.

"No—that's not it."

"Be logical," he said. "Everyone was a suspect. Who could I trust?"

"Me," she said, pushing the tangles of hair away from her face. "You knew I was innocent—at least you knew that much."

He studied her. She looked beautiful in the hazy light cast by the lantern, her sensual curves outlined in the skimpy camisole and shorts she wore. She also looked strong and capable, but Nick's first instinct was to protect her. It was a fierce sort of protectiveness that had always hit him right in the gut, and it did so now.

"Look, anything could've happened tonight," he said. "I wasn't about to risk you in that."

"You still won't admit the truth, will you? The fact is, you just don't want to admit you could possibly need someone else—for any reason whatsoever." She turned as if to go.

"Dana...Jarrett may be a crazy SOB, but he's right about one thing. It was good for you to see what a drunk can really be like. It's not something you can live with. The truth is...a drunk can't even live with himself most of the time."

She bent her head for a moment. "When I saw you lying there like that, I felt so... betrayed. That was the worst of it—the sense of betrayal. As if somehow you owed it to me to be sober." Now she lifted her head and gazed at him somberly. "What made you decide to stop drinking this time around, Nick? I wish you'd at least tell me that. You said you couldn't do it for a woman—not even for this Kathryn you loved. So what *did* make you stop?"

He didn't want to talk about it, but maybe he owed Dana at least this one answer. He rubbed his shoulder again. "After Kathryn left, I indulged myself—the pressure was off. I got drunk every night, not doing much else with my life.... Then I simply realized I had a choice. I could either go on soaking my brains in alcohol—or not. It didn't seem like a great choice either way, but there it was. If you're expecting me to share some earth-shattering revelation, Dana—forget it. I didn't think life would suddenly be fantastic if I stayed sober. I just knew I wanted a little of my self-respect back. And somehow it was easier to stay sober without Kathryn around—without the burden of all her expectations. I've found that my own expectations for myself are more than enough to handle."

"I see." Dana's voice was curiously flat. "You don't want any woman to intrude on your sobriety—or your cynicism. But I won't be intruding much longer, Nick. I've decided... I've decided to accept Alan's counterproposal. I'm going to write back to him and tell him that I'll marry him."

Nick wasn't prepared for the punch in the gut those words gave him. "If it's really what you want," he said without conviction. "I'm glad for you, Dana."

"I'm turning into a cynic, too," she said quietly. "I'm finally learning that I can't have everything I want—so I'll just take what I *can* get. I'm not going to pine for something impossible." With that, she left.

Nick sat down heavily on the cot. He reached over and picked up the machete that had fallen to the ground during his struggle with Jarrett. The blade was very sharp, the handle the texture of timeworn bone. It was the machete that had been stolen from him weeks ago. Who knew what had been going on in Jarrett's mind even then, what distortions of resentment and bitterness had impelled his actions.

Who knew what went on in anyone's mind or heart . . . ? Nick's own included.

CHAPTER SEVENTEEN

PAT PROWLED AMONG THE palm trees along the beachfront. "Hurry up," she whispered frantically to Dana. "We're going to lose him!"

"Robert is right there in full view," Dana pointed out. "I can't believe I'm doing this. It was bad enough rooting through Robert's belongings. Now you want to spy on him. We have enough to worry about with Jarrett still lurking around somewhere—"

"Forget Jarrett. He's probably long gone by now. But what's Robert *doing?* He's just standing there now, staring at that boat. Although I'd say it qualifies as a yacht, really. Very impressive. Very impressive, indeed...."

Dana stopped listening and leaned against a coconut palm. At this moment she didn't care if twenty coconuts plummeted down on top of her. Since the fracas with Jarrett the night before, she hadn't slept or relaxed a bit. For one thing, she was still trying to digest the fact that Jarrett, in spite of his air of earnest gentility, had been the culprit all along. Inspector Maciel had a team scouring the jungle for signs of him, to no avail. He was also keeping guard on the boats at the landing dock. Nonetheless, Jarrett had obviously been resourceful thus far; it was possible he had already escaped.

Meanwhile, Nick maintained his vigilance at the temple, aided by Anton Montano. He still believed that it was only a matter of time before Jarrett would appear at the temple, intent on sabotage, and he'd summarily dispatched the rest of his crew to the village, arguing that they'd be safer there. As usual, he was doing everything his own way—on his own terms.

More than anything, Dana resented Nick's power—over her and over her heart. In the past twenty-four hours alone, she'd allowed him to pull her into a maelstrom of emotion. Believing that the project had been shut down and she would have to leave Nick, then believing he was drunk, then finding out everything had been part of his own private plan....

She'd almost hated him after that. Certainly she'd hated his domination of her feelings. And so, without further deliberation, she'd opened her mouth and told Nick that she was going to marry Alan. She hadn't stopped to question her impulse—but it was almost as if she'd hoped to use the idea of Alan as a talisman against Nick's power.

Some talisman... Nick's reaction to her announcement had been so guarded that she couldn't even guess at *his* real feelings. Added to that was Dana's disgust at herself. Had she become so desperate that she would even *consider* marrying Alan? What about her new life and the self-respect it had given her? Would she turn away from that, in a wild attempt to free herself of Nick Petrie? Dammit, even now the man held sway over her thoughts, over her senses....

Of course, she hadn't yet posted her answer to Alan, although part of her actually felt relieved at the thought of returning to her old life. Alan might not be the most imaginative, passionate man in the world, but once he decided on something he followed it through. She knew that much about him. She knew that she could have a comfortable relationship with him....

The other part of her ached stubbornly for Nick Petrie, the least comfortable man she'd ever known. But where did that get her? Nick had already made it unmercifully clear that he would not let her into his life. A night or so of shared passion—that was all he'd allowed.

Her discouraging reverie was broken by the sound of Pat's voice; trust Pat not to stay quiet for long. "Look—Robert's moving closer to that boat. And those islanders aren't any too happy about it. Maybe they're mistaking him for Jarrett."

Dana made an effort to concentrate on Robert. He had approached the small, elegant yacht moored at the dock, and two island men had instantly converged on him. Robert began to engage in a rather intense conversation with them. He was fluent in Spanish as well as French and English, a fact that only seemed to add to the aura of mystery surrounding him. Robert was an educated, cultured man—or at least he gave a good imitation of one. It seemed a lot of people were adept at pretense. The night before, Nick had certainly convinced everyone he was drunk, and Dana still hated the memory of it.

"We have to get closer," Pat said. "We have to hear what's going on." She scuttled to another cluster of palms, and Dana trudged after her. Robert apparently satisfied the two men that he was not the criminal in question, and then he turned around and gazed into the palms.

"Pat, Dana—you might as well come out," he called in a long-suffering tone. "The two of you should never become private detectives. You're no good at sneaking around."

Pat looked discomfited, but she emerged from her cover and walked over to Robert. Dana had no choice but to do the same. Pat immediately began trying to exonerate herself.

"This is a public beach, you know. Dana and I are just out for a stroll. If you happen to be here, too, Robert, it's hardly our—"

"Oh, for goodness' sake," Dana snapped. "Robert knows exactly what we're doing. The only question is why I let myself get involved."

Pat stared at her with an injured expression. "Really, Dana. You're becoming more impossible to live with by the minute. I don't understand why you're so cranky. And, Robert, why on earth *do* you keep staring at that boat? It's lovely, I'll grant you that, but what's it to you?"

Robert stroked his beard—a most luxuriant beard by now. "She's found me," he murmured distractedly as he went on considering the sleek white yacht. "I don't know how she managed it, but she's found me."

"She...who?" Pat began to look worried. "What are you talking about?"

Robert didn't answer. He simply crossed the dock and went up the gangplank of the yacht. When Pat followed him, he didn't protest or try to stop her; he simply seemed to have forgotten her presence. Dana hesitated for a moment, but then she, too, went aboard. Anything was better than standing about, brooding over Nick Petrie.

Robert seemed very familiar with the boat. He walked along the deck as if he knew exactly where he was going. And the yacht was gorgeous. There could simply be no other word for it—all burnished wood fashioned in graceful lines. The slatted deck chairs alone were impressive and came complete with their own lushly padded cushions.

"Whoever owns this boat is loaded," Pat murmured.

"I own the boat," Robert said over his shoulder. It seemed he was still keeping tabs on Pat, after all.

"I don't know whether or not to believe you," Pat grumbled. "I really wonder if I believe anything you—" She broke off abruptly as a woman emerged from the cabin—a woman, in fact, as gorgeous as the boat itself. Her raven black hair fell in soft natural waves to her shoulders, offsetting the creamy white of her complexion. Her eyes were a deep, luminous gray. She wore an elegant silk dress in a subtle shade of pearl that surely had been chosen to complement her eyes, and it did the job well. But hers was a cool, subdued beauty that seemed a bit out of place in the torrid air of Isla Calamar.

The woman gazed at Robert and spoke to him in French. She made the language sound as soft and cool and elegant as she herself appeared. Robert answered quickly, also in French. He stepped next to the woman and kissed her on the cheek. Turning then, he behaved with polite formality as he switched to English.

"Marie, I should like you to meet two of my... associates. Dana Morgan and Pat Aldridge. Dana, Pat... this is Marie Calder, my fiancée."

Marie was not only beautiful—she was gracious. She greeted Pat and Dana with a quiet courtesy, offering her hand to each of them. Pat, however, only made a small sound of dismay.

Dana understood the dismay. It had to be awful for Pat, learning in such an unexpected manner that Robert possessed a fiancée. And not just any fiancée, either... Marie Calder shimmered like an exquisitely understated diamond. In contrast, Pat herself was like a bright chunk of costume jewelry. She stood there with her sunburn still flaming, her sandy hair flying in wisps, her coral blouse rumpled—and her expression openly miserable.

Robert, too, seemed aware of the contrast. He glanced back and forth between Pat and Marie, his expression one of puzzlement. Dana could only guess at what he was thinking.

"Well, Marie," he said at last. "Pat, Dana and I were just discussing the matter of detective work. And you, my dear, must be a very good detective if you managed to find me on this little island."

Marie gave a delicate shrug. "I won't weary you with the details at the moment. Your... friends, surely they don't wish to hear."

"Don't mind Pat and Dana," Robert said airily. "Their curiosity is infinite—there is no detail about my life too small for their amusement. You can speak of anything to them."

Dana was starting to feel very uncomfortable. She could sense the undercurrents of tension between Robert and his fiancée. Certainly he didn't seem overjoyed to see her. Not to mention how odd it was that he'd come to this island without even letting Marie know where he was....

As far as Dana was concerned, Robert and his beautiful fiancée should just be left to themselves. "Pat and I will be going now," she said firmly. "It was nice to meet you, Marie—"

"I don't mind staying," Pat interrupted, using a belligerent tone that didn't bode well.

"See... What did I tell you? I fascinate them. By all means, sit down and relax," Robert said sarcastically. To all appearances, he was now playing a somewhat acerbic host. Before Dana quite knew how it had happened, she was seated in a cluster of chairs with the others, and a deckhand in a crisp white uniform had appeared with a tray of iced tea. It was all very civilized, and just a little too bizarre for Dana's taste: the warm breeze stirring, the sky arching overhead in a pure, brilliant blue, the waves of the Caribbean lapping against the sides of the boat... and Robert holding court with three women. As he leaned back and sipped from his glass, he actually seemed to be enjoying himself.

"So how did you find me?" he asked Marie.

She sipped from her own glass, her slim, well-shaped legs crossed at the knee. "Someone on this island was making inquiries about you, Robert. In turn, I began to make my own inquiries."

Robert nodded. "I imagine it was Nick poking about in my background. Somehow he has never trusted me."

Pat spoke up. "Well, you can hardly blame him. You've been deliberately mysterious all along." She turned to Marie. "Robert never even told us about you. You can imagine our curiosity now that suddenly...suddenly you're here." Pat clenched both hands around her glass, but she hadn't taken even a sip of tea.

Marie gazed steadily back at her. "Robert and I have been engaged for two years now, and we are to be married in a month's time. I felt it necessary to collect the groom, you see."

"No, I don't see," Pat muttered. "What kind of man takes off without even letting his fiancée know where he's going? What kind of man doesn't even tell anyone he *has* a fiancée, and that he's about to be married?"

"What kind of man, indeed?" Marie echoed in her soft, melodious voice. Both women turned and stared accusingly at Robert. Dana stared at him, too. She wouldn't mind hearing the answer to *this* one.

Robert, incredibly, still seemed to be enjoying himself. He was like a magician smugly deciding whether or not he would reveal his magic tricks. "It's all quite simple, really," he said. "As I tried explaining to Nick, I decided that I needed to take a sort of sabbatical from my everyday life. Archaeology seemed the perfect solution."

"You told me only that you had to leave for a time," Marie said. "Why, Robert? How could you do such a thing?"

He finally had the grace to look just a little nonplussed. "Marie, my dear—"

"Don't keep saying that—'my dear.' It means nothing . . . worse than nothing." Marie's eyes were truly luminous now, brimming as they did with tears. The woman deserved a little privacy in which to berate Robert.

This time Dana was determined to get Pat out of here. She set down her own glass of untouched tea, hauled Pat to her feet, made the necessary excuses and then conducted Pat down the gangplank. She didn't stop until they were among the palms again, far away from the lovely white yacht.

"Why did you do that?" Pat demanded. "We were just starting to get to the interesting part."

"You're even more of a busybody than I'd suspected, Pat. Besides, I can't help but like Marie, and I figured she needed to preserve some dignity. I figure the same about you. Can't you see what Robert's doing? He actually enjoys having two women in a tizzy over him! Don't give him the satisfaction."

Pat sighed heavily. "There's still so much I don't understand. I mean, Robert ran away from his own fiancée, and then he did his best to make us all wonder about him.... What could possibly be his intention?"

"He told me once that if we knew the truth about him, we might consider his life boring and mundane, even though he's wealthy. Maybe Robert just felt that he had to spice things up a little...." Now Dana was the one who sighed, taking off her hat and fanning herself with it. "I can understand that, I suppose. I wanted to spice up my own life, and that's why I came to this island. The trouble is, adding a little spice is something that can get out of control before you know it."

Pat didn't seem to be listening. "How am I going to compete with that woman?" she wailed. "She and Robert look like they were cloned from the same beauty gene. Besides, she's not only stunning, she's *nice.*"

"And that's what makes it all the worse," Dana said. "Robert ran away from her, but he didn't make a clean break. He seems to be using Marie ... keeping her as a convenience. That way he could tell you he had 'prior commitments.'"

"He's supposed to marry her in a month!" Pat slumped against the trunk of a coconut palm. "What am I going to do?"

Dana didn't have an answer to that. Right now she realized she was doing something just a little too similar to Robert's ploys. Maybe she hadn't sent Alan an answer yet, but she was using him—using him in one final, desperate attempt to protect herself from Nick Petrie. Alan deserved better than that, surely. But Dana didn't want to face the pain of loving Nick.... She just didn't want to face it head-on.

Oh, yes, she loved him. There was no longer any use in denying that. The knowledge filled her with a poignant, almost unbearable hurt: she loved Nick Petrie.

And now she could only ask the same question Pat had. What on earth was she going to do?

NICK SAT IN THE TENT he'd rigged up at the temple site—a big, thick sheet of canvas stretched over a frame and anchored to the ground with stakes and guylines. Canvas was a lot less breathable than the palm thatch of the island huts, and Nick felt the sweat trickling down his back. Nonetheless, this was his best chance at solitude for the moment. Outside, he could hear the murmur of voices, Pat's as usual the most vociferous.

Nick couldn't manage to get rid of his crew—that was the problem. Only Daniel seemed determined to stay away from Nick these days. But Robert, Tim, Pat and Dana all refused to remain in the village. They argued that they belonged at the temple site as much as Nick did. Unfortunately, they were only making his life more difficult. Two nights had passed since Jarrett's escape, and the man hadn't yet shown himself. That he would show eventually, Nick had no doubt. For some unfathomable reason, Jarrett seemed to feel he had a score to settle with Nick. He'd strike again, sooner or later, and being ready for him would be a whole hell of a lot easier if the others would just stay at the village. Dana, especially... She'd be safer there, with Inspector Maciel keeping an eye on things and the rest of the islanders on alert, too. Dana needed to leave Nick alone so he could do his job.

Dana... What would it take to get her out of his mind—out of his soul? Every instinct told him he shouldn't be involved with her. He'd already proved that he was lousy at relationships. First he'd pared Meg from his life, and then Kathryn. Paring down—he was good at that. He didn't need to accumulate people anymore. Not a wife, not a child...not a family. He was better off alone, and he knew it. Maybe being alone was even necessary for his survival. So how did he get Dana out of his head?

Just then Pat came ducking under the door flap of the tent and stared at Nick in a challenging manner. She plunked herself down on a camp stool across from him. "I need to talk," she declared.

Nick rattled his survey maps of the temple. "I'm busy right now, Pat. Let it wait—"

"No, I have to know something right away." She took a deep breath. "I understand that you investigated Robert's background. You started asking questions about him, who knows where."

"I got some leads on him through the Institute," Nick conceded.

"Have you been investigating the rest of us, too?"

"I checked some of you out, yes. It was only reasonable to try finding any clue I could to our problems here. So what's your complaint, Pat?"

She held her hands tightly in her lap. "Just come out with it," she said. "I'm sure you checked into *my* background, too. What did you find?"

He hesitated a few seconds.

"You know, don't you?" she said, her voice ragged. "You know about the time I was hospitalized for depression, and all the rest of it."

Nick had rung up quite a phone bill these past few weeks. He knew the Institute wouldn't be any too pleased about that. He'd learned, among other things, that Robert was the successful owner of a shipping firm based in Paris and London, that Jarrett had spent some twenty years teaching at the same small university in Oklahoma, that Tim lived alone in Fort Collins, Colorado and no one had anything to say about him, good or bad—and, yes, that Pat had been hospitalized for depression while attending graduate school in Arizona. There was only one person Nick *hadn't* checked up on.... Dana. He disliked poking into other people's lives and had done so only out of necessity. Probing around in Dana's life would have been going too far. He already knew too much about her, too much about how she thought and felt.

But now he had to deal with Pat, who continued to gaze at him combatively.

"Once you found out about me, you probably thought *I* was the culprit," she said. "After all, they had to lock me away so I wouldn't hurt myself. When you learned that, maybe you thought I was capable of anything."

She was showing fortitude by confronting him on this, and he had to be honest in return. "Not really, Pat," he said. "Your background may not be stable, but for some reason you never struck me as the murderous type."

"Yes, of course. I see." She seemed to stiffen a little.

Honesty wasn't such an easy thing. He'd no doubt end up saying something Pat wouldn't really want to hear, but Nick went on anyway. He didn't know how to be other than blunt and straightforward. "From everything I learned and everything I've observed about you... I could tell you'd turn any anger upon yourself before you'd harm someone else."

"Then you know I tried to commit suicide." Pat could be blunt, too, it seemed.

"I'd gathered as much."

She held her hands together all the more tightly, staring down at them. Her voice was very low, yet it carried pain. "Sometimes... sometimes all your perceptions get tilted. At first you *know* they're tilted and you try to make them right again.... You try to tell yourself that you should be happy, and that what you do every day should make sense. But then you just get so tired, and somehow you just can't try anymore. You end up feeling smaller and smaller...."

Nick listened. He'd never felt quite the way she'd described, and he could only guess at the reasons she'd gone through her own particular torment. But he did know something about a different type of pain and about getting tired of fighting yourself every day.

"Listen, Pat," he said inadequately. "The important thing is that you pulled out of it. You didn't give in."

Now her head came up, her posture defensive, as if she already regretted exposing her weaknesses to him. "I want to live. I've decided that I'll never, *ever* try to hurt myself again."

She seemed to be waiting for some confirmation from him, but he didn't know how to give her that. He wasn't one for trite reassurances. Pat seemed to be the kind of person who could be both enthralled and repelled by herself. Either way, Pat was fiercely wrapped up in her own life; Nick just hoped she could find a little peace of mind in it all. Hell, he was looking for his own peace of mind more and more these days.

At last Pat stood and pushed aside the tent flaps, glancing back at him for a moment.

"Can I trust you not to tell the others? Especially not Robert...."

He gave her a hard look. "What do you think, Pat?"

She didn't answer for a moment. "Yeah... I suppose it was stupid even to ask." Pat turned to leave, then stopped herself. "You're really making it tough on Dana, aren't you? Give her a break, Nick. She's not as strong as you think." With that, Pat ducked out of the tent.

CHAPTER EIGHTEEN

"WE'RE STARTING TO break through," Nick said in a taut voice. "I could swear it's shifting."

Dana didn't feel a darn thing shifting. She slumped against the carved limestone slab that she and Nick were attempting to push inward. The muscles in her arms and legs ached, and she was damp with perspiration. It was already late at night, but still Nick wouldn't give up. He was determined to keep working, no matter that he'd been at it for hours or that he ought to give his wounded shoulder a rest. Since his tussle with Jarrett, Nick even refused to wear his sling, paying no heed to the doctor's admonishments. And now he continued to push with his good shoulder against this large stone slab.

Dana supposed that the slab could actually be termed a door. Earlier this evening, great excitement had prevailed among the crew when the last of the rubble in the temple stairway had been breached. More steps had been revealed, leading downward to a narrow landing...which was sealed by this thick stone door. The crew had already expended great effort and time in trying to move the door, managing to chisel out the mortar seal around its edges. That in itself had been a painstaking, grueling job. At last, exhausted and hungry—Tim already having fallen asleep on the stone steps—and their excitement ebbing, the others had declared a sort of mutiny on Nick, demanding a time-out. Now only Dana remained at Nick's side. In the light of the one small lantern, she studied the strained, intense lines of his face.

"Give it rest," she said. "After a night's sleep, we'll all be fresh. We'll manage it in the morning."

He actually stopped for a moment, gazing back at her. "Why are you still here?" he asked. "You could have gone with the rest of them."

She turned away, not knowing how to answer his question. Certainly she couldn't tell him about the need deep inside her, the need that compelled her to be near him, whatever the circumstances. And she certainly couldn't tell him that she loved him. It would be too humiliating, too hurtful, to have him reject her all over again.

"Dana." He reached out and forced her to look at him once more, cupping his hand against her cheek. His fingers were more roughened than ever and caked with limestone dust. She didn't care. It seemed such a long while since he had touched her, and she pressed her own hand against his. Apparently even that was too much. Abruptly he broke the contact between them, stepping away from her as far as he was able in this confined space.

"I keep forgetting that you belong to another man."

"I don't *belong* to anyone," she said sharply. "I'm sure you'd like to think that I do, however. It gives you the perfect excuse to dismiss me from your life."

"You said you were going to marry the guy."

She still hadn't mailed her answer to Alan. She hadn't called him on the phone, either—as might be expected of a joyful fiancée. But she didn't tell Nick that.

"Would it make you happy if I *did* marry him?" she asked. "For once...just once, I wish you'd let me know what you're feeling. Can't you give me that much, Nick?"

His features tightened still more in the wavering light, and he didn't answer for a long time. Dana knew she was becoming pathetic, begging for any crumb Nick could give her. Didn't she have any dignity left at all? She'd never known that love could do this...reduce her to such irrevocable need and desire, such improbable hope. That was the worst of it—even after the way Nick had shut himself off from her, she still clung to her shabby hopes.

At last he spoke, his voice grating against the night. "I sure as hell don't want you to marry someone else, Dana. But I don't have any right to tell you not to do it. I can't offer you anything in replacement."

"You hold to your principles, don't you, Nick?" Her own voice was brittle. "Just like Daniel. The two of you have finally managed to push each other away completely. Now all you have to do is push *me* away, once and for all, and the job will be done."

He studied her, his eyes a very dark blue as the lantern sent its flickering light over him. "Are you going to do it, then?" he asked. "Are you really going to marry this guy?"

"Alan has all the right qualifications," she said. "He's a stockbroker on his way up. He's ambitious. He's even dependable, once he decides what he wants."

"Sounds like you two are made for each other."

Made for each other... Right. She turned from Nick again. There were some things that would be too humiliating to tell him—such as the fact that in four years with Alan she'd never experienced the passion she could feel in one minute with Nick. To go back to Alan...it would be like returning to the desert after she'd had a taste of this mysterious tropical island....

Suddenly Dana was angry. A glimpse of paradise wasn't enough. And as to whether she'd actually go ahead and marry Alan, after all—that was none of Nick Petrie's damn business. Now Dana was the one who strained against the stone door. If it was going to move, why didn't it just move?

She could sense Nick watching her, but after a pause he redoubled his efforts. They worked in tense silence for several moments and then Dana heard it—the slightest rasp of stone scraping stone as the door gave just a little.

"It's happening," she said. "You were right...."

Nick didn't answer, all his focus concentrated on the door. They worked together without speaking, their labored breathing the only sound in the passageway, punctuated now and then by another scraping noise as they made infinitesimal progress in budging the door.

Slowly, agonizingly, they proceeded. They couldn't use such helpful devices as crowbars, for they couldn't risk damaging the stone. But slowly, a fraction of an inch at a time, the door pivoted inward. Finally, there was just enough space for one person to squeeze through at a time.

Dana's heart pounded from all the exertion and from a feeling of almost unbearable suspense. "We should tell the others," she said breathlessly.

Nick put a staying hand on her arm. "No," he said. "We'll go through together first—just the two of us."

She hesitated, a jumble of sensations competing inside her: an odd foreboding mingled with an equally odd exhilaration. No one had been through this doorway in centuries, and now she had a chance to do so with Nick. Yes, just the two of them. . . .

Her heart pounding even more, Dana watched as Nick squeezed through the opening. Then, picking up the lantern, she followed him.

Yet more steps led down from the landing. The passage was still so cramped that Nick and Dana had to travel single file, crouched over as they went. The air was stuffy, unused, closing in around them. Then, before Dana was quite ready for it, they emerged into a vaulted chamber. The lantern light swept eerily over the frescoes on the walls. The colors were vivid—gold, black, a crimson bright as blood. They depicted figures that seemed to jump out at Dana—men draped regally in robes of animal skin and crowned with the grimacing heads of jaguars, women mantled in white and adorned with elaborate bracelets and necklaces. Dana's gaze was riveted by one figure in particular—a young girl plunging a knife into her own breast, an expression almost of rapture on her face. Dana shivered, but Nick took the lantern from her and was already moving deeper into the chamber.

He stopped before a large rectangular burial case fashioned of masonry. Dana came up beside him and found herself gripping his hand.

"You were right all along," she murmured a bit shakily. "This is a burial chamber, no question about it."

"We haven't found the real tomb yet," he answered, his own voice hushed. "Most likely the sacrificial victims were interred here."

"Sacrificial..." But Dana already knew from reading Nick's books that no Maya of importance was buried in solitude. Others had to be killed so their spirits could guard the deceased. Dana shivered again. She could not believe they had gone willingly to their deaths.

Now she saw the items arranged before the burial site: precisely molded figurines, clay vases and pots painted with intricate figures and symbols, small ornaments of jade and shell, bottles fashioned of soapstone. Perhaps some mourner all those centuries ago had laid these offerings to honor the dead.

Shadows engulfed Dana as Nick went on. She hurried to stay beside him—and now, it seemed, he found what he was really looking for.

Deep inside the chamber, he set down the lantern and knelt beside another limestone slab set into the floor. It was a work of art in itself, carved with intricate designs in bas-relief. Nick studied the designs intently.

"This is the lid of a sarcophagus," he said, his voice grown reverent. "It will take some doing to lift it up, but I can guess at what we'll find underneath—the mummy of a Mayan noblewoman."

"How can you be so sure it's a woman?"

He gestured at the lid. "An image of her is carved right here on the stone. And these glyphs are the signs of a titled woman. Some important Mayan rulers have been known to be female. It's appropriate—right now we're inside a shrine to a goddess."

Dana leaned over the sarcophagus so she could study the portrait etched in stone. This Mayan woman wore a fringed robe that was richly embossed. Her jeweled and feathered headdress was ornate, a long-tailed quetzal bird soaring above it. The woman cradled a fan in one hand and she looked pensive, gazing into some unknown distance. Across the ages, something reached to Dana. The woman's expression, after all, was one of yearning... one of longing unfulfilled. How well Dana herself could understand that feeling.

Dana sat back on her heels, quite overwhelmed. "I wonder how she died. I wonder if she's the one who begged Ixchel for a child...."

"We'll learn more about her. The clues are all here, waiting to be deciphered."

Dana gazed across the sarcophagus at Nick. Now he fairly radiated intensity, his features molded with strength and decisiveness even in the wavering light of the lantern.

"Congratulations," she murmured. "You have what you want here... the discovery you dreamed about."

He gazed back at her, there in the ancient chamber, and a different sort of intensity seemed to take him over.

"I don't have everything I want, Dana. Not by a long shot—"

He didn't get a chance to finish. Suddenly the light of the lantern was snuffed out, plunging the chamber into darkness.

Dana heard Nick's brusque exclamation, then a scuffling sound. She scrambled to her feet, only to have a terrible pain explode on the side of her head. Now the darkness truly engulfed her.

DANA WASN'T SURE how much later she awakened, but darkness still shrouded her. A gag had been stuffed into her mouth, nearly choking her, and the side of her head throbbed wickedly. When she tried to move, she found her legs and arms bound with rope. She lay curled on an uneven surface of stone and at first panic swept through her, drenching her in a clammy sweat. It took every ounce of willpower she possessed to calm herself, to force herself to think clearly. Very well, she could tell she was no longer inside the burial chamber, for the warm night air wafted over her. But where was she—

"Hello, Dana." It was Jarrett's voice, close to her ear.

She tried to move again, struggling against the ropes. Never had she felt so powerless, so abjectly at someone else's mercy. At first the panic threatened to sweep over her again, but then she experienced pure rage as she fought to free herself.

Jarrett continued to crouch over her. "Easy," he said. "I have you at last...." His courtly tone seemed almost a parody now. Dana stopped struggling, if only to conserve her energy. She glanced around wildly, trying at least to learn where she was. She could see stars in the distance, that was all. When she tried to speak, the gag jammed into her mouth and prevented her from uttering any sound. Jarrett had thought of everything.

She felt something metallic press against her forehead and knew that it was the muzzle of a gun.

"Now," said Jarrett, still so close to her she could feel his breath on her face. "I'm going to remove your gag. If you attempt to scream or draw attention in any way...I'll have to kill you. Do you understand, Dana?"

She nodded once, her heartbeat racing. It seemed essential at this moment to keep fear from claiming her entirely. Somehow she had to retain a calm, rational center that would allow her a chance of escape. Oh, God, let there *be* a chance....

Jarrett loosened the strap of cloth tied behind her head and removed the rag stuffed into her mouth. At least this gave her some measure of relief. She swallowed, her throat raw.

"Jarrett—" she whispered hoarsely, intent on reasoning with him. But then, before she could twist her face away, he bent closer and kissed her full on the mouth.

Dana shuddered with revulsion. Jarrett's lips had a peculiar softness, a slackness to them. When he raised his head, she could just faintly see his outline.

"I've been watching these past few days," he said. "I've watched you and Petrie.... The two of you haven't been getting along so well, have you? It's much better that you're here with me."

It was awful to think that Jarrett had been lurking in the jungle all this time, watching the rest of them. But knowing that was the least of Dana's problems right now.

"Jarrett, it's not too late—you haven't really hurt anyone yet—"

"Not by choice," he said, almost in a conversational tone. "Too bad I only got Petrie in the shoulder—I wanted to kill him."

"Why?" she whispered.

"Why not?" Jarrett countered, a chilling edge to his voice now. "He's a washed-up drunk. Damned if I'll let him get credit for my discovery. Damned if I'll let him have you." He pressed the gun next to her forehead again, moving the barrel against her skin in a macabre caress.

"If you want me, then why would you try to kill me?" she asked with reckless desperation. "You contaminated that water, knowing anyone might drink it—including me. And when you shot at Nick, you could have taken me out, too—"

"I was in control the entire time. I'm still in control. Don't forget that, Dana." He leaned over her once more, moving his lips against her cheek. She clenched her jaw, her head throbbing until she thought it would burst. She tried to wrench away from Jarrett's touch—only to have him press the gun barrel even deeper into her flesh. She heard the small, ominous click as he cocked the revolver.

"Don't underestimate me," he murmured. "I just might do it, you see. I just might pull the trigger, after all. Petrie has had his hands all over you. That's reason enough."

Dana lay very still, as ice-cold as if she herself had been entombed in the temple for centuries. She had no doubt that Jarrett could, indeed, pull that trigger. In another second or two she might very well be dead. She confronted the knowledge, refusing to flinch from it. And somehow that alone gave her strength.

She wasn't dead yet—that was all that mattered. Jarrett hadn't won . . . not yet.

FROM THE EDGE OF the jungle Nick doubled back toward the temple, the breath burning in his lungs. He'd already wasted too much time and he cursed despairingly. If anything happened to Dana...he couldn't even finish the thought. He just knew he had to find her and he prayed it wasn't too late.

Jarrett had been very clever so far. He'd chosen his moment and had acted quickly and efficiently. He'd managed to extinguish the lantern in the tomb and attack Nick almost simultaneously, knocking him semi-unconscious. Then Jarrett had spirited Dana away. When Nick emerged from the tomb, he'd yelled for his crew, only to find that not one of them had seen anything unusual. It was as if Jarrett were the ghost rumored to haunt the temple, unseen by mortal eyes. Nick had sent everyone fanning out in a search, but finding Jarrett and Dana in the depths of night seemed a hopeless proposition, particularly if they had disappeared into the jungle.

Nick, however, couldn't afford to give up hope—not where Dana was concerned. Now he was following a hunch. If Jarrett was truly clever, he might stay near the temple itself, where he was least expected to be.

Reaching the temple at last, Nick quickly searched the tomb chamber again. He found nothing beyond those remnants of the ancient dead. With a heavy feeling he climbed out again, panning his flashlight across the exterior of the temple...and a few steps up he saw Dana's floppy-brimmed hat. He grabbed it, remembering that she'd been wearing it in the tomb. Dana and her ridiculous hat...

Nick switched off his flashlight and gazed toward the top of the temple pyramid, and he could've sworn he detected a shadow of movement up there. Maybe he was only imagining it—maybe it was just the night playing games with him—but Nick began crawling stealthily up the terraced steps.

As he neared the altar room at the very pinnacle, he was rewarded by the sound of Jarrett's voice through the darkness. A second later, Nick heard Dana's answering murmur. It sounded faint, but at least she was still alive. Relief flooded through Nick. Only now would he admit to himself how much he'd feared for her safety. Thank God she was still alive—

Nick crept along the side of the altar room until he reached one of the archways. As he peered inside, the darkness of night was both a help and a hindrance. It allowed him to remain hidden, but it also revealed little. Nick saw only vague shapes and he squandered a few more precious seconds as he ascertained that Dana was lying on the altar stone, Jarrett poised above her. It appeared as if Jarrett was trying to re-create a gruesome scene from centuries past: the Mayan sacrificial victim stretched over the altar, the priest standing ready to cut out her heart. Except that Jarrett's weapon wasn't an ancient knife of obsidian; Nick saw the glimmer of gunmetal. He moved swiftly, silently into the room, intent on taking Jarrett by surprise—

"Hello, Petrie," Jarrett said calmly. "No closer, please."

Nick froze where he was, assessing the situation. Now he could tell that Dana was heavily bound with ropes and Jarrett was aiming the gun right at her heart. The symbolism of what Jarrett was doing obviously hadn't escaped him. He was staging all this for his own benefit—and perhaps for Nick's and Dana's benefit, as well.

"What good will killing someone do you now?" Nick asked quietly. "It's not too late, Jarrett."

"Funny, Dana said the same thing. But it is too late, you see. I'm the one in charge. It was never you, Petrie. Don't you get it? I've been calling the shots all along."

"Fine," Nick said, his own voice very calm. "You've made your point. You've kept the entire project off-balance—"

"Don't try throwing me a bone, Petrie. I'm not here to be placated by a has-been like you. It's my project. And Dana's mine, too—"

It was then that Dana acted. Somehow she managed to heave herself over the stone, knocking into Jarrett and causing him to stumble backward. The gun went off, the sound shattering the air. Lord, if the bullet had hit Dana—

Nick lunged at Jarrett and pounded his face, drawing back his fist for one blow after another. Pain ripped through his shoulder, but that only increased Nick's fury. At last Jarrett slumped to the ground, the gun sliding out of his hand. Nick grabbed it.

"Dana—"

"I'm fine," she said in a scratchy voice. "Just fine..."

Jarrett appeared to be unconscious, but Nick wasn't taking any chances. Quickly he worked at untying Dana, and in short order he'd trussed Jarrett up in the ropes. Jarrett groaned, but then he lapsed back into unconsciousness. He wouldn't be going anywhere soon.

Only now did Nick allow himself to take Dana into his arms, savoring her warmth, her softness and—yes—her strength.

"Are you sure you're all right?" he asked, gathering her close.

"All in one piece," she said shakily, leaning against him, wrapping her own arms around him. "Hold me, Nick. Just hold me, and don't ever stop."

Maybe he couldn't offer her any promises, but he could damn well hold her.... He could hold her as if he never *would* let her go. And at last he gave in to what he'd denied himself all this time. He tilted Dana's face up to his and kissed her with all the passion and tenderness only she could evoke in him.

CHAPTER NINETEEN

THIS TIME ELENA HAD put just a little too much chili powder into the rice. The taste of it scorched Nick's mouth, but he wasn't about to say anything. Neither was Anton, it seemed; he simply pushed the rice to one side of his plate and tried to look involved with his beans.

Elena ate a forkful of the rice off her own plate. "I like things a little spicy, myself," she said defensively. "Chili pepper is good for the sinuses. Helps you breathe—did you know that, Nicolás?"

"I'm sure breathing well right now," he admitted.

Anton took this as an opportune moment to change the subject. "Our friend Jarrett—he has finally been shipped to the mainland?"

"Our friend, indeed," Nick said ironically. "Yes, Inspector Maciel escorted him over this morning. Apparently he'll be transferred to the States soon, and the Institute will file charges against him there."

Elena popped an extra tortilla onto her husband's plate. "So, what's the story with Jarrett?" she asked. "I'll admit I never did like him much, but—"

"Listen to you," Anton said with a smile. "You always told me you thought Jarrett was a true caballero—a true gentleman."

Elena peered imperturbably at Anton's plate. "Eat the rice and let Nicolás speak."

Nick eased back in his chair and gazed out at the jade-blue waters of the Caribbean. Today he envied the Montanos again. They lived in their small, simple hut, surrounded by beauty—surrounded by each other's love. But could anything ever really be this uncomplicated? Nick wondered about that....

Unwillingly, he brought himself back to the subject of Jarrett. "From what I can piece together, Jarrett's one of those people who feels he only got a second-rate go at life. Working for me tipped the scales, I guess.... I became the target for all his resentment. He didn't want to be second anymore, especially not to me—someone with the reputation of a has-been drunk."

"He was wrong," Elena pronounced decisively. "Nicolás, you're a fine man. You should forget the past and look to the future now."

Nick shifted in his chair, still trying to puzzle out the whole thing with Jarrett. He remembered something Pat had said, when attempting to explain her own problems. She'd talked about the world becoming tilted, perceptions distorting more and more. And that was how Nick pictured Jarrett—viewing the world from the tilted angle of his own bitterness.

It seemed that at first Jarrett had simply planned to disrupt the dig, hoping, in the process, to discredit Nick. Such a course of action possessed its own logic, admittedly: if it appeared that Nick was unable to control the project, the Institute might very well look to Jarrett as second-in-command. Perhaps Jarrett had, indeed, surmised on his own that a tomb lay beneath the temple.

With such an important discovery at stake, he'd have good reason to try taking over.

In the beginning, then, Jarrett had instigated his plan well. He'd staged the attack on himself so that he would look innocent, and he'd proceeded to sabotage the dig in a subtle manner. Then, however, something had pushed him over the edge—right over the edge to attempted murder. Most probably it had been Nick's announcement that he planned to excavate the temple. And Dana herself had obviously been a catalyst.

Dana. Thinking about her was like probing an open wound; it plagued Nick worse than the ache in his shoulder. It should be enough now to know that she was safe and well. It should be more than enough—but, dammit, somehow it wasn't....

Elena whisked his plate away and served him with a dessert of *churros*—bits of dough that had been fried and dusted liberally with sugar. Nick had no complaints about this portion of the meal. When he finished, he stood reluctantly to leave. He studied both Anton and Elena.

"You've been good friends," he said. "You stuck with me through all this. I wouldn't have blamed you if you'd just stayed away."

Anton put his arm around his wife. "I kept Elena safe—that was all that mattered."

"I kept *you* safe," Elena said tartly. "Just remember that."

They sat there together, united in love, each of them convinced that their love was all-powerful, invincible. Either they were very naive...or very lucky.

"We'll have a lot more work to do at the temple," Nick said. "I hope you're willing to be part of it."

"We'll be there," Anton said. "You can count on us."

Nick believed it. He turned to go, only to have Elena speak up again. She didn't mince words, that was for certain.

"Nicolás, when are you going to allow yourself some happiness? Why are you so stubborn? Do you believe that it's wrong to be happy?"

It was a deceptively simple question, yet it stumped Nick. "I don't know," he said at last. "I just don't know."

As far as Dana was concerned, Nick Petrie had become more high-handed than ever. This afternoon, for example, she disliked the way he had ordered his crew to convene for a meeting in front of the field huts. He behaved like a corporate executive marshaling his subordinates before him and expecting the proper respect. She gazed at him sourly as he paced back and forth. He certainly seemed full of energy, his lean, powerful frame manifesting a new vitality. His gaze swept over Pat, Tim and Robert...then lingered on Dana with just a hint of skepticism. Even when he looked at her like that— somehow she still loved him. Her love, it seemed, was a burden of exquisite pain. She didn't know how to rid herself of it. Of course, for a few brief moments the other night, Dana had thought her pain would turn to joy. Nick had dispensed with Jarrett there in the altar room, and afterward he had taken Dana in his arms. He had kissed her as she'd longed to be kissed...and then, damn him, he'd withdrawn from her once more.

Nick had begun to speak. "As you all know by now," he said, "the Mesoamerica Institute has decided to extend our tenure on the island. They rightfully agree that the tomb has much to tell us about Mayan life and Mayan art. Depending on our ability to decipher the inscriptions and murals, this could be quite a breakthrough.''

"The understatement of the year," Pat added sotto voce.

Nick paused to glance at Pat and, despite the frown on his face, Dana could see the enthusiasm lighting his eyes. The zeal had returned to Nick's face—the same vigor and intensity that had been captured in those early photos from his books. He had his career back on track, there could be no doubt about that. Dana thought about the exciting accomplishment that had taken place only this morning. By means of jacks and thick wooden levers, Nick had supervised the cautious lifting of the sarcophagus lid. Inside had been an awe-inspiring sight: the bones of the Mayan noblewoman, still wrapped in a shroud and bearing traces of the red cinnabar sprinkled on her at burial. A beautiful diadem and mask of jade mosaic adorned her face and she had been covered with bracelets and necklaces of shell, slate and mother-of-pearl. In contrast to all this wealth of jewelry, a single plain bead of unpolished jade had been placed in the mouth opening of the woman's mask so that she could obtain food while traveling through the afterlife.

A prickle went down Dana's spine as she thought about that long-dead noblewoman. In some ways it still seemed sacrilege to disturb her tomb.... In others it seemed that learning more about the woman and her people would be a means to honor her.

Nick was going on, his tone ironic now. "We've barely started work on the tomb, but already the division of spoils has been made. All the artifacts we uncover, of course, remain in the possession of the Mexican government, although the Institute will get full credit for their discovery and be allowed to supervise a touring expedition of certain finds. Fortunately, the Institute isn't interested only in the tomb. We'll be continuing to excavate farming sites on the island. All of this means that we'll have more funds and a larger crew." His gaze swept over them again. "Things will be changing around here. We'll have a lot more activity. Regardless of the new workers . . . I'm inviting each of you to stay on with me. You deserve to be in on this discovery all the way through."

He stopped, perhaps waiting for an automatic chorus of assent. No one spoke, however—no one eagerly accepted Nick's offer. Tim stared down at his own feet while Robert pursed his lips in a abstracted manner. Even Pat was silent, darting a glance now and then at Robert. As for Dana herself . . . well, she hardly knew what answer to give Nick. How could she actually stay on the island and work with him when he couldn't seem to return her love? She'd only be letting herself in for more heartache and pain. On the other hand, could she actually return to Alan? What appalled Dana was the fact that she *was* contemplating that possibility. Alan's letter still lay crumpled in her pocket, unanswered . . . a tangible sign that she was still desperate enough to seek any escape from her own feelings. She'd actually consider marrying a man she didn't love, in a futile attempt to blot out the man she *did* love. . . .

Nick was studying her with a rather questioning frown, but then he stirred and addressed the entire group. "Don't everyone jump on the bandwagon at once," he said dryly. "I'll be around if any of you decide you want to continue with our work." Apparently the meeting was dismissed after that, because Nick disappeared into his "office"—the larger of the field huts.

Pat immediately dragged Dana to one side. She seemed particularly worked up. "I can't believe how cool Nick is playing it. I mean, you'd think he'd be jumping up and down with excitement. The Institute is actually going to pry open its coffers—it'll pour funds into this project for real now. After all, the discovery of that tomb is going to put the Institute on the map, give it some prestige for once. Heck, this is going to give *Nick* all sorts of prestige—and anyone working with him gets to share in that." She paused for breath, and Dana managed to wedge in a word or two.

"I don't understand, Pat. If everything you say is true, why didn't you tell Nick right away that you wanted to stay on?"

Pat showed her ability for instant mood swings; now she looked disheartened. She gazed across the clearing toward Robert, who had settled down on a tree stump, seemingly losing himself in his own thoughts.

"If I stay here . . . it might just be too complicated. If Robert goes back to France with Marie, I'll just be haunted by memories of him. If *he* decides to stay— well, that'll be even worse. I don't know how I can be around him much longer. . . . I've made a real mess of things, I'm afraid."

Pat appeared to be in genuine distress, and Dana stared at her. "What do you mean? It's no crime to fall in love with a man—"

"It's more than that," Pat said, turning so that she wasn't looking at Robert anymore. "It's been driving me crazy—the way Robert goes to spend time with his fiancée on that wretched yacht of his.... So last night I did something really stupid. Oh, Dana—I wanted to get his attention, so I told him everything about myself. All the horrid things in my past... You see, I once tried to kill myself, Dana. Things got so bad inside, I actually tried to do it. And now I've told Robert. I just spilled it all out. I didn't keep a single thing hidden! I don't know what came over me, but I wish I'd just kept my stupid mouth shut."

Dana had seen Pat in turmoil many a time, but this was something new. For once, she didn't seem to be overdramatizing.

"I'm sorry about your problem, Pat. I had no idea," Dana said gently. "But when you told Robert... what did he have to say?"

"Nothing—that's the whole point. He just took it all in like he was watching some B-grade horror movie and then he told me very politely that he had to turn in early. After that... he just left. It was so humiliating. I'll bet Marie doesn't have any awful secrets like mine. I'll bet she's been perfectly well-adjusted her entire life."

"It's best that you were open with Robert. There's no sense hiding anything—"

"Come off it, Dana. Would you tell Nick every rotten detail about yourself?"

Dana stiffened. "I don't see what Nick has to do with it."

Pat gave her a commiserating glance. "You're in pretty much the same fix as me, and you might as well admit it. You're in love with a guy who's holding out on you. Maybe the reasons are different, but everything else is pretty much the same."

Dana wanted to argue...but she couldn't. She and Pat were in the same predicament, all right. Too bad that having company didn't make Dana feel any better.

Pat moved her hand in a restless gesture. "I never thought I'd say this—but I don't like this dig having prestige. I wish things could just be the way they were before. Our little group and no one else. Robert and me fighting...and me not knowing a thing about any fiancée of his."

"I can't believe you're getting nostalgic," Dana chided. "You're forgetting about all the trouble Jarrett caused, and the fact that he could have actually killed one of us."

The sun pressed down with its usual heat. Pat took out a handkerchief, blotted her face with it and then stuffed it willy-nilly back into her pocket.

"Even with Jarrett—I want the old days back," she insisted. "Sure, we made an oddball group, but we had a lot in common. We were all trying to run away from something in our lives. It's different now—I guess we know it's no use running anymore. Well, I'd rather go on believing it *is* possible."

It struck Dana that Pat had just made a very astute observation. They'd all been trying to escape, in one fashion or another. Dana herself had wanted to throw off an existence that had become too predictable, too safe. In much the same way, Robert had wanted to evade a life that had grown dull and unsatisfying, despite its wealth and privilege. Tim had been trying to hide out from his parents' unmet expectations; Pat, it appeared, had been trying to run away from emotional problems in her past. And for all Jarrett's vicious behavior, Dana could understand that he, too, had been attempting to escape something—his own ineffectualness and lack of power.

They'd all come to this little island thinking they would change their lives. It had been a heavy burden, perhaps, to place on Isla Calamar. In the end maybe it was impossible to wish for so much. Maybe, as Pat had pointed out, it was impossible to run away from yourself.

Dana pulled off her hat and creased the brim. Then she jammed the hat back onto her head. The joke was on *her*, all right. She'd come to this island, but she couldn't outrun her own need for love and constancy from a man. Worst of all, she yearned for love and constancy from the man least likely to give them to her...proud, stubborn, solitary Nick Petrie.

DANA WAS SITTING IN the courtyard of the hotel when Tim came by, lugging his suitcase. It was a rather atrocious suitcase, large, bulky and covered with an unfortunate paisley design. It made him look as if he were reluctantly dragging along someone's old sofa.

He stopped beside Dana. "I'm ready to leave," he said, a bit unnecessarily. A day earlier Tim had informed Nick that he wouldn't be staying on with the project. He was the first of the group to make a decision about it, one way or another. Dana realized she was going to miss Tim. As far as she was concerned, he hid a lot of talent behind a seemingly listless exterior. She just hoped he didn't waste his life over his parents' disappointment in him.

Now she rose from her wicker chair. "I'll walk with you down to the landing," she offered.

Tim didn't say anything, and she took that as acquiescence. Together they left the hotel and went through the village toward the dock. Dana knew this was her last chance to influence Tim. He probably wouldn't appreciate it, but she had to go ahead anyway—before it was too late.

"Look, Tim," she said forcefully. "Let me tell you right now, you're making a big mistake if you don't pursue this artist thing—"

"Relax," he said, a beleaguered expression on his face. "I've been giving it a lot of consideration and I realize that drawing is something I like to do. Maybe I don't really care a whole lot whether people think I'm good at it or not—I like the doing of it. So... I've already decided I'm going to sign up for an art class or two next semester. You don't need to make a big deal about it, though. It's just some lousy classes, all right?"

His announcement had taken the steam out of her argument, but she didn't mind. It seemed that Tim, at least, wasn't running away from himself quite so much anymore.

"I'm happy for you," she said. "You really are talented, Tim. And with time, I'll bet you—"

"Dana, give it a rest, will you? Let me just figure it out one step at a time."

She knew when to keep her mouth shut. Without saying anything more, she glanced at Tim. He was still gangly and awkward in manner, but she saw the suggestion of manhood in his face. Some people came to maturity later than others, it seemed, but Tim might just be on his way.

They arrived at the landing, where Robert's trim white yacht continued to preside among the lesser craft. The ferry to the mainland was ready to take off and Dana debated whether or not to give Tim a farewell hug. She settled for giving him a firm, no-nonsense handshake.

"I hope we stay in touch," she said.

"Yeah, sure," he muttered. He started to climb aboard the ferry, but then he stopped, struggled with the fastenings on his suitcase and popped it open. He took out a sheet of drawing paper and thrust it at Dana.

"Goodbye," he said. He relocked the suitcase, apparently in a great hurry to leave now. He seemed relieved when the captain of the ferry cast off immediately.

As the boat chugged away from the landing, taking Tim with it, Dana stared down at the sheet of paper he'd given her. She saw a pencil sketch of herself—a very evocative sketch, indeed. In a style that was bold and economical at once, Tim had captured her in profile, gazing at some unknown object with intense reflectiveness. The expression of wanting on her face was unmistakable. Dana studied her own portrait with a growing sense of heartache. She knew, without a doubt, that Tim had captured her at a moment when she'd been gazing straight at Nick.

CHAPTER TWENTY

DANA WAS STILL STANDING on the dock, clutching that portrait of herself, when Pat came wandering along. Luckily, Pat was absorbed in her own problems at the moment and didn't ask to see what Dana was holding. Instead, she stopped to gaze mournfully at Robert's yacht.

"He's probably on that thing with Marie right now. I wish he'd just be done with it and sail away with her! Then I could get on with my life."

Dana quickly rolled up Tim's sketch and tucked it under her arm. "Don't wait around for Robert to make the decisions. Take charge yourself, Pat. That's the only thing to do."

Pat didn't seem to be listening. She simply went on staring at the yacht like a supplicant hoping for some improbable benediction. It was very annoying, because Dana realized that she herself had spent too much time waiting and hoping these past few days. She needed to follow her own advice and take charge of the situation. Feeling a sudden, welcome sense of determination and energy, she turned to go.

Just then, however, Robert emerged from the cabin of the boat and came strolling down the gangplank. He observed Pat and Dana with his usual air of amusement.

"Well, well," he said. "If it isn't Sherlock Holmes and Dr. Watson. What clues are the two of you ferreting out today?"

Pat scowled at him. "For your information, Robert, we're not the slightest bit interested in what you might be doing."

"I'll tell you anyway," he said imperturbably. "I was just saying my farewells to Marie. She's heading back for France tomorrow, and I wanted to wish her smooth sailing."

Pat looked confused. "You mean—you're not going with her..."

Robert's own expression was bland. "For someone so nosy, you can be remarkably dense. No, I am not returning with Marie."

Pat folded her arms in a defensive stance. "You're still engaged to her, I'm sure."

"It appears that Marie has broken the engagement." Robert gave a regretful shrug. "She doesn't understand why I wish to remain on this island and she cannot picture herself staying here with me. It is unfortunate. I enjoyed having a fiancée...at a distance."

Pat, for one brief moment, allowed herself to look blissful. Immoderately blissful... Dana found it alarming that a few casual words from Robert could cause such a reaction in Pat. Then, thank goodness, Pat reverted to form.

"You're staying on this island, Robert? What for— what's your game?"

He smiled complacently. "I realized that without me here, Pat, who would you spy on? Whose belongings would you rifle through in the dead of night? Who would you accuse of any number of nefarious activities?''

''I can't believe I actually have to go on tolerating your presence,'' Pat declared. ''I don't know how I'll manage it. I really don't...''

The two of them went off down the pier, engrossed in their own bickering. At the end of the pier, however, Robert glanced over his shoulder and gave Dana a quick wink. Then he took Pat's arm in a possessive manner... and went right on arguing with her.

IT WAS A FEAST DAY in the village, which made it even more difficult for Nick to find Daniel. The streets were crowded with merrymakers. To celebrate the birthday of the island's patron saint, dancers in bright costumes replete with feathers and bells darted across the cobblestones. Incense perfumed the air and candles flickered in the deep recesses of the church. It made for an intriguing mixture of Mayan and Spanish social custom, but at the moment Nick wasn't into analyzing that. He just wanted to find Daniel.

At last, as he crossed the plaza one more time, he located the kid. Daniel, it seemed, was still trying to sell those strings of wooden beads. He had them spread out on his scrap of blue plastic, but he had no customers at the moment. Everyone was more interested in celebrating with ''bombs''—the colorful hollowed-out eggs that exploded with confetti when cracked. When you least expected it, someone would crack one over your head, the confetti covering you in a shower of paper dust.

Nick watched as Daniel stood beside his meager wares. It occurred to him that Daniel ought to be grabbing some of those eggs and dashing about with the other island kids to cause mayhem. Instead he was stuck here, trying to earn a few pesos. Had he ever known a real childhood? It was impossible to tell.

At last Nick stepped forward. "Thought I'd join the festivities, Daniel."

The kid gave him a skeptical glance. "You're not the fiesta type, Señor Petrie."

Nick had to admit that Daniel had a point there. "Look, I need to talk to you."

"I'm busy right now," Daniel said stiffly.

"I can see that. But this is important, what I have to say to you."

Daniel looked unconvinced. He seemed to waver for a moment, but then abruptly he gathered up his beads in the sheet of plastic and headed down the street. Maybe he was trying to get away from Nick or maybe he was just leading the way to a more private area for their discussion. Nick decided to assume the latter. He kept pace with Daniel—and now they had, indeed, reached a side street where there was a lot less commotion going on.

Nick settled down on the curb. After another moment of hesitation, Daniel sat down, too, although at a distance from Nick. His young face had settled into stony lines, as if he would be willing to listen but not to approve. Nick realized this was going to be even more difficult than he'd thought. Where the hell did he begin?

Maybe he just had to start at the most painful place. "Daniel, I had a boy once—a son."

Daniel turned a fraction of an inch toward Nick, although his expression remained guarded. Nick forced himself to continue.

"He was a good kid. Maybe a little excitable at times ... but nobody should die because of that. Josh was riding his bike out on the street where we'd forbidden him to go. Some damn truck was going too fast and swerved into him." Nick stopped there. It had happened eight years ago, but still it was too vivid in his mind. Meg's sobbing phone call, his own rush home by plane, Josh's small, inert body already whisked away to the hospital and then to the morgue, where the stale odor of death had pervaded the atmosphere. . . .

"I'm an alcoholic, Daniel," Nick said quietly. "I don't know if you understand how bad that can be. Anyway, I didn't know how to handle the death of my son. I started drinking even more than usual and I blew my marriage. Things pretty much went downhill from then on."

Daniel wrapped his arms around his thin legs. "It's too bad about your son. But why are you telling me this?"

Nick grimaced; he should've known that Daniel wouldn't waste any time on inconsequentials. "It's something I wish I'd told you about before. The reason I'm doing it now ... It has a lot to do with Dana." Nick surprised himself on that one—he hadn't expected to bring Dana into it. But he'd only spoken the truth.

Daniel grew instantly wary. "Why her ... *la rubia?*" he asked in a tone of distrust.

"She thinks you and I are a lot alike, Daniel. She thinks we're too damn stubborn and too proud of being on our own. I'm pretty sure she also thinks we're scared."

Daniel looked contemptuous of that idea. "I'm not afraid of anything," he said.

"I am," Nick admitted quietly. "Dana's made me see it, whether I want to or not. For a long time I've been afraid of letting anybody get close to me again. I didn't want to care about anyone the way I cared about my son...." Dana had made him see it, all right. With her own stubbornness, her warmth, her passion, her hopefulness in new beginnings. . . .

Nick rubbed his bad shoulder. Hell, he didn't know if he could ever really believe in new beginnings himself. He was just feeling his way along today, and not doing a very good job of it.

He glanced at Daniel. The kid was staring straight ahead, with that familiar, defensive jut to his chin. Now it was time for some hard-core negotiating, and Nick didn't fool himself about it. This wasn't going to be easy for either one of them.

"The truth is, I missed out on raising my son. I missed out on having someone to follow in my footsteps. So I've been thinking. Since I don't have anyone in my life right now... Well, neither do you." Nick paused, then plunged ahead.

"Here's the deal. I'm missing something in my life. I suspect you're missing something, too, Daniel. So I adopt you. I get another chance with a son. In return, you put up with me as a father. Hell, I'm not saying that I'm anything to shout about. I still want a drink every day of my life, and I'm not always reasonable." Nick gave Daniel a considering glance. "Anyway, I'm saying that I'm no prize, but that's the deal."

Nick felt as if he'd jumped off a cliff and he didn't know what he'd find at the bottom. Daniel was tough.

He'd probably think of a dozen reasons not to go for this.

The kid went on staring straight ahead, but he seemed to be undergoing some type of struggle within. He was young, in spite of everything, and he couldn't disguise the conflicting emotions on his face—hope, perhaps, as well as fear. It was the hope that got to Nick, the unexpected wistfulness in Daniel's expression.

"You'd be doing me a big favor if you agreed to be my son," Nick said. "A great honor, really."

Daniel stood, as if determined to leave. But then his shoulders tensed, and suddenly he looked as if he was about to cry.

"It may seem selfish, Daniel," Nick said gruffly, "but I'm asking this for myself as much as anything else." He was trying his best to allow the kid a way to give in without sacrificing his pride. At the same time, however, Nick was only speaking the truth.

Nick stood, too, and put a hand on Daniel's shoulder. "Look, it's okay to need somebody. Of course, I'm just starting to figure that out myself. But the way I see it—it's never too late, Daniel. It's never too late to let someone else into your life."

The kid scrunched his eyes tight, but still a few tears managed to escape. Awkwardly Nick pulled Daniel into his arms.

"Deal, Daniel?"

There was no response, but Nick just held on.

Then, after a long moment, "Deal, Señor Petrie," came Daniel's muffled voice.

Nick closed his own eyes in relief. He couldn't believe it—he was going to be a father once again. He just couldn't believe it.

"No sense in being so formal," he said after a second. "Now that we've entered into a partnership, and all. Anton and Elena call me Nicolás. What do you think about that?"

Daniel wormed his way out of Nick's embrace. "Nicolás," he said tentatively. "I have to get back to work now, Señor Nicolás. Tomorrow morning I'll meet you at the dig. We can . . . we can begin our partnership then."

Nick studied Daniel closely. He'd wiped his cheeks with the back of his hand, and now only his dark eyes betrayed any hint of emotion. The kid was making a supreme effort to regain some composure, and if he needed to set some of the terms himself, that was only fair.

"Fine, Daniel. I'll see you tomorrow."

Nick didn't know the proper etiquette to observe on acquiring a son—particularly when the son was determined to treat the whole thing as a sort of business transaction. He and Daniel—they had a lot to learn, it appeared. But there'd be time for that.

"*Hasta luego*—until later," Nick said.

"*Hasta luego.*" Daniel took his wares and hurried down the street. At the corner he looked back once, briefly . . . as if to make sure Nick was still there.

"I'm not going anywhere, kid," Nick murmured to himself. "You're not exactly getting a bargain with me . . . but I'm not going anywhere. At least you can count on that."

DANA MADE HER WAY across the crowded plaza. A marimba band was playing from the gazebo, and several couples were dancing to the lighthearted beat.

Children darted about, laughing and shouting. Everyone seemed so happy on this fiesta day, but Dana felt only a heaviness deep inside. She couldn't join in the celebration, not when she'd never felt less like celebrating....

She knew what she had to do, however. There was no other choice for her. Even if it meant she would never again see Nick Petrie, the man she loved... Even so, she had to leave this island. *Because* of Nick, she had to leave. She couldn't bear the heartache of seeing him every day and knowing he didn't love her in return. And so she'd made her plans. Now it was only a matter of carrying them out.

Dana glanced across the street and saw young Daniel striding along with a purposeful air, a bundle of some sort tucked under his arm. She hadn't known whether or not she would get to say goodbye to him. This would probably be her only chance, and she went to intercept him.

"Daniel—"

He looked up at her. She expected his usual aloof manner, but instead he seemed filled with an unusual excitement.

"La rubia..." he said distractedly. He appeared eager to be on his way.

"Daniel—I'm leaving the island tomorrow morning. Before I go... I'll wish you good luck." She wanted to wish him a whole lot more than that, but she didn't know quite how to put it into words.

"Luck...I'm already having good luck," Daniel said with satisfaction. "Tomorrow Señor Petrie is going to start being my father."

"Your father?" Dana echoed, wondering if she'd heard right.

"Yes," Daniel said. "And I'm going to be his son. It's like being partners. We figured it all out this morning."

Dana gazed at him with a growing sense of wonderment. Nick and Daniel, actually figuring things out between them—actually realizing that they were meant to be together....

Daniel shifted from one foot to the next, as if still anxious to be off. At this moment, he had an expression on his face that Dana hadn't seen there before. His dark eyes brimmed with it, in fact. It was happiness. Plain, ordinary, kidlike happiness.

Dana smiled, and put out her hand. "Congratulations, Daniel."

He hesitated, but then allowed a brief handshake. He started to leave, only to turn back.

"I hope you have good luck, too," he said. He spoke with the magnanimity of one whose good fortune allowed him to be generous. And then, for just a second, he smiled at Dana. She realized it was the first time she'd ever seen him smile. It suited him. Watching him, the heaviness inside Dana lightened just a little.

Daniel turned, and this time he went darting off. He was obviously intent on getting ready to start his brand-new life... his new life as Nick Petrie's son.

THE GLASS OF TEQUILA looked innocent enough. It sat in the center of Nick's table, untouched. Nick stared at it. He'd ordered it to prove he could face his greatest fear, thinking he'd take one look at the drink, then just stand up and walk away. But then the craving had started....

If Nick wanted to be brutally honest right now, he'd admit that he was scared—damn scared. His earlier sense of exhilaration over Daniel had given way to apprehension. He was going to be a father again, but would he do the job right? He didn't want to fail Daniel. He couldn't afford to fail, not this time around.

And then...then there was Dana. Lovely, warm Dana Morgan, who still haunted every one of Nick's thoughts. Letting Daniel into his life had been the first step for him. It was where he'd had to start. He'd realized that no true healing could begin for him until he'd faced his sorrow over Josh and done something about it. That "something," it turned out, meant opening his heart to another son....

So he'd managed that much. Self-doubts and all, he *was* going to be a father again. But could he take the next step? Did he have enough to give Dana what she deserved? Because she deserved a hell of a lot more than a crabby ex-drunk staring at a glass of tequila....

"Nick." It was Dana's voice, firm and matter-of-fact, but with that unexpected thread of huskiness. It seemed as if, once again, he'd called her to him with the very insistence of his thoughts. He leaned back in his chair and gazed at her. She wore her sleeveless denim blouse and colorful island skirt. The material swirled enticingly around her legs and he remembered the night she'd come to his room. If anything, however, she was more lovely, more enticing now, her skin a golden brown, her sunlit hair falling in ripples down her back.

Without waiting for an invitation, she pulled out a chair and sat beside him. Frowning, she gazed at the glass of tequila. He waited for her to say something about it, but she surprised him. After a long moment, she glanced away from it as if she refused to acknowledge its existence any further.

"I ran into Daniel a little while ago," she said. "He seemed . . . hopeful. Actually, he seemed very hopeful, now that you're going to be his dad."

"Daniel and I . . . we're both ornery enough to belong together."

"That's the understatement of the year," she remarked. "But I'm glad for the two of you. More than glad." Then, a long moment later, she spoke again. "I came to say goodbye, Nick."

That made him sit up. "You haven't said anything before about leaving. I started to assume . . . well, that you were going to stay."

"You were wrong," she said with some asperity. "I'm leaving on the first ferry out in the morning."

He wasn't ready to see her go. Hell, *that* was an understatement. He didn't want her to go at all. He'd forbidden himself to have her, but he needed her nearby— he knew that much.

Neither one of them said anything for some time. Dusk had started to drift downward, streaking the sky with lavender and rose. Across the street in the plaza, couples still danced in honor of this feast day, the marimba band casting its light, silvered notes on the air. Dana tapped her fingers on the table in a restless counterpoint to the beat.

"So you're really going to marry that guy," Nick said at last.

"No," she answered calmly. "I'm not. I posted a letter to Alan today. I told him I appreciated the offer, but I couldn't possibly marry him. I don't love him, you see, and I'm not going to use him just because—well, I'm not going to use him, that's all. I don't need to marry someone in order to...escape."

Hope stirred in Nick, and now he leaned toward her. "Dana, you don't have to leave. You can stay and work here. There's a place for you—"

"Dammit, Nick Petrie." Now she glared at him, the fire in her showing. "Don't you think I have any pride of my own? Do you think I'm going to wait around on the off chance you'll make love to me again—is that it?"

Once again, he wasn't handling things well. "Look, it just doesn't seem right for you to leave. In some ways, I think you belong on this island as much as I do."

She gave a humorless laugh. "You're really something, Nick. You want me to stay...as long as you can make clear we'll have no commitment between us. That makes it so easy, so convenient for you." She stood and pushed her chair back toward the table, as if to erase any sign that she'd been sitting there. Afterward, she gazed at him steadily.

"I'll tell you something, Nick. It so happens that I love you. It's taking a lot of courage for me to admit that out loud, when I know how little difference it will make with you. But I'm doing it anyway. It's also going to take a lot of courage to walk away from you—but I'm going to do that, too. I told you once that I'm no martyr, and that's still true. I love you, but somehow I'm going to make a decent, satisfying life for myself away from this island. Away from *you*. Goodbye, Nick." With that she turned and did, indeed, walk away from him, moving with the tall, graceful posture that was second nature to her, hair flowing out behind her like a golden banner.

Nick watched her go, and then he glanced at the glass of booze in front of him. Slowly he picked up the glass, slowly he brought it toward him . . . and slowly he up-ended it, pouring its contents over the sidewalk. Then he set down the glass, pushed back his chair and went after Dana.

She was already striding along the beach by the time he caught up to her.

"Go away, Nick," she said furiously, not looking at him. "We've already said everything."

"That was a pretty good speech you gave," he acknowledged. "A pretty nice exit, too—I sort of hate to ruin it. But I have a few things to say, myself."

She didn't stop. She went on, the waves of the sea lapping near her feet. "I don't want to hear it. Just let it be, Nick."

"I love you, too, Dana."

Now she did stop, swiveling around to face him. If he'd thought to bowl her over with his announcement, he was mistaken. She gazed at him with an expression of open distrust.

"Hell," he said grouchily. "I've probably loved you since that first time you were sick in the bushes. I just didn't want to admit it. I couldn't admit it.... I'd stopped believing that love was much good for anything."

He saw the sorrow that flickered across her face. "What's different now?" she asked softly.

He drew her into his arms, holding her close. She felt so good next to him . . . more than good. "It's all because of you," he murmured against her hair. "You've made me pretty damn uncomfortable, the way you've poked and prodded all my emotions. I wanted to stop feeling hope or love or anything else—but you wouldn't let me. So finally I asked Daniel to be my son. I got that far." He paused for a moment. "But then you left me sitting at that table and I saw the choice, crystal clear. I could let you go—or I could decide to be happy. It was that simple."

For the second time today, Nick felt a deep, quiet sense of relief. Opening his heart to Daniel—to another son—had, indeed, been the first step for him. Now he'd just taken the next very important step. It seemed to Nick that in the past few moments he'd finally brought a blurred image into sharp, vivid focus: the image of what his life could be if he truly allowed Dana into it. A warm life, all his old loneliness banished...and, yes, a happy life. Now that he'd seen it so clearly, he couldn't turn away from it.

Dana, however, had gone rigid in his arms, as if doing her very best to resist him. He could understand that. Up until now, he hadn't given her much reason to trust him. He hadn't trusted himself, that was the real problem.

He went on holding her, wondering how to explain what she needed to know. He'd kept back too much, for too long a time. That had to change.

"Dana...sweetheart." He tried out the endearment, realizing that it felt a little awkward. He guessed that he just needed practice with this type of thing. "Dana, you're right—closing myself off from others was the easiest thing to do, a hell of a lot easier than admitting I needed someone."

Dana hadn't relaxed much in his arms. Her face was turned away from him and he couldn't read her expression, couldn't gauge her reaction. No matter—now that he had her, he wasn't letting go.

He caressed the silken strands of her hair, telling her all the rest of it. "Breaking up with Meg... Maybe that would've been inevitable, even if Josh hadn't died. We never had the best foundation for a marriage. We were never really in tune with each other. Then Kathryn came along. I probably allowed myself to get involved with her in the first place because I knew she didn't have the power to touch me too deeply. So that breakup was inevitable sooner or later, too. But then *you* came along, Dana... and I knew almost from the first minute I saw you that you were the one who could touch me too deeply. Do you blame me for fighting you so much?"

At last she spoke. "Yes," she said. "I blame you, all right."

Gently he turned her face so that she had to look at him. "I was fighting for survival. Up until you, the only way I knew how to survive was to be alone. But tonight, when you told me you were leaving... I couldn't let you go. I couldn't be without you anymore. It was just that simple."

"You keep saying that," she grumbled. "Nothing's that simple."

"Maybe not. Maybe we have a whole lot of complications between us we haven't even thought about yet. Then again, maybe complications aren't such a bad thing...."

"Oh, Nick." Suddenly she wrapped her arms around him, holding him with her own fierceness. "It's complicated, all right. But if we could just work it all out together. Everything—"

"Not everything," he said. "Some things I take responsibility for alone. You can't keep me sober, Dana. Only I can do that. I've managed so far, and I just have to go on managing."

She pulled back a little and gazed at him in the last shimmering light of the day. Lord, she was beautiful, as well as warm and sensual and strong. No other woman he'd known possessed her courage and spirit. No other woman was like her in any way.

He bent his head with the intention of kissing her, but apparently she had something else on her mind.

"You're incredibly stubborn, Nick Petrie. Won't you admit there's *something* we can do together—some way we can help each other through life a little?"

"There is something," he admitted. "You could try parenthood with me. I could use the help, believe me."

"Nick—it's not going to be easy for Daniel to share you with me, I can guarantee that...."

"With some help, he'll realize there's enough love to go around. I'm starting to realize that myself. Think you can take the two of us on?"

She seemed to give the matter some consideration. "You're both incredibly difficult," she said. Her smile was rueful. "You know, I came to this island looking for adventure and work that could mean something to me. I'm getting a whole lot more than I bargained for! Not just an adventurous new career, but a thirteen-year-old son and a most aggravating man to love."

"You told me once that you felt a connection to me," he reminded her. "As if we'd known one another in some other lifetime."

"Could be that the connection's getting stronger all the time." Her voice grew a little huskier, her dark brown eyes even richer in color. "Truth is, though, it's this lifetime that concerns me now. This lifetime with you, Nick...."

He couldn't hold off any longer. He lifted her face toward him, capturing her mouth, possessing it as his.

When they broke apart a long, breathless moment later, it seemed that Dana still had something on her mind.

"I swore I'd never ask a man this question again," she muttered. "But Nick—for goodness' sake, will you marry me?"

He grinned. "What...no candles, no music, no romantic dinner for two?" Then, before she could get worked up..."Yes," he said. "Yes, Dana, I'll marry you."

And as Nick held Dana even more closely than before, he recognized the long-forgotten emotion stealing over him.

It was happiness.

 HARLEQUIN SUPERROMANCE®

WOMEN WHO DARE
They take chances, make changes
and follow their hearts!

Too Many Bosses
by Jan Freed

According to Alec McDonald, Laura Hayes is "impertinent,
impulsive, insubordinate and totally lacking in self-discipline"—
all negatives in an employee. Mind you, he also has to admit that
she has the legs of a Las Vegas showgirl.

According to Laura Hayes, Alec McDonald is "a pompous
bigot who considers Kleenex standard issue for his female
employees." But while these are negatives in a boss, Laura
doesn't intend to remain his employee for long, because it's
obvious that Alec needs Laura—in his business and in his life.

Within twenty-four hours of their first meeting, Laura and Alec
are partners in a new business. *Equal* partners. Yet two bosses
is one too many for any business—especially when the boss is
falling in love with the boss!

Watch for *Too Many Bosses* by Jan Freed.
Available in May 1995, wherever Harlequin books are sold.

Bestselling Author

Jasmine Cresswell

May 1995 brings you face-to-face with her
latest thrilling adventure

Desires & Deceptions

Will the real Claire Campbell please stand up?
Missing for over seven years, Claire's family has
only one year left to declare her legally dead and
claim her substantial fortune—that is, until a woman
appears on the scene alleging to be the missing
heiress. Will DNA testing solve the dilemma? Do
old family secrets still have the power to decide
who lives and dies, suffers or prospers, loves or
hates? Only Claire knows for sure.

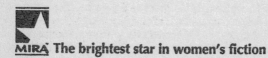

HARLEQUIN SUPERROMANCE®

**He's sexy, he's single...and he's a father!
Can any woman resist?**

Coming in May 1995

Finding Father
By Anne Marie Duquette

Nina Delacruz, age nine, refuses to believe that her father, a world-famous mountain climber who disappeared in Alaska, is never coming back. She insists someone will find him, even though her mother, Mercedes, says it's impossible.

April Montgomery, age eleven, lost her mother as an infant, and now she's withdrawing from her father, too. April's been keeping a secret from Cass, one that she knows will hurt him deeply. If he finds out, maybe he won't love her anymore....

These two families are brought together by a dog—a dog they both claim is theirs. And as it turns out, that's the best thing that could have happened. Because, with Mercedes's help, Cass can become the father both girls need. And the lover, friend and husband *Mercedes* needs.

Look for *Finding Father* in May, wherever Harlequin books are sold.

FM-4

HARLEQUIN SUPERROMANCE®

presents

EVERY MOVE YOU MAKE
By Bobby Hutchinson

This May, meet the first of our FOUR STRONG MEN:

Mountie Joe Marcello. He was hot on the trail of his
man, but what he got was...a woman. Schoolteacher
Carrie Zablonski found herself in the wrong place at the
wrong time, and when Joe learned there was more to the
lady than met the eye—and she was quite an eyeful—he
assigned himself as her personal guardian angel. Trouble
was, Carrie didn't *want* his protection....

Look for *Every Move You Make* in May 1995,
wherever Harlequin books are sold.

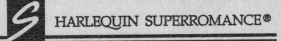

HARLEQUIN SUPERROMANCE®

presents

a new book by

Bestselling Author Janice Kaiser

MONDAY'S CHILD

Kelly Ronan was on vacation; Bart Monday was on the lam. When the two met in Thailand, more than sparks began to fly. Chased by a rain of bullets, they swam to relative safety, dodging snakes and pirates on a small but dangerous island. It wasn't Kelly's idea of a dream vacation, but her mother had always told her she needed a little excitment in her life....

Look for *Monday's Child* in May 1995,
wherever Harlequin books are sold.

MCHILD

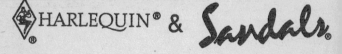

HARLEQUIN®

PRESENTS
RELUCTANT BRIDEGROOMS

Two beautiful brides, two unforgettable romances...
two men running for their lives....

My Lady Love, by Paula Marshall, introduces
Charles, Viscount Halstead, who lost his memory
and found himself employed as a stableboy by the
untouchable Nell Tallboys, Countess Malplaquet.
But Nell didn't consider Charles untouchable—
not at all!

Darling Amazon, by Sylvia Andrew, is the story of
a spurious engagement between Julia Marchant
and Hugo, marquess of Rostherne—an engagement
that gets out of hand and just may lead Hugo to
the altar after all!

Enjoy two madcap Regency weddings this May,
wherever Harlequin books are sold.

HARLEQUIN®

Don't miss these Harlequin favorites by some of our most distinguished authors!

And now, you can receive a discount by ordering two or more titles!

HT #25607	PLAIN JANE'S MAN by Kristine Rolofson	$2.99 U.S./$3.50 CAN.	☐
HT #25616	THE BOUNTY HUNTER		
	by Vicki Lewis Thompson	$2.99 U.S./$3.50 CAN.	☐
HP #11674	THE CRUELLEST LIE by Susan Napier	$2.99 U.S./$3.50 CAN.	☐
HP #11699	ISLAND ENCHANTMENT by Robyn Donald	$2.99 U.S./$3.50 CAN.	☐
HR #03268	THE BAD PENNY by Susan Fox	$2.99	☐
HR #03303	BABY MAKES THREE by Emma Goldrick	$2.99	☐
HS #70570	REUNITED by Evelyn A. Crowe	$3.50	☐
HS #70611	ALESSANDRA & THE ARCHANGEL		
	by Judith Arnold	$3.50 U.S./$3.99 CAN.	☐
HI #22291	CRIMSON NIGHTMARE		
	by Patricia Rosemoor	$2.99 U.S./$3.50 CAN.	☐
HAR #16549	THE WEDDING GAMBLE by Muriel Jensen	$3.50 U.S./$3.99 CAN.	☐
HAR #16558	QUINN'S WAY by Rebecca Flanders	$3.50 U.S./$3.99 CAN.	☐
HH #28802	COUNTERFEIT LAIRD by Erin Yorke	$3.99	☐
HH #28824	A WARRIOR'S WAY by Margaret Moore	$3.99 U.S./$4.50 CAN.	☐

(limited quantities available on certain titles)

	AMOUNT	$
DEDUCT:	**10% DISCOUNT FOR 2+ BOOKS**	$
ADD:	**POSTAGE & HANDLING**	$
	($1.00 for one book, 50¢ for each additional)	
	APPLICABLE TAXES*	$_____
	TOTAL PAYABLE	$_____
	(check or money order—please do not send cash)	

To order, complete this form and send it, along with a check or money order for the total above, payable to Harlequin Books, to: **In the U.S.:** 3010 Walden Avenue, P.O. Box 9047, Buffalo, NY 14269-9047; **In Canada:** P.O. Box 613, Fort Erie, Ontario, L2A 5X3.

Name:_____

Address:_____ City:_____

State/Prov.:_____ Zip/Postal Code:_____

*New York residents remit applicable sales taxes.
Canadian residents remit applicable GST and provincial taxes.

HBACK-AJ2